A HOME FOR
THE HIGHLAND CATTLE
and
THE ANTHEAP

Doris Lessing

edited by Jean Pickering

broadview literary texts

National Library of Canada Cataloguing in Publication

Lessing, Doris, 1919–
    A home for the highland cattle ; and, The antheap / Doris Lessing ; edited by Jean Pickering

(Broadview literary texts)
Includes bibliographical references.
ISBN 1-55111-363-5

    I. Pickering, Jean.   II. Title.   III. Series.   IV. Title: The antheap.

PR6023.E833H64 2003   823'.914   C2003-903710-X

Broadview Press Ltd. is an independent, international publishing house, incorporated in 1985. Broadview believes in shared ownership, both with its employees and with the general public; since the year 2000 Broadview shares have traded publicly on the Toronto Venture Exchange under the symbol BDP.

We welcome comments and suggestions regarding any aspect of our publications – please feel free to contact us at the addresses below or at broadview@broadviewpress.com.

North America
Post Office Box 1243, Peterborough, Ontario, Canada K9J 7H5
3576 California Road, Orchard Park, NY, USA 14127
Tel: (705) 743-8990; Fax: (705) 743-8353;
e-mail: customerservice@broadviewpress.com

UK, Ireland, and continental Europe
Plymbridge Distributors Ltd.
Estover Road
Plymouth PL6 7PY UK Tel: (01752) 202301; Fax: (01752) 202333
e-mail: orders@plymbridge.com

Australia and New Zealand
UNIREPS, University of New South Wales
Sydney, NSW, 2052
Tel: 61 2 9664 0999; Fax: 61 2 9664 5420
email: info.press@unsw.edu.au

www.broadviewpress.com

This book is printed on acid-free paper containing 30% post-consumer fibre.

Series Editor: Professor L.W. Conolly
Advisory editor for this volume: Michel W. Pharand
Typesetting and assembly: True to Type Inc., Mississauga, Canada.

Certified Eco-Logo
30% Post.

PRINTED IN CANADA

Contents

Acknowledgments

I wish to thank Doris Lessing for what I've learned from her over the forty years I've been reading her work, which has engaged my mind and heart; for her vast and varied body of work; for her sensitivity to ideological currents and changing ideas. She has consistently been aware of historical events as they unfold and new character types as they emerge in response to the historical situation. Certainly she is one of the great observers and reporters of our time. I also wish to thank her for her generosity in answering my questions.

I wish to thank Broadview Press for inviting me to do this edition of Doris Lessing's *A Home for the Highland Cattle* and *The Antheap*, two of her short novels that have been out of print for over a quarter century. They are two short chapters in the story of how the British went to Africa, how they lived there, and how they left, a story that, as the newspapers daily remind us, has not yet played out.

I am grateful to Jan Byrd, supervisor of the Madden Interlibrary Loan Department at California State University, Fresno, for her indefatigable efforts to procure hard-to-get texts, and to Anthony Chennells and Paul Schlueter for their quick, full answers to my questions. In particular, I wish to thank Suzanne Kehde for her help at all stages of assembling this book, from discussion of Lessing's works and selection of materials for the appendices, to sustained proofreading of both scanned materials and my text.

Introduction

We learn, through the word, who we are *not*, who we might yet become.

———Caryl Emerson[1]

Texts and Contexts

When readers sit down to read, they bring to the texts at hand the sum of their experience: their responses to previous reading, to family and community interactions, to national and world events. These responses form the contexts, necessarily unstable, in which they will read the works before them. The relation between reader and text, however, is more complex than this description suggests. Hans Robert Jauss postulates a three-way relationship of author, text and reader. Resisting the traditional dominant role of the author in determining significance, he calls attention to the triangular relationship of "author, work and public [in which] the last is no passive part, no chain of mere reactions, but itself an energy formative of history. The historical life of a literary work is unthinkable without the active participation of its addressees." He presupposes "a dialogical ... relationship ... between work, audience, and new work."[2] Books, like children, come into a world that already has expectations of them, in the case of fiction expectations about form, representation, plot, significance, enjoyability. Through successive readings by all kinds of readers—critics, authors, literary historians—a literary work takes its place in a "horizon of expectations": a book acquires a reading history, accumulates a mixed bag of reputations based on the experiences and opinions of previous readers, reviewers, critics, teachers, theologians, and so forth.

Thus the horizon of expectations is no more stable than the individual reading context. It too is subject to changing literary

---

1 "Outer Word and Inner Speech: Bakhtin, Vygotsky, and the Internalization of Language," *Bakhtin: Essays and Dialogues on His Work* (Chicago: Chicago UP, 1986), 36.
2 "Literary History as a Challenge to Literary Theory," tr. Timothy Bahti. *The Critical Tradition: Classic Texts and Contemporary Trends*, ed. David H. Richter (Boston, MA: Bedford, 1998), 935-37.

fashions—including ways of reading—to national and cultural differences, to history. *In Pursuit of Doris Lessing: Nine Nations Reading*[1] illustrates this phenomenon. "Nine different Lessings emerge from these essays, forcing us to question received propositions about the universality of literature and the stability of the text," according to the dust jacket. These "different Lessings" also bring to the fore issues of the relationships between the texts and contexts of both reading and writing.

I read *Nine Nations* with particular interest because it implicitly spoke to my own situation. Soon after I emigrated from Britain to the United States at the height of the Red Scare, I met in a Kansas university town a woman who disapprovingly told me, "We're just back from Europe, and do you know, the people over there would rather do *anything* than fight another war." I heard other expressions of the Manichean proclivity that enabled McCarthyism: "Better dead than red," was a popular slogan. From this experience with those who had judged Europe through a worldview grounded in the remote, safe, prosperous Middle West, I eventually formulated a proposition: the sparser the historical detail, the greater the inclination to myth. I later recognized my proposition as a version of the binary opposition—any totalizing discourse that divides the entire field into opposing factions, no conscientious objectors allowed. In all her work Lessing has questioned such binary thinking. Her most famous novel, *The Golden Notebook*,[2] names the following binaries, all of which are interrogated and deconstructed by the end of the novel: "Bound. Free. Good. Bad. Yes. No. Capitalism. Socialism. Sex. Love...." (44). These binaries are some of the "false dichotomies" Lessing has seen "at the heart of our culture," which, she says in her preface to the second edition of *The Golden Notebook*, "must not compartmentalise" (x). Binarism is not only the consequence of the lack of historical specificity, it also promotes it. When the present ignores history, it falls back on essentialist ideas of human nature as perceived by the collective (Lessing's term both for institutions like the educational system and for voluntary groups like the Girl Scouts), whose thinking is necessarily binary, and abandons the individual reader to act as arbiter of and model for representations of the "universal" human being.

---

1   Claire Sprague, ed. (London: Macmillan, 1990). Hereafter abbreviated as *Nine Nations*.

2   New York: Bantam, 1973. (First edition: London: Michael Joseph; New York: Simon and Schuster, 1962.)

Of particular interest for readers of *A Home for the Highland Cattle* and *The Antheap* is Eve Bertelsen's essay on Lessing's South African reception, "The Quest and the Quotidian,"[1] which gives a decade-by-decade account of the most important events in Rhodesia and South Africa that relate to Lessing's work. Lessing was well-known in South Africa, "a troublesome and famous local girl." Her affiliation with the quasi-Communist Left Study Group and her divorce from Frank Wisdom, with whom she left their children—manifestations of her repudiation of the middle class into which she had been born—were "items of common conversation" (42). South African reviewers seem to have perceived her as a traitor to her (and their) class, just as her brother and an old neighbor of the Taylers saw her as a traitor to the family (Seligman 6-9, 15-16).[2] Both reviewers and family saw her work as "thinly fictionalised autobiography" (Bertelsen 42).

> Their personal knowledge of Doris Lessing was not the only determinant of this reception. She and they had lived through the same events, and their different reactions to this common historical experience were perhaps even more influential. They recognized the events she represented, but her representation, at odds with their perceptions, offended them. Lessing's Rhodesian experiences of the 1940s [on which her African fiction published in the fifties, including *Cattle* and *Antheap*, was based] engage all of the important elements of the period: racism; the threat to white ascendancy posed by both socialism and African nationalism, and the personal dilemmas of whites as they attempt to align their European values and sensibilities with both the stark reality of the land itself and new threats to their controlling interests. To the South African reviewer Lessing's fictional representations are thus urgent, compelling and of personal concern. (43)

"The reviewers," says Bertelsen, "all applaud her 'promise' and eagerly anticipate from her pen.... the 'Great South African Novel....'" It is her treatment of the material they all recognize that they denounce. Their disagreement with Lessing's views was often couched in the terms of aesthetic criticism: "Lessing has not produced a pure work of art; it is mainly meant to convey social judgements" (45). Bertelsen's account makes clear the degree to which Lessing has always been a contrarian, vigorously opposing the received wisdom of the culture she resentfully grew up in.

---

1   *Nine Nations.*
2   "The Four-Faced Novelist," *Modern Fiction Studies* 26, 1980.

Doris Lessing has published two volumes of autobiography. The first, *Under My Skin*,[1] gives her reflections on her life up to 1949. She lists the books and authors she remembers reading as a young child: "I was reading the easier bits in the books in the heavy bookcase. The classics. The classics of that time, all in dark red leather covers, with thin-as-skin pages, edged with gold. Scott. Stevenson. Kipling. Lamb's *Tales from Shakespeare*. Dickens.... *Plain Tales from the Hills*. *The Jungle Book*, *Oliver Twist*" (82). Later, for three or four years, her mother ordered books for her from London, among them Bunyan's works and biographies of great men from Napoleon to Cecil Rhodes (88). She read a range of children's classics from *The Swiss Family Robinson* and *Lobo, the Wolf* to *Alice in Wonderland*, *Black Beauty*, and *Biffel, a Trek Ox*. Later yet, she read war memoirs and histories, and *All Quiet on the Western Front*, questioned by her mother but approved by her father, who "identifi[ed] with the German soldiers, betrayed like the English tommies by their generals ..." (110).

In an interview in 1964, Lessing told Roy Newquist that she had read "The best—the classics of European and American Literature. One of the advantages of not being educated was that I didn't have to waste time on the second-best.... I could have been educated—formally that is—but I felt some neurotic rebellion against my parents who wanted me to be brilliant academically. I simply contracted out of the whole thing and educated myself" (5). Lessing stopped going to school when she was fourteen, but the habit she then acquired of educating herself through constant wide reading has continued all her life. While she has always read whatever has been to hand, she has been particularly influenced by nineteenth-century novelists: "For me the highest point of literature was the novel of the nineteenth century; the work of Tolstoy, Stendahl, Dostoevsky, Balzac, Turgenev, Chekov; the work of the great realists. I define realism as art which springs so vigourously and naturally from a strongly-held, though not necessarily intellectually-defined, view of life that it absorbs symbolism."[2] She began to write in her teens and, since publishing *The*

---

1 *Volume One of My Autobiography, to 1949* (London and New York: HarperCollins), 1994.
2 "The Small Personal Voice," *A Small Personal Voice* (1957), ed. Paul Schlueter (New York: Vintage Knopf, 1975), 4.

Grass is Singing[1] in 1950, for over fifty years has supported herself entirely by her writing.

Lessing, accustomed to flouting the restrictions her mother thought proper to "nice children," escaped to bush and veld, where she spent hours roaming either alone or with her brother. Much of her early fiction uses what she observed on these expeditions. In her preface to *African Stories*[2] she has said that "the chief gift from Africa to writers, white and black, is the continent itself, which for some people is like an old fever, latent and always in their blood; or like an old wound throbbing in the bones as the air changes" (viii). It has occupied her writer's imagination all her life. "And while the cruelties of the white man towards the black man are among the heaviest counts in the indictment against humanity, colour prejudice is not our original fault, but only one aspect of the atrophy of the imagination that prevents us from seeing ourselves in every creature that breathes under the sun" (viii). After *Grass*, a novel that exposes settler society for its cruelties and hypocrisies, she published *This Was the Old Chief's Country*,[3] two volumes of *African Stories*, and *Five*,[4] all of which, with the exception of one short novel, are set in Africa, as are the first four volumes of *Children of Violence*, a five-volume sequence covering the years from 1934 to an unspecified time in an apocalyptic future. Anna Wulf, the writer–character in *The Golden Notebook*, recording in the black notebook her recollections of Africa during World War II, ponders the "lying nostalgia" (64) overlaying her novel, *The Frontiers of War*. Africa has continued to appear in later works, in the *Canopus in Argos: Archives* series,[5] *Mara and Dann*,[6] and the *Sweetest Dream*.[7]

While Lessing learned to love the land, she also learned to regard the Rhodesian English-settler society as a trap, a confinement, a

---

1 London: Michael Joseph; New York: Crowell.
2 London: Michael Joseph, 1964; New York: Simon and Schuster, 1965.
3 London: Michael Joseph, 1951; New York: Crowell, 1952. Short stories.
4 *A Home for the Highland Cattle* and *The Antheap* first appeared in *Five: Short Novels* (London: Michael Joseph, 1953).
5 Vol.1 *Re: Colonised Planet 5, Shikasta*. London: Jonathan Cape; New York: Knopf, 1979. Vol. 2 *The Marriages Between Zones, Three, Four, and Five*, 1981; Vol. 3 *The Sirian Experiments*, 1982; Vol. 4 *The Making of the Representative for Planet 8*; Vol. 5 *Documents Relating to the Sentimental Agents in the Volyen Empire*, 1983.
6 London and New York: HarperCollins, 1999.
7 London: Flamingo, 2001.

prison, which she thought a consequence of the need constantly to maintain the appearance of racial superiority. She was particularly appalled by the treatment of the blacks. Anna Wulf remarks, "The white people in Central Africa ... used to say, 'Well, of course, the blacks will drive us into the sea in fifty years time.' They used to say it cheerfully. In other words, 'We know what we are doing is wrong'" (43–44). This sentiment appears again in *African Laughter: Four Visits to Zimbabwe*: "I remember as a child hearing farmers remark, with the cynical good nature that is the mark of a certain kind of bad conscience: 'One of these days they are all going to rise and drive us into the sea'" (5). In 1949 Lessing emigrated to Britain, thus escaping both her parental home and colonial culture.

Lessing wrote *Cattle* and *Antheap* half a century ago during her first years in London, then a drab, ruined city, with wasteland left from the bombing, and a citizenry inured to the scarcity of consumer goods, to electricity brown-outs and food rationing. On street corners loitered spivs, men of irregular work habits without any visible source of income, who dressed in American-style clothing and adopted accents inflected with American vowels. Lessing has written about this London in *In Pursuit of the English: A Documentary*[1] and in the first chapters of *The Four-Gated City*.[2] Against the backdrop of this crowded northern city, the spacious lands and skies of Southern Rhodesia must have gleamed bright in memory. Although the jerry-built city of Salisbury (now Harare) in *Cattle* and the open-face goldmine in *Antheap* are squalid settings, there are details that contradict the squalor. Salisbury is "a city of gardens" (12), though a hodge-podge of flimsy "villas" without a sewage system—at night the carts come along the "sanitary lanes" to empty the lavatory buckets.[3] It fails to live up to what the Founder—Cecil Rhodes—intended, but the citizens retain "a vision of that city we all dream of, that shapely city without stain or slum"—the City of the Imagination that was to play an important role in Lessing's subsequent work. A description of Cecil Rhodes Vista is luxurious technicolor: "The street ... was double-lined with trees, first jacaranda, fine green lace against the blue sky, and behind heavy dark masses of the cedrilatoona. All the way down the street were bursts of colour, a drape of purple bougainvil-

---

1 London: McGibbon and Kee, 1960; New York: Simon and Schuster, 1961.
2 Vol. 5 of *Children of Violence*.
3 *Under My Skin* 242.

laea, the sparse flowers of the hibiscus." Descriptions like this are bathed in the golden glow of the nostalgia that comes from the regret for a lost time as well as a lost place; it appears when the lost object is gone forever and the writer's worldview has shifted to a point where the unobtainable lost object has become exotic in the imagination. Lessing's description embodies what Anthony Chennells has called "the impulse to Eden," which in *Cattle* is "foiled as soon as the immigrant arrives in the colony" (27).

Writing Contexts/Reading Contexts

Various scholars familiar with Lessing's work have kindly suggested documents for the appendices for this edition. I wish to thank them all for the considerable time they spent preparing their suggestions. The contextual materials, however, are my choice, and as such are the result of this one reader's conception of both the short novels themselves and the documents in the appendices. I have selected those that seem to me the most useful, here defined as the most specific and the nearest to the time of writing and to the time in which the novels are set. Always mindful of the importance of context, I have tried to find contemporary documents using words and ideas occurring in the novels; this approach, I thought, would do away with the need for out-of-context generalized explanations. Ultimately, of course, my choice comes from the way I read not only these novels but also Lessing's entire body of work.

Appendix A contains excerpts from interviews in which Lessing answers questions on her writing, her relations with Africa, and her education. I also looked for details to flesh out the chronology of her life, an explanation of how her parents came to emigrate to Rhodesia, for example. I included her description of the eccentricity of British emigrants, the consequence of the enlarged sense of themselves fostered by the spaciousness of Africa because I think her observation has a larger application. Her reference to the large spaces of the western United States makes it clear she thinks this phenomenon is not confined to Africa. But it may have other causes besides wide-open spaces; it seems to have something to do with the act of emigration, now a growing concern when large populations leave their homelands for economic or political reasons. I chose the Bertelsen piece because it touches on an important current issue in literary studies. The interviewer presses Lessing on the implicit opposition between historical specificity and generalization—what Bertelsen perhaps sees as a conflict between constructionist and essentialist views of the human being. This is an opposition Lessing rejects, as does Anna Wulf, who practices holding in her mind simultaneously the images of both a drop of water and the turning earth. Another way of saying this might be that Lessing yearns for both the historical and the transcendental.

The book reviews I have selected for Appendix B come from both British and American sources. The four short novels set in Africa were included in *African Stories* and *Collected African Stories*.[1] I have chosen three reviews of *African Stories* from U.S. publications. J.D. Scott, an English novelist and critic, was based in Washington D.C. at the time of the review. Mary Ellman writes with an eye to her U.S. readers, establishing an extended comparison between the treatment of Africans and African Americans. Edward Hickman Brown, a native of South Africa, sees as Lessing's most important characteristic "the intrinsic truth of these tales."

The last, from *The Guardian Weekly*, reviews Lessing's *Collected African Stories* and Dan Jacobson's *Inklings*, another book of short stories with an African setting published in 1973. Gabriel Pearson compares these two collections in regard to both material and technique. Dealing with these two writers together prompts him to observe that "traditional realism seems in its deepest assumptions about human nature recalcitrantly European and constitutes precisely the literary equivalent of the settler and the suburban culture which at once occupies and refuses the land." Realism is both an expression of and a figure for European culture—and more, an agent of the oppression it describes. Just as Europeans expropriated the land and the labor of the indigenous inhabitants for their own ends, so the dominant European modes of fiction colonize black lives and black lands.

Appendix C includes stories by black African women writers that would have been a feature of the context in which Lessing wrote *Cattle* and *Antheap*. Neither Mabel Dove Danquah nor Efua Sutherland writes in the tradition of European realism. Danquah's "Anticipation" and Sutherland's "New Life at Kyerefaso," both about the relations of men and women in contemporary matrilineal Akan-Asante society, make little reference to the white presence in Ghana.

---

1   London: Michael Joseph, 1973.

Lastly, Appendix D contains historical documents. Sheer abundance made choice difficult. Material for the other appendices, in each case bounded by a narrower time frame, was sparser and more tightly linked to Lessing. She has said only so much about what she has written, only so much about the relationship of her life experience to *Cattle* and *Antheap*; only a limited number of reviews of them were published, only so much fiction produced by contemporary African writers. There are however (as with any enterprise involving empire and commerce) numerous official records and numerous histories written from those records. Almost everything I looked at seemed to have some point of contact with Lessing's African fiction. Moreover, I had a fuller agenda for this appendix. I wanted my choices to suggest a historical narrative, to reveal contemporary frames of mind, and to illustrate the complexity of race relations with the vast differences of personality and opinion contending beneath the surface of that simplifying phrase.

I should perhaps explain how I became aware of the existence of this vast mass of material. Although I was well acquainted with the material available for the other appendices, I knew virtually nothing about the history of Rhodesia. My university library has an excellent selection of books on the country's early years, the bibliographies of which pointed me to yet earlier books, Vindex's *Cecil Rhodes: His Political Life and Speeches, 1881-1900* (1900), for example. I also consulted the bibliographies of more recent works written by professional historians that contained details of original research in manuscripts, private papers, and government reports. Books published in the late fifties and early sixties were particularly useful for pointing me toward material from the recent past about which Lessing had written in *Cattle* and *Antheap*. The reports from various Commissions of Enquiry cited in Richard Gray's *The Two Nations: Aspects of the Development of Race Relations in the Rhodesias and Nyasaland*[1] have been particularly informative.

Ultimately I had to omit such gems as the Glen Grey Bill speech of Cecil Rhodes, then Prime Minister of the Cape Colony, on the "Native Question" (1894) and the lecture of H. Marshall Hole, Civil Commissioner and Magistrate, Salisbury, urging young adventurous Englishmen with a few hundred pounds to emigrate to Rhodesia (1900). Both eloquently portray frames of mind and pat-

---

1   Oxford: Oxford UP, 1960.

terns of thought then current in Southern Africa, but they are long on rhetoric and short on historical detail.

Reports of Commission Inquiries provide an interesting corollary to historical narrative. The "Report on Urban Conditions in Southern Rhodesia" (1943), reprinted in *African Studies* (vol. 4, 1945: 9-22), was easily available. The *Report on the Commission of Inquiry regarding the Social Welfare of the Coloured Community of Southern Rhodesia* (1946) came to me on microfilm that contained other shreds and patches of Rhodesian government papers from the forties and fifties, including a remarkable promotional booklet featuring smiling blacks engaged in various work and recreational activities. Though the print-out from that forty-five year old microfilm was so lined and shadowed it was unscannable, I could not pass up the information, which I have not seen anywhere else.

The voices of the commission members conducting these inquiries are earnest, self-confident, and not at all self-reflective. They grapple with enormous problems and in so doing reveal the unspoken premises for the principles—the ideologies—on which they make their recommendations. They take care to distinguish between the black population and the coloured (children of African mothers and white fathers as well as Indian and Chinese immigrants). They seem to be trying to jockey both groups into the British class system, much as Rhodes did in his Glen Grey speech, where he touts the blacks' willingness to work—an activity perhaps held in less esteem by the blacks and the British working-class than by their would-be masters.

Although both inquiries took testimony from black as well as white witnesses, none appears in either report. I am therefore including three letters by black miners that describe the privations of minework during the twenties. One absence I deeply regret. From Gray's *Two Nations* I discovered that the Standing Committee on Domestic Service of the Federation of the Women's Institutes of Rhodesia had written at least one report on the servant problem. I thought it might provide some excerpts that would add greatly to the reading context for *Cattle*, but I could not obtain a copy.

Clearly, reading these historical documents will not replicate— will not even approach—the historical commonality Bertelsen describes. The documents can be only a gesture towards the writing context of these two novels. Perhaps, though, they will stimulate a reading context that, more than receptive, will actively embrace the texts.

Metaphors and Metonymies

The structuralist linguist Roman Jakobson has pointed out that there are two fundamental ways of organizing discourse, by similarity (metaphor) and by contiguity (metonymy). Poetry leans toward metaphor, prose toward metonymy; further, "romanticism [not only romantic poetry] is linked with metaphor and realism with metonymy."[1] Narrative, moving forward by contiguity, is predominantly metonymic.

Jakobson holds that "a competition between these devices [metaphor and metonymy] is manifest in any symbolic process" (60). *Cattle* and *Antheap* each has a strong narrative line, to be expected in realist fiction. Time, place and event are identifiable, characters' motives explained, cause and effect securely connected. Each narrative unfolds in an "organic" way. However, in each of these novels an object of metonymic importance gradually accrues metaphoric resonance until it is a significant vehicle of meaning as well as of the narrative line. I am here reading Jakobson's "competition" as a cooperative act, although the idea of contest persists between the two questions readers ask of a text: *What happens? What does it mean?* Readers will rate the relative importance of these questions according to whether their symbolic processes are more inclined to metaphor or to metonymy.

A Home for the Highland Cattle

When World War II ended in 1945, there were some nine million displaced persons in refugee camps in Europe. Housing was an international concern. In London, 109,000 houses had been destroyed by bombs and V-rockets;[2] none had been built; new families were being established; babies postponed during the war years were now being born. Burdened by an economy undermined by war debts, Britain was still in the grip of wartime austerity. In the spring of 1949 I went abroad on my first school trip. Paris was a miracle. I was stunned by the absence of war damage—only later did I realize that the deep pocks on the walls of the house we stayed

---

1 "The metaphoric and the metonymic poles," *Modern Criticism and Theory*, ed. David Lodge (London: Longman, 1988), 60.
2 Angus Calder, *The People's War: Britain 1939-1945* (London: Jonathan Cape, 1969), 563.

in had been caused by machine gun fire—and the huge array of consumer goods, including cream pastries and chocolate in every boulangerie. Food rationing was still in force in Britain; for weeks I'd dreamed that I was trying to catch squadrons of flying éclairs with a butterfly net.

On my way to school one morning some months later, I saw my first political advertisement—a picture of a trowel full of cement and the caption *The Conservatives would let you build a house now.* Inured to propaganda by six years of official pronouncements I'd overheard grown-ups trying to decode, I couldn't credit such an optimistic vision of the future. With everything from butter to shoes still in short supply, I thought, how could they expect to fulfill such promises?

This is the situation from which Marina and Philip Giles have recently emigrated. They are not the only ones looking for housing. All the characters in *Cattle* are searching for homes. One might say that they are all displaced persons.

The residents of 138 Cecil John Rhodes Vista are a little community—a microcosm of Rhodesian society—riven by issues of race and class. The picture of the highland cattle focuses these issues. Marina, loathing the picture, sees it as an embodiment of a disagreeable past—indeed, associates it with Victorianism, its very Scottishness tying it to Queen Victoria herself, famously enamored of things Scottish. Mrs. Skinner, owner of the picture, associates it with her grandmother and with the Empire. The picture encapsulates the cluster of ideas—the ideology—that supports Mrs. Skinner's views on the proper relationship of whites and blacks.

Charlie, Marina's servant—a fixture of the dwelling Marina subrents from Mrs. Skinner—comes from a tribe for whom cattle, not lands, are the supreme marker of wealth and status—and more, the giving and receiving of cattle on marriage establishes important kinship ties, thus conveying social recognition to the bridegroom. With Marina's connivance, he presents the picture as *lobola*[1] to the father of his second wife. The old man accepts the picture but, mourning the passing of the glory days, launches into a sad, loving description of the "five fine cattle" he himself had painstakingly driven across country and presented to his own father-in-law as bride-price for Theresa's mother. Charlie seems to conflate the pic-

---

1 Bridewealth: payment by the groom to his father-in-law, traditionally in cattle.

ture's representation of cattle with the cattle themselves; his father-in-law, however, understands it as a figure for the loss of his whole culture.

Marina's hatred of the picture, Mrs. Skinner's fondness for it, Charlie's desire to possess it, his father-in-law's sorrow on being presented with it: all are tied in complex ways to issues of class and race.

Marina and Philip are identifiable as upper-middle class by their speech patterns, noted by Mrs. Black, who asks Marina if she has "swallowed a dictionary"; by Marina's clothing, her straw summer hat and her white gloves; and by Philip's professional status. Their given names have a certain upper-class resonance: *Marina*, never a common English name, recalls Princess Marina of Greece, Duchess of Kent, made popular by her stoic behavior in 1942 on the Duke's death in the course of his wartime duties as a Royal Air Force captain. At the time of writing, *Philip* was even more in the limelight as Prince Philip of Greece, now the Duke of Edinburgh, had married Princess Elizabeth (now Queen of the United Kingdom) in 1952. Both names thus have an elitist flavor unmistakable to their neighbors.

Other residents of 138 Cecil John Rhodes Vista, either prewar settlers of long standing, or born in Africa, are revealed as lower-class by their speech patterns—"I had to have the police to him" says Mrs. Skinner—and occupations: haberdasher's assistant or railway-engine driver, for example. The women argue over cups of borrowed sugar. All regard Marina and Philip as *Fabians*, whose efforts to do right by the "natives" will undermine the rightful position of the whites. The residents' place in the class system (which doesn't exist in Africa, of course, but the nuances of which the settlers certainly understand) has risen by the sheer fact of immigration. Purely by virtue of being white, they now have a whole new class below them—two classes, in fact, as the *Report of the Commission of Enquiry regarding the Social Welfare of the Coloured Community of Southern Rhodesia* shows, the coloured out-trumping the blacks in legal standing.

Although Marina despises Victorian attitudes, she manifests some characteristics of upper-class Victorian women. She is a "stern reformer," vigilant to do good. She is sure that acting alone she can make a difference. She treats Charlie well, to the surprise and dismay of the Gileses' neighbors: she pays him more than the going rate, buys him an iron bedstead because she cannot bear that her servant should sleep on a blanket on a cement floor, and presses him to marry Theresa when he impregnates the girl. Philip too is a would-be reformer, a soil expert who complains about the Africans' abuse of the land. Traditionally Africans depleted the soil by keeping too many cattle and migrating when the land would no longer support their herds. He has no patience with *lobola*: it encourages the preference for ten mangy over five thriving kine. The clear parallel between the "natives" and the British immigrants escapes him.

The Antheap

Lessing deploys the central metaphor of *Antheap* in even more complex ways. There are two antheaps, the literal (metonymic) antheap, the "high anthill" on which Dirk builds the shed where his books and Tommy's sculptures will be stored, and "the enormous [metaphoric] ant-working" of the Macintosh mine. Throughout the novel these two play off each other.

Tommy notices that the anthill on which the shed is built is "very much alive." It is working in the "substance of life." Living organism and regenerative force seem to be Lessing's primary associations with antheap. In *Pursuit of the English*, she describes sitting in her tiny room in London: "Under the roof it was like sitting on the top of an anthill, a tall sharp peak of baked earth that seems abandoned, but which sounds, when one puts one's ear to it, with a continuous vibrant humming" (90). In a review of Eugène Marais's *The Soul of the White Ant* Lessing elaborates this idea: "Marais's analogy of the termitary with the human body, an organism of which the queen ant is the soul, or breath, invisibly controlling workers, soldiers, the fungus gardens, the galleries, hard outer shell (skin, streams of blood, organs) is only a jumping-off point for inspired speculation. A termitary *is* an animal.... [Marais] offers a vision of nature as a whole, whose parts obey different time laws, move in affinities and linkages we could learn to see, parts making wholes on their own level...."[1] This transcendental vision based on the antheap recalls Chennells's observation that *Cattle* has an "impulse to Eden." This impulse surfaces again in *Antheap*, to be as quickly squelched. Macintosh has made his mine the cheapest possible way, without digging shafts or roofing tunnels, hiring "hun-

---

1   "Ant's Eye View: A Review of *The Soul of the White Ant*," *A Small Personal Voice* 146.

dreds of African labourers" who "shovel[ed] up the soil ... so that there was soon a deeper hollow, then a vast pit, then a gulf like an inverted mountain." Tommy recognizes this inversion; already having noticed that the men working far below are "ants and flies," he perceives the mine as "an enormous ant-working, as brightly tinted as a fresh ant-heap." This perception is followed by a feeling that "he had left a golden age of freedom behind." Lessing has identified artists as "traditional interpreters of dreams and nightmares,"[1] which role Tommy here fills. He makes a frieze, a satiric representation of the mine that Mr. Macintosh instantly recognizes. He "saw the great pit, the black little figures tumbling and sprawling over into the flames, and he saw himself, stick in hand, astride his two legs at the edge of the pit...." (254). Tommy has seen the mine as Hell and effectively communicated his vision to the responsible party.

In Tommy's representation, Mr. Macintosh is a figure for the entire imperial enterprise. A famous *Punch* cartoon depicts Cecil Rhodes standing just so. Lessing herself has made the connection between this posture and the Founder. In the second volume of her autobiography, she describes a gynecologist thus: "Then he stands square on his planted legs like Cecil Rhodes staring north at the continent of Africa from Cape Town...."[2]

The metonymic and the metaphoric antheaps work contrapuntally, each carrying an increasing symbolic weight as the narrative progresses. The mine becomes associated with money, expropriation, machinery, destruction, segregation, (forced) labor, age/the past; the anthill with knowledge, art, liberation, nature, cooperation, renewal, youth/the future.

Lessing and Others

An introduction is an envoy, a harbinger, a greeter. Ushering in the main event, it must resist closure, at the same time acknowledging the gap that lies between reader and text. The London Underground exhorts the unwary traveler, "Mind the gap!" In lieu of such exhortation, to bridge the gap I offer observations by Lessing and other commentators:

---

1 "The Small Personal Voice" 35.
2 *Walking in the Shade, ...1949 to 1962* (London and New York: Harper-Collins, 1997), 327.

From Lessing's review of Laurens van der Post's *The Lost World of the Kalahari*:[1]

"[T]he emotional impulse behind nearly all white writing [about Africa] ... is a nostalgia, a hunger, a reaching out for something lost ... an unappeasable hunger for what is out of reach. All white-African literature is the literature of exile: not from Europe, but from Africa."

From Lawrence Vambe's *From Rhodesia to Zimbabwe*:[2]

"[W]ith such a great rush of new settlers into the country immediately after the war, ... [t]here emerged a very vocal liberal element, which derived its inspiration from the Socialist movement in Britain. These people openly campaigned for a common front between the working-class Africans and Europeans in their struggle for economic justice. [One of]the leading exponents of this revolutionary school of thought was Mrs Doris Lessing, the well-known British novelist...."

From Jenny Taylor's "Introduction: Situating Reading":[3]

"[B]y the time *The Golden Notebook* came out[, Lessing's] reputation rested primarily on her status as a radical white Rhodesian exile and a committed realist writer. Her African writing offered both a satire of the crumbling Empire's expatriate delusions and of the 'sickness of dissolution' of Rhodesian white supremacy to a liberal English readership."

From Martin Green's "The Dream of Empire: *Memoirs of a Survivor*":[4]

"Lessing's protagonist [in *Memoirs of a Survivor*] speaks for all those who bore the 'white man's burden,' whether in the colonies or at home, including those who rebelled against it. We can hear in her voice the echo of T.S. Eliot's. We can hear the weariness of the responsible class. Above all, we can hear the end of empire."

---

1 *New Statesman* 56, November 15, 1958, 7.
2 London: Heinemann; Pittsburgh, PA: University of Pittsburgh Press, 1976, 161.
3 *Notebooks/Memoirs/Archives: Reading and Rereading Doris Lessing*, ed. Jenny Taylor (London: Routledge and Kegan Paul, 1982), 2.
4 Claire Sprague and Virginia Tiger, eds., *Critical Essays on Doris Lessing* (Boston: Hall, 1986), 37.

From Rebecca O'Rourke's "Doris Lessing: Exile and Exception":[1]
"The African short stories, particularly in her later prefaces, evidence an obvious link between Africa and her writing. But they are not the only point of engagement: the documentary accounts in *In Pursuit of the English* and *Going Home*[2] are one form it takes; the *Children of Violence* series and the black notebook in *The Golden Notebook*, another. Finally, in *Canopus in Argos: Archives*, colonisation is a subject writ large—the African experience becomes a mirror for the universe."

From Ellen Cronan Rose's "From Supermarket to Schoolroom: Doris Lessing in the United States":[3]
"Doris Lessing loves paradox and champions ambiguity. If I were asked to write her epigraph, I'd unhesitatingly choose a sentence first articulated by Charles Watkins in her *Briefing for a Descent into Hell* and repeated in numerous interviews by Lessing: 'It isn't either or at all, it's and, and, and, and, and.'"

From Gayle Greene's *Doris Lessing: The Poetics of Change*:[4]
"I'm intrigued by her play with endings, the ways she finds of resisting narrative closure and devising open, nonteleological forms that render processes of working through and point a way beyond teleology. I'm struck by images and metaphors that intimate the existence of another world glimmering just beyond this one, beyond our senses and capacities, a world attainable through wonder."

From Earl Ingersoll's *Doris Lessing: Conversations*:[5]
"Ingersoll: You don't seem to have had very much patience with us academics.
Lessing: I don't know. I seem always to be meeting academics and visiting with them and going to their universities and quarreling with them. What more do you want?"

---

1 *Notebooks/Memoirs/Archives*, 221.
2 London: Michael Joseph, 1957; New York: Ballantine, 1968.
3 *Nine Nations* 84.
4 Ann Arbor: University of Michigan Press, 1994, 33.
5 Earl G. Ingersoll, ed. Princeton: Princeton University Press, 1944; London (British title: *Putting the Questions Differently*) HarperCollins, 1996, 237.

From Lessing's chat-room discussion of *Mara and Dann*[1]
"[M]y private theory is that we, the human race, are story-tellers above all. We tell each other stories all the time, and at night we tell ourselves stories. Dreams are stories...."

---

1   bn.com Live: Chat Transcripts, January 20, 1999, 2.

Doris Lessing: A Brief Chronology

1919 Birth of Doris May Tayler in Kermanshah, Persia (now Iran) to British subjects Emily Maude Tayler, a nurse, and Alfred Cook Tayler, a bank clerk.

1921 Birth of Harry, Doris's brother.

1924 Taylers move to Southern Rhodesia (now Zimbabwe) to farm maize.

1926-32 Doris goes to Roman Catholic Convent School in Salisbury.

1932-33 Spends a year at the Girls' High School in Salisbury, the last of her formal schooling.

1934-36 Works as an au pair in Salisbury.

1937 Works as a telephone operator.

1939 Marries Frank Wisdom, a civil servant. Birth of son, John.

1941 Birth of daughter, Jean.

1942 Joins the Left Book Club, a quasi-Communist group.

1943 Divorces Frank Wisdom.

1945 Marries Gottfried Lessing, a refugee from the Nazis. Works as a typist.

1947 Birth of son, Peter.

1947-48 Works on first novel, *The Grass is Singing*. Publishes four short stories in *Trek*, a local journal.

1949 Divorces Gottfried Lessing; sails to London with Peter.

1950 Publishes *The Grass is Singing*.

1951 *This Was the Old Chief's Country* (short stories).

1952 *Martha Quest* (first volume of *Children of Violence*).

1953 *Five: Short Novels*. First play, *Before the Deluge*, produced in London.

1954 *A Proper Marriage* (second volume of *Children of Violence*). Somerset Maugham Award of the Society of Authors.

1956 *Retreat to Innocence*. Visits Africa; discovers she has been declared a "prohibited immigrant."

1957 *Going Home* (reportage of African trip); *The Habit of Loving* (short stories).

1958 *A Ripple From the Storm* (third volume *Children of Violence*). *Each His Own Wilderness* performed at the Royal Court Theatre, London.

1959 *Fourteen Poems*.

1960 *In Pursuit of the English. The Truth About Billy Newton* (play) produced in Salisbury, U.K.

1962	*The Golden Notebook. Play With a Tiger* produced in London.
1963	*A Man and Two Women* (short stories).
1964	*African Stories*. Begins studying Sufism.
1965	*Landlocked* (fourth volume of *Children of Violence*).
1966	Translation of *The Storm* (play by Alexander Ostrovsky), produced by National Theatre, London. Production of television plays *Please Do Not Disturb* and *Care and Protection*.
1967	*Particularly Cats. Between Men*, television play adaptation from short story.
1969	*The Four-Gated City* (final volume of *Children of Violence*). Tours United States: visits State University of New York, at Buffalo and Stony Brook, and University of California, Berkeley.
1971	*Briefing For a Descent into Hell*.
1972	*The Story of a Non-Marrying Man and Other Stories*.
1973	*The Summer Before the Dark. Complete African Stories*, 2 vols: *The Sun Between Their Feet* and *This Was the Old Chief's Country*.
1974	*The Memoirs of a Survivor. The Small Personal Voice* (collected essays). Second trip to the United States.
1976	Awarded French Prix Medici for Foreigners.
1978	*Complete British Stories*, 2 vols: *To Room Nineteen* and *The Temptation of Jack Orkney*.
1979	*Re: Colonised Planet 5, Shikasta* (first volume of *Canopus in Argos: Archives*).
1980	*The Marriages Between Zones Three, Four, and Five* (second volume of *Canopus*).
1981	*The Sirian Experiments* (third volume of *Canopus*).
1982	*The Making of the Representative for Planet 8* (fourth volume of Canopus). Receives the Shakespeare Prize of the West German Hamburger Stiftung and the Austrian State Prize for European Literature. Trips to Spain, Africa, and Japan.
1983	*Documents Relating to the Sentimental Agents in the Volyen Empire* (fifth volume of *Canopus*). *The Diary of a Good Neighbour* (published under the name *Jane Somers*).
1984	*If the Old Could ...* (published under the name *Jane Somers*). Third U.S. tour.
1985	*The Good Terrorist. Prisons We Choose to Live Inside* (The Massey Lectures, Canadian Broadcasting Corporation).

1986	Receives the W.H. Smith Literary Award and the Italian Mondello Prize.
1987	*The Wind Blows Away Our Words.*
1988	*The Fifth Child.* Receives the Italian Grizane Cavour Prize. Opera *The Making of the Representative for Planet 8* (libretto by Lessing, music by Philip Glass) premiers at Houston. Trip to Africa.
1989	Receives Honorary Doctorate of Letters from Princeton.
1992	*London Observed: Stories and Sketches* (published in U.S. as *The Real Thing: Stories and Sketches*). *African Laughter: Four Trips to Zimbabwe.*
1994	*Under My Skin: Volume One of My Autobiography, to 1949.*
1995	*Playing the Game* (a graphic novel with illustrations by Charlie Adlard). *Spies I Have Known and Other Stories.* Receives James Tait Black Prize, Los Angeles Times Book Prize, and Honorary Degree from Harvard.
1996	*Love, Again. The Pit.*
1997	*Walking in the Shade, Volume Two of My Autobiography, 1949 to 1962.* Opera *The Marriages Between Zones Three, Four, and Five* (libretto by Lessing, music by Philip Glass) premiers at Heidelberg.
1999	*Mara and Dann, an Adventure. Problems, Myths and Stories* (monograph). Appointment as a Companion of Honour, bestowed by HRH Queen Elizabeth II.
2000	*Ben, in the World. The Old Age of El Magnificato* (reissue of *Particularly Cats* with additional chapter).
2001	*The Sweetest Dream.*

A Note on the Text

The texts of *A Home for the Highland Cattle* and *The Antheap* are those included in *Five: Short Novels* (Penguin Books, in association with Michael Joseph, 1960). The spellings and punctuation therein have been retained.

A HOME FOR THE HIGHLAND CATTLE

These days, when people emigrate, it is not so much in search of sunshine, or food, or even servants. It is fairly safe to say that the family bound for Australia, or wherever it may be, has in its mind a vision of a nice house, or a flat, with maybe a bit of garden. I don't know how things were a hundred or fifty years ago. It seems, from books, that the colonizers and adventurers went sailing off to a new fine life, a new country, opportunities and so forth. Now all they want is a roof over their heads.

An interesting thing, this: how is it that otherwise reasonable people come to believe that this same roof, that practically vanishing commodity, is freely obtainable just by packing up and going to another country? After all, headlines like: World Housing Shortage, are common to the point of tedium; and there is not a brochure or pamphlet issued by immigration departments that does not say (though probably in small print, throwing it away, as it were) that it is undesirable to leave home, without first making sure of a place to live.

Marina Giles left England with her husband in just this frame of mind. They had been living where they could, sharing flats and baths and kitchens, for some years. If someone remarked enviously: 'They say that in Africa the sky is always blue,' she was likely to reply absentmindedly: 'Yes, and won't it be nice to have a proper house after all these years.'

They arrived in Southern Rhodesia, and there was a choice of an immigrants' camp, consisting of mud huts with a communal water supply, or a hotel; and they chose the hotel, being what are known as people of means. That is to say, they had a few hundred pounds, with which they had intended to buy a house as soon as they arrived. It was quite possible to buy a house, just as it is in England, provided one gives up all idea of buying a home one likes, and at a reasonable price. For years Marina had been inspecting houses. They fell into two groups, those she liked, and those she could afford. Now Marina was a romantic, she had not yet fallen into that passive state of mind which accepts (as nine-tenths of the population do) that one should find a corner to live, anywhere, and then arrange one's whole life around it, schooling for one's children, one's place of work, and so on. And since she refused to accept it, she had been living in extreme discomfort, exclaiming: 'Why should we spend all the capital we are ever likely to have, tying ourselves down to a place we detest!' Nothing could be more reasonable, on the face of it.

But she had not expected to cross an ocean, enter a new and

indubitably romantic-sounding country, and find herself in exactly the same position.

The city, seen from the air, is half-buried in trees. Sixty years ago, this was all bare veld; and even now it appears not as if the veld encloses an area of buildings and streets, but rather as if the houses have forced themselves up, under and among the trees. Flying low over it, one sees greenness, growth, then the white flash of a high building, the fragment of a street that has no beginning nor end, for it emerges from trees, and is at once reabsorbed by them. And yet it is a large town, spreading wide and scattered, for here there is no problem of space: pressure scatters people outwards, it does not force them perpendicularly. Driving through it from suburb to suburb, is perhaps fifteen miles—some of the important cities of the world are not much less; but if one asks a person who lives there what the population is, he will say ten thousand, which is very little. Why do so small a number of people need so large a space? The inhabitant will probably shrug, for he has never wondered. The truth is that there are not ten thousand, but more likely 150,000, but the others are black, which means that they are not considered. The blacks do not so much live here, as squeeze themselves in as they can—all this is very confusing for the newcomer, and it takes quite a time to adjust oneself.

Perhaps every city has one particular thing by which it is known, something which sums it up, both for the people who live in it, and those who have never known it, save in books or legend. Three hundred miles south, for instance, old Lobengula's kraal[1] had the Big Tree. Under its branches sat the betrayed, sorrowful, magnificent King in his rolls of black fat and beads and gauds, watching his doom approach in the white people's advance from the south, and dispensing life and death according to known and honoured customs. That was only sixty years ago....

This town has The Kopje.[2] When the Pioneers were sent north, they were told to trek on till they reached a large and noble mountain they could not possibly mistake; and there they must stop and build their city. Twenty miles too soon, due to some confusion of mind, or perhaps to understandable exhaustion, they stopped near a small and less shapely hill. This has rankled ever since. Each year, when the ceremonies are held to honour those pioneers, and the

---

1   A village settlement round a cattle enclosure.
2   A kopje: a hill with large granite boulders at the top.

vision of Rhodes who sent them forth, the thought creeps in that this is not really what the Founder intended....[1] Standing there, at the foot of that kopje, the speechmakers say: Sixty years, look what we have accomplished in sixty years. And in the minds of the listeners springs a vision of that city we all dream of, that planned and shapely city without stain or slum—the city that could in fact have been created in those sixty years.

The town spread from the foot of this hill. Around it are the slums, the narrow and crooked streets where the coloured people eke out their short swarming lives among decaying brick and tin. Five minutes walk to one side, and the street peters out in long, soiled grass, above which a power chimney pours black smoke, and where an old petrol tin lies in a gulley, so that a diving hawk swerves away and up, squawking, scared out of his nature by a flash of sunlight. Ten minutes the other way is the business centre, the dazzling white blocks of concrete, modern buildings like modern buildings the world over. Here are the imported clothes, the glass windows full of cars from America, the neon lights, the counters full of pamphlets advertising flights Home—wherever one's home might be. A few blocks further on, and the business part of the town is left behind. This was once the smart area. People who have grown with the city will drive through here on a Sunday afternoon, and, looking at the bungalows raised on their foundations and ornamented with iron scrollwork will say: In 1910 there was nothing beyond this house but bare veld.

Now, however, there are more houses, small and ugly houses, until all at once we are in the thirties, with tall houses eight to a block, like very big soldiers standing to attention in a small space. The verandas have gone. Tiny balconies project like eyelids, the roofs are like bowler hats, rimless. Exposed to the blistering sun, these houses crowd together without invitation to shade or coolness, for they were not planned for this climate, and until the trees grow, and the creepers spread, they are extremely uncomfortable. (Though, of course, very smart.) Beyond these? The veld again, wastes of grass clotted with the dung of humans and animals, a vlei[2] that is crossed and criss-crossed by innumerable footpaths where the natives walk in the afternoons from suburb to suburb, stopping to snatch a mouthful of water in

---

1   All ellipses in *Cattle* and *Antheap* are Lessing's.
2   A valley.

cupped palms from potholes filmed with irridescent oil, for safety against mosquitoes.

Now, this is something really quite different. Where the houses, only twenty minutes walk away, stood eight to a block, now there are twenty tiny, flimsy little houses, and the men who planned them had in mind the cheap houses along the ribbon roads of England. Small patches of roofed cement, with room, perhaps, for a couple of chairs, call themselves verandas. There is a hall a couple of yards square—for otherwise where should one hang one's hat? Each little house is divided into rooms so small that there is no space to move from one wall to the other without circling a table or stumbling over a chair. And white walls, glaring white walls, so that one's eyes turn in relief to the trees.

The trees—these houses are intolerable unless foliage softens and hides them. Any new owner, moving in, says wistfully: It won't be so bad when the shrubs grow up. And they grow very quickly. It is an extraordinary thing that this town, which must be one of the most graceless and inconvenient in existence, considered simply as an association of streets and buildings, is so beautiful that no one fails to fall in love with it at first sight. Every street is lined and double-lined with trees, every house screened with brilliant growth. It is a city of gardens.

Marina was at first enchanted. Then her mood changed. For the only houses they could afford were in those mass-produced suburbs, that were spreading like measles as fast as materials could be imported to build them. She said to Philip: 'In England, we did not buy a house because we did not want to live in a suburb. We uproot ourselves, come to a reputedly exotic and wild country, and the only place we can afford to live is another suburb. I'd rather be dead.'

Philip listened. He was not as upset as she was. They were rather different. Marina was that liberally-minded person produced so plentifully in England during the thirties, while Philip was a scientist, and put his faith in techniques, rather than in the inherent decency of human beings. He was, it is true, in his own way an idealist, for he had come to this continent in a mood of fine optimism. England, it seemed to him, did not offer opportunities to young men equipped, as he was, with enthusiasm and so much training. Things would be different overseas. All that was necessary was a go-ahead Government prepared to vote sufficient money to Science—this was just common sense. (Clearly, a new country was likely to have more common sense than an old one.) He was prepared to make gardens flourish where deserts had been. Africa appeared to him eminently suitable for this treatment; and the more he saw of it, those first few weeks, the more enthusiastic he became.

But he soon came to understand that in the evenings, when he propounded these ideas to Marina, her mind was elsewhere. It seemed to him bad luck that they should be in this hotel, which was uncomfortable, with bad food, and packed by fellow immigrants all desperately searching for that legendary roof. But a house would turn up sooner or later—he had been convinced of this for years. He would not have objected to buying one of those suburban houses. He did not like them, certainly, but he knew quite well that it was not the house, as such, that Marina revolted against. Ah, this feeling we all have about the suburbs! How we dislike the thought of being just like the fellow next door! Bad luck, when the whole world rapidly fills with suburbs, for what is a British Colony but a sort of highly-flavoured suburb to England itself? Somewhere in the back of Marina's mind has been a vision of herself and Philip living in a group of amiable people, pleasantly interested in the arts, who read the *New Statesman* week by week, and held that discreditable phenomena like the colour bar, and the black-white struggle could be solved by sufficient goodwill ... a delightful picture.

Perhaps they could buy a house through one of the Schemes for Immigrants? He would return from this Housing Board or that, and say in a worried voice: 'There isn't a hope unless one has three children.' At this, Marina was likely to become depressed; for she still held the old-fashioned view that before one has children, one should have a house to put them in.

'It's all very well for you,' said Marina. 'As far as I can see, you'll be spending half your time gallivanting in your lorry from one end of the country to the other, visiting native reserves and having a lovely time. I don't mind, but I have to make some sort of life for myself while you do it.' Philip looked rather guilty; for in fact he was away three or four days a week, on trips with fellow experts, and Marina would be very often left alone.

'Perhaps we could find somewhere temporary, while we wait for a house to turn up?' he suggested.

This offered itself quite soon. Philip heard from a man he met casually that there was a flat available for three months, but he wouldn't swear to it, because it was only an overheard remark at a sundowner party—Philip followed the trail, clinched the deal and returned to Marina. 'It's only for three months,' he comforted her.

138 Cecil John Rhodes Vista was in that part of the town built before the sudden expansion in the thirties. These were all old houses, unfashionable, built to no imported recipe, but according to the whims of the first owners. On one side of 138 was a house whose roof curved down, Chinese fashion, built on a platform for protection against ants, with wooden steps. Its walls were of wood, and it was possible to hear feet tramping over the wooden floors even in the street outside. The other neighbour was a house whose walls were invisible under a mass of golden shower—thick yellow clusters, like smoky honey, dripped from roof to ground. The houses opposite were hidden by massed shrubs.

The sidewalks were of dusty grass, scattered with faggots of dogs' dirt, so that one had to walk carefully. Outside the gate was a great clump of bamboo reaching high into the sky, and all the year round weaver-birds' nests, like woven grass cricket balls, dangled there bouncing and swaying in the wind. Near it reached the angled brown sticks of the frangipani, breaking into white and creamy pink, as if a young coloured girl held armfuls of blossom. The street itself was double-lined with trees, first jacaranda, fine green lace against the blue sky, and behind heavy dark masses of the cedrilatoona. All the way down the street were bursts of colour, a drape of purple bougainvillaea, the sparse scarlet flowers of the hibiscus. It was very beautiful, very peaceful.

Once inside the unkempt hedge, 138 was exposed as a shallow brick building, tin-roofed, like an elongated barn, that occupied the centre of two building stands, leaving plenty of space for front and back yards. It had a history. Some twenty years back, some enterprising businessman had built the place, ignoring every known rule of hygiene, in the interests of economy. By the time the local authorities had come to notice its unfitness to exist, the roof was on. There followed a series of court cases. An exhausted judge had finally remarked that there was a housing shortage; and on this basis the place was allowed to remain.

It was really eight semi-detached houses, stuck together in such a way that standing before the front door of any one, it was possible to see clear through the two rooms which composed each, to the back yard, where washing flapped over the woodpile. A veranda enclosed the front of the building: eight short flights of steps, eight front doors, eight windows—but these windows illuminated the front rooms only. The back room opened into a porch that was screened in by dull green mosquito gauze; and in this way the architect had achieved the really remarkable feat of producing, in a country continually drenched by sunlight, rooms in which it was necessary to have the lights burning all day.

The back yard, a space of bare dust enclosed by parallel hibiscus hedges, was a triumph of individualism over communal living. Eight separate wood piles, eight clothes-lines, eight short paths edged with brick leading to the eight lavatories that were built side by side like segments of chocolate, behind an enclosing tin screen: the locks (and therefore the keys) were identical, for the sake of cheapness, a system which guaranteed strife among the inhabitants. On either side of the lavatories were two rooms, built as a unit. In these four rooms lived eight native servants. At least, officially there were eight, in practice far more.

When Marina, a woman who took her responsibilities seriously, as has been indicated, looked inside the room which her servant shared with the servant from next door, she exclaimed helplessly: 'Dear me, how awful!' The room was very small. The brick walls were unplastered, the tin of the roof bare, focusing the sun's intensity inwards all day, so that even while she stood on the threshold, she began to feel a little faint, because of the enclosed heat. The floor was cement, and the blankets that served as beds lay directly on it. No cupboards or shelves: these were substituted by a string stretching from corner to corner. Two small, high windows, whose glass was cracked and pasted with paper. On the walls were pictures of the English royal family, torn out of illustrated magazines, and of various female film stars, mostly unclothed.

'Dear me,' said Marina again, vaguely. She was feeling very guilty, because of this squalor. She came out of the room with relief, wiping the sweat from her face, and looked around the yard. Seen from the back, 138 Cecil John Rhodes Vista was undeniably picturesque. The yard, enclosed by low, scarlet-flowering hibiscus hedges, was of dull red earth; the piles of grey wood were each surrounded by a patch of scattered chips, yellow, orange, white. The colourful washing lines swung and danced. The servants, in their crisp white, leaned on their axes, or gossiped. There was a little black nurse-girl seated on one of the logs, under a big tree, with a white child in her arms. A delightful scene; it would have done as it was for the opening number of a musical comedy. Marina turned her back on it; and with her stern reformer's eye looked again at the end of the yard. In the spaces between the lavatories and the servants' rooms stood eight rubbish cans, each covered by its cloud of flies, and exuding a stale, sour smell. She walked through them into the sanitary lane. Now, if one drives down the streets of such a city, one sees the trees, the gardens, the flowering hedges: the streets form neat squares. Squares (one might suppose) filled with blossoms and greenness, in which the houses are charmingly arranged. But each block is divided down the middle by a sanitary lane, a dust lane, which is lined by rubbish cans, and in this the servants have their social life. Here they go for a quick smoke, in the middle of the day's work; here they meet their friends, or flirt with the women who sell vegetables. It is as if, between each of the streets of the white man's city, there is a hidden street, ignored, forgotten. Marina, emerging into it, found it swarming with gossiping and laughing natives. They froze, gave her a long suspicious stare, and all at once seemed to vanish, escaping into their respective back yards. In a moment she was alone.

She walked slowly back across the yard to her back door, picking her way among the soft litter from the wood piles, ducking her head under the flapping clothes. She was watched, cautiously, by the servants, who were suspicious of this sudden curiosity about their way of life—experience had taught them to be suspicious. She was watched, also, by several of the women, through their kitchen windows. They saw a small Englishwoman, with a neat and composed body, pretty fair hair, and a pink and white face under a large straw hat, which she balanced in position with a hand clothed in a white glove. She moved delicately and with obvious distaste through the dust, as if at any moment she might take wings and fly away altogether.

When she reached her back steps, she stopped and called: 'Charlie! Come here a moment, please.' It was a high voice, a little querulous. When they heard the accents of that voice, saw the white glove, and noted that *please*, the watching women found all their worst fears confirmed.

A young African emerged from the sanitary lane where he had been gossiping (until interrupted by Marina's appearance) with some passing friends. He ran to his new mistress. He wore white shorts, a scarlet American-style shirt, tartan socks which were secured by mauve suspenders, and white tennis shoes. He stopped before her with a polite smile, which almost at once spread into a grin of pure friendliness. He was an amiable and cheerful young man by temperament. This was Marina's first morning in her new home, and she was already conscious of the disproportion between her strong pity for her servant, and that inveterately cheerful face.

She did not, of course, speak any native language, but Charlie spoke English.

'Charlie, how long have you been working here?'

'Two years, madam.'

'Where do you come from?'

'Madam?'

'Where is your home?'

'Nyasaland.'

'Oh.' For this was hundreds of miles north.

'Do you go home to visit your family?'

'Perhaps this year, madam.'

'I see. Do you like it here?'

'Madam?' A pause; and he involuntarily glanced back over the rubbish cans at the sanitary lane. He hoped that his friends, who worked on the other side of the town, and whom he did not often see, would not get tired of waiting for him. He hoped, too, that this new mistress (whose politeness to him he did not trust) was not going to choose this moment to order him to clean the silver or do the washing. He continued to grin, but his face was a little anxious, and his eyes rolled continually backwards at the sanitary lane.

'I hope you will be happy working for me,' said Marina.

'Oh, yes, madam,' he said at once, disappointedly; for clearly she was going to tell him to work.

'If there is anything you want, you must ask me. I am new to the country, and I may make mistakes.'

He hesitated, handling the words in his mind. But they were difficult, and he let them slip. He did not think in terms of countries, of continents. He knew the white man's town—this town. He knew the veld. He knew the village from which he came. He knew, from his educated friends, that there was 'a big water' across which the white men came in ships: he had seen pictures of ships in old magazines, but this 'big water' was confused in his mind with the great lake in his own country. He understood that these white people came from places called England, Germany, Europe, but these were names to him. Once, a friend of his who had been three years to a mission school, had said that Africa was one of several continents, and had shown him a tattered sheet of paper—one half of the map of the world—saying: Here is Africa, here is England, here is India. He pointed out Nyasaland, a tiny strip of country, and Charlie felt confused and diminished, for Nyasaland was what he knew, and it seemed to him so vast. Now, when Marina used the phrase 'this country' Charlie saw, for a moment, this flat piece of paper, tinted pink and green and blue—the world. But from the sanitary lane came shouts of laughter—again he glanced anxiously over his shoulder; and Marina was conscious of a feeling remarkably like irritation. 'Well, you may go,' she said formally; and saw his smile flash white right across his face. He turned, and ran back across the yard like an athlete, clearing the woodpile, then the rubbish cans, in a series of great bounds, and vanished behind the lavatories. Marina went inside her 'flat' with what was, had she known it, an angry frown. 'Disgraceful,' she muttered, including in this condemnation the bare room in which this man was expected to fit his life, the dirty sanitary lane bordered with stinking rubbish cans, and also his unreasonable cheerfulness.

Inside, she forgot him in her own discomfort. It was a truly shocking place. The two small rooms were so made that the interleading door was in the centre of the wall. They were more like passages than rooms. She switched on the light in what would be the bedroom, and put her hands to her cheek, for it stung where the sun had caught her unaccustomed skin through the chinks of the straw of her hat. The furniture was really beyond description! Two iron bedsteads, on either side of the door, a vast chocolate-brown wardrobe, whose door would not properly shut, one dingy straw mat that slid this way and that over the slippery boards as one walked on it. And the front room! If possible, it was even worse. An enormous cretonne-covered sofa, like a solidified flower bed, a hard and shiny table stuck in the middle of the floor, so that one must walk carefully around it, and four straight, hard chairs, ranged like soldiers against the wall. And the pictures—she did not know such pictures still existed. There was a desert scene, done in coloured cloth, behind glass; a motto in woven straw, also framed in glass, saying: '*Welcome all who come in here, Good luck to you and all good cheer.*'

There was also a very large picture of highland cattle. Half a dozen of these shaggy and ferocious creatures glared down at her from where they stood knee-deep in sunset-tinted pools. One might imagine that pictures of highland cattle no longer existed outside of Victorian novels, or remote suburban boardinghouses—but no, here they were. Really, why bother to emigrate?

She almost marched over and wrenched that picture from the wall. A curious inhibition prevented her. It was, though she did not know it, the spirit of the building. Some time later she heard Mrs Black, who had been living for years in the next flat with her husband and three children, remark grimly: 'My front door handle has been stuck for weeks, but I'm not going to mend it. If I start doing the place up, it means I'm here for ever.' Marina recognized her own feeling when she heard these words. It accounted for the fact that while the families here were all respectable, in the sense that they owned cars, and could expect a regular monthly income, if one looked through the neglected hedge it was impossible not to conclude that every person in the building was born sloven or slut. No one really lived here. They might have been here for years, without prospect of anything better, but they did not live here.

There was one exception, Mrs Pond, who painted her walls and mended what broke. It was felt she let everyone else down. In front of *her* steps a narrow path edged with brick led to her segment of yard, which was perhaps two feet across, in which lilies and roses were held upright by trellis work, like a tall, green sandwich standing at random in the dusty yard.

Marina thought: Well what's the point? I'm not going to *live* here. The picture could stay. Similarly, she decided there was no sense in unpacking her nice curtains or her books. And the furniture might remain as it was, for it was too awful to waste effort on it. Her thoughts returned to the servants' rooms at the back: it was a disgrace. The whole system was disgraceful....

At this point, Mrs Pond knocked perfunctorily and entered. She was a short, solid woman, tied in at the waist, like a tight sausage, by the string of her apron. She had hard red cheeks, a full, hard bosom, and energetic red hands. Her eyes were small and inquisitive. Her face was ill-tempered, perhaps because she could not help knowing she was disliked. She was used to the disapproving eyes of her fellow tenants, watching her attend to her strip of 'garden'; or while she swept the narrow strip across the back yard that was her path from the back door to her lavatory. There she stood, every morning, among the washing and the woodpiles, wearing a pink satin dressing-gown trimmed with swansdown, among the clouds of dust stirred up by her yard broom, returning defiant glances for the disapproving ones; and later she would say: "Two rooms is quite enough for a woman by herself. I'm quite satisfied."

She had no right to be satisfied, or at any rate, to say so....

But for a woman contented with her lot, there was a look in those sharp eyes which could too easily be diagnosed as envy; and when she said, much too sweetly: 'You are an old friend of Mrs Skinner, maybe?' Marina recognized, with the exhaustion that comes to everyone who has lived too long in overfull buildings, the existence of conspiracy. 'I have never met Mrs Skinner,' she said briefly. 'She said she was coming here this morning, to make arrangements.'

Now, arrangements had been made already, with Philip; and Marina knew Mrs Skinner was coming to inspect herself; and this thought irritated her.

'She is a nice lady,' said Mrs Pond. 'She's my friend. We two have been living here longer than anyone else.' Her voice was sour. Marina followed the direction of her eyes, and saw a large white door set into the wall. A built-in cupboard, in fact. She had already noted that cupboard as the only sensible amenity the 'flat' possessed.

'That's a nice cupboard,' said Mrs Pond.

'Have all the flats got built-in cupboards?'

'Oh, no. Mrs Skinner had this put in special last year. She paid for it. Not the landlord. You don't catch the landlord paying for anything.'

'I see,' said Marina.

'Mrs Skinner promised me this flat,' said Mrs Pond.

Martha made no reply. She looked at her wrist-watch. It was a beautiful gesture; she even felt a little guilty because of the pointedness of it; but Mrs Pond promptly said: 'It's eleven o'clock. The clock just struck.'

'I must finish the unpacking,' said Marina.

Mrs Pond seated herself on the flowery sofa, and remarked: 'There's always plenty to do when you move in. That cupboard will save you plenty of space. Mrs Skinner kept her linen in it. I was going to put all my clothes in. You're Civil Service, so I hear?'

'Yes,' said Marina. She could not account for the grudging tone of that last, apparently irrelevant question. She did not know that in this country the privileged class was the Civil Service, or considered to be. No aristocracy, no class distinctions—but alas, one must have something to hate, and the Civil Service does as well as anything. She added: 'My husband chose this country rather than the Gold Coast,[1] because it seems the climate is better, even though the pay is bad.'

This remark was received with the same sceptical smile that she would have earned in England had she been tactless enough to say to her charwoman: Death duties spell the doom of the middle classes.

'You have to be in the Service to get what's going,' said Mrs Pond, with what she imagined to be a friendly smile. 'The Service gets all the plums.' And she glanced at the cupboard.

---

1 Now Ghana.

'I think,' said Marina icily, 'that you are under some misapprehension. My husband happened to hear of this flat by chance.'

'There were plenty of people waiting for this flat,' said Mrs Pond reprovingly. 'The lady next door, Mrs Black, would have been glad of it. And she's got three children, too. You have no children, perhaps?'

'Mrs Pond, I have no idea at all why Mrs Skinner gave us this flat when she had promised it to Mrs Black....'

'Oh, no, she had promised it to me. It was a faithful promise.'

At this moment another lady entered the room without knocking. She was an ample, middle-aged person, in tight corsets, with rigidly-waved hair, and a sharp, efficient face that was now scarlet from heat. She said peremptorily: 'Excuse me for coming in without knocking, but I can't get used to a stranger being here when I've lived here so long.' Suddenly she saw Mrs Pond, and at once stiffened into aggression. 'I see you have already made friends with Mrs Pond,' she said, giving that lady a glare.

Mrs Pond was standing, hands on hips, in the traditional attitude of combat; but she squeezed a smile on to her face and said: 'I'm making acquaintance.'

'Well,' said Mrs Skinner, dismissing her, 'I'm going to discuss business with my tenant.'

Mrs Pond hesitated. Mrs Skinner gave her a long, quelling stare. Mrs Pond slowly deflated, and went to the door. From the veranda floated back the words: 'When people make promises, they should keep them, that's what I say, instead of giving it to people new to the country, and civil servants....'

Mrs Skinner waited until the loud and angry voice faded, and then said briskly: 'If you take my advice, you'll have nothing to do with Mrs Pond, she's more trouble than she's worth.'

Marina now understood that she owed this flat to the fact that this highly-coloured lady decided to let it to a stranger simply in order to spite all her friends in the building who hoped to inherit that beautiful cupboard, if only for three months. Mrs Skinner was looking suspiciously around her; she said at last: 'I wouldn't like to think my things weren't looked after.'

'Naturally not,' said Marina politely.

'When I spoke to your husband we were rather in a hurry, I hope you will make yourself comfortable, but I don't want to have anything altered.'

Marina maintained a polite silence.

Mrs Skinner marched to the inbuilt cupboard, opened it, and

found it empty. 'I paid a lot of money to have this fitted,' she said in an aggrieved voice.

'We only came in yesterday,' said Marina. 'I haven't unpacked yet.'

'You'll find it very useful,' said Mrs Skinner. 'I paid for it myself. Some people would have made allowances in the rent.'

'I think the rent is quite high enough,' said Marina, joining battle at last.

Clearly, this note of defiance was what Mrs Skinner had been waiting for. She made use of the familiar weapon: 'There are plenty of people who would have been glad of it, I can tell you.'

'So I gather.'

'I could let it tomorrow.'

'But,' said Marina, in that high formal voice, 'you have in fact let it to us, and the lease has been signed, so there is no more to be said, is there?'

Mrs Skinner hesitated, and finally contented herself by repeating: 'I hope my furniture will be looked after. I said in the lease nothing must be altered.'

Suddenly Marina found herself saying: 'Well, I shall of course move the furniture to suit myself, and hang my own pictures.'

'This flat is let furnished, and I'm very fond of my pictures.'

'But you will be away, won't you?' This, a sufficiently crude way of saying: 'But it is we who will be looking at the pictures, and not you,' misfired completely, for Mrs Skinner merely said: 'Yes, I like my pictures, and I don't like to think of them being packed.'

Marina looked at the highland cattle and, though not half an hour before she had decided to leave it, said now: 'I should like to take that one down.'

Mrs Skinner clasped her hands together before her, in a pose of simple devotion, compressed her lips, and stood staring mournfully up at the picture. 'That picture means a lot to me. It used to hang in the parlour when I was a child, back Home. It was my granny's picture first. When I married Mr Skinner, my mother packed it and sent it especial over the sea, knowing how I was fond of it. It's moved with me everywhere I've been. I wouldn't like to think of it being treated bad, I wouldn't really.'

'Oh, very well,' said Marina, suddenly exhausted. What, after all, did it matter?

Mrs Skinner gave her a doubtful look: was it possible she had won her point so easily? 'You must keep an eye on Charlie,' she

went on.'The number of times I've told him he'd poke his broom-
handle through that picture....'

Hope flared in Marina.There was an extraordinary amount of
glass. It seemed that the entire wall was surfaced by angry, shaggy
cattle. Accidents did happen....

'You must keep an eye on Charlie, anyway. He never does a
stroke more than he has to. He's bred bone lazy.You'd better keep
an eye on the food too. He steals. I had to have the police to him
only last month, when I lost my garnet brooch. Of course he swore
he hadn't taken it, but I've never laid my hands on it since. My husband gave him a good hiding, but Master Charlie came up smiling, as usual.'

Marina, revolted by this tale, raised her eyebrows disapprovingly. 'Indeed?' she said, in her coolest voice.

Mrs Skinner looked at her, as if to say: 'What are you making
that funny face for?' She remarked: 'They're all born thieves and
liars.You shouldn't trust them further than you can kick them. I'm
warning you. Of course, you're new here. Only last week a friend
was saying, I'm surprised at you letting to people just from England, they always spoil the servants, with their ideas, and I said:
'Oh, Mr Giles is a sensible man, I trust him.' This last was said
pointedly.

'I don't think,' remarked Marina coldly,'that you would be well-
advised to trust my husband to give people "hidings."' She delicately isolated this word.'I rather feel, in similar circumstances, that
even if he did, he would first make sure whether the man had, in
fact, stolen the brooch.'

Mrs Skinner disentangled this sentence and in due course gave
Marina a distrustful stare. 'Well,' she said, 'it's too late now, and
everyone has his way, but of course this is my furniture, and if it is
stolen or damaged, you are responsible.'

'That, I should have thought, went without saying,' said Marina.

They shook hands, with formality, and Mrs Skinner went out.
She returned from the veranda twice, first to say that Marina must
not forget to fumigate the native quarters once a month if she did-
n't want livestock brought into her own flat ... ('Not that I care if
they want to live with lice, dirty creatures, but you have to protect
yourself ...'); and the second time to say that after you've lived in a
place for years, it was hard to leave it, even for a holiday, and she
was really regretting the day she let it at all. She gave Marina a final
accusing and sorrowful look, as if the flat had been stolen from her,
and this time finally departed. Marina was left, in a mood of defi-

ant anger, looking at the highland cattle picture, which had assumed, during this exchange, the look of a battleground. 'Really,' she said aloud to herself, 'Really! One might have thought that one would be entitled to pack away a picture, if one rents a place....'

Two days later she got a note from Mrs Skinner, saying that she hoped Marina would be happy in the flat, she must remember to keep an eye on Mrs Pond, who was a real trouble-maker, and she must remember to look after the picture—Mrs Skinner positively could not sleep for worrying about it.

Since Marina had decided she was not living here, there was comparatively little unpacking to be done. Things were stored. She had more than ever the appearance of a migrating bird who dislikes the twig it has chosen to alight on, but is rather too exhausted to move to another.

But she did read the advertisement columns every day, which were exactly like those in the papers back home. The *accommodation wanted* occupied a full column, while the *accommodation offered* usually did not figure at all. When houses were advertised they usually cost between five and twelve thousand—Marina saw some of them. They were very beautiful; if one had five thousand pounds, what a happy life one might lead—but the same might be said of any country. She also paid another visit to one of the new suburbs, and returned shuddering. 'What!' she exclaimed to Philip. 'Have we emigrated in order that I may spend the rest of life gossiping and taking tea with women like Mrs Black and Mrs Skinner?'

'Perhaps they aren't all like that,' he suggested absentmindedly. For he was quite absorbed in his work. This country was fascinating! He was spending his days in his Government lorry, rushing over hundreds of miles of veld, visiting native reserves and settlements. Never had soil been so misused! Thousands of acres of it, denuded, robbed, fit for nothing, cattle and human beings crowded together—the solution, of course, was perfectly obvious. All one had to do was—and if the Government had any sense—

Marina understood that Philip was acclimatized. One does not speak of the 'Government' with that particular mixture of affection and exasperation unless one feels at home. But she was not at all at home. She found herself playing with the idea of buying one of those revolting little houses. After all, one has to live somewhere....

Almost every morning, in 138, one might see a group of women standing outside one or other of the flats, debating how to rearrange the rooms. The plan of the building being so eccentric, no solution could possibly be satisfactory, and as soon as everything had been moved around, it was bound to be just as uncomfortable as before. 'If I move the bookcase behind the door, then perhaps ...' Or: 'It might be better if I put it into the bathroom....'

The problem was: Where should one eat? If the dining-table was in the front room, then the servant had to come through the bedroom with the food. On the other hand, if one had the front room as bedroom, then visitors had to walk through it to the living-room. Marina kept Mrs Skinner's arrangement. On the back porch, which was the width of a passage, stood a collapsible card-table. When it was set up, Philip sat crouched under the window that opened inwards over his head, while Marina shrank sideways into the bathroom door as Charlie came past with the vegetables. To serve food, Charlie put on a starched white coat, red fez, and white cotton gloves. In between courses he stood just behind them, in the kitchen door, while Marina and Philip ate in state, if discomfort.

Marina found herself becoming increasingly sensitive to what she imagined was his attitude of tolerance. It seemed ridiculous that the ritual of soup, fish and sweet, silver and glass and fish-knives, should continue under such circumstances. She began to wonder how it all appeared to this young man, who, as soon as their meal was finished, took an enormous pot of mealie porridge off the stove and retired with it to his room, where he shared it (eating with his fingers and squatting on the floor) with the servant from next door, and any of his friends or relatives who happened to be out of work at the time.

That no such thoughts entered the heads of the other inhabitants was clear; and Marina could understand how necessary it was to banish them as quickly as possible. On the other hand ...

There was something absurd in a system which allowed a healthy young man to spend his life in her kitchen, so that she might do nothing. Besides, it was more trouble than it was worth. Before she and Philip rose, Charlie walked around the outside of the building, and into the front room, and cleaned it. But as the wall was thin and he energetic, they were awakened every morning by the violent banging of his broom and the scraping of furniture.

On the other hand, if it were left till they woke up, where should Marina sit while he cleaned it? On the bed, presumably, in the dark bedroom, till he had finished? It seemed to her that she spent half her time arranging her actions so that she might not get in Charlie's way while he cleaned or cooked. But she had learned better than to suggest doing her own work. On one of Mrs Pond's visits, she had spoken with disgust of certain immigrants from England, who had so far forgotten what was due to their position as white people, as to dispense with servants. Marina felt it was hardly worth while upsetting Mrs Pond for such a small matter. Particularly, of course, as it was only for three months....

But upset Mrs Pond she did, and almost immediately.

When it came to the end of the month, when Charlie's wages were due, and she laid out the twenty shillings[1] he earned, she was filled with guilt. She really could not pay him such an idiotic sum for a whole month's work. But were twenty-five shillings, or thirty, any less ridiculous? She paid him twenty-five, and saw him beam with amazed surprise. He had been planning to ask for a rise, since this woman was easy-going, and he naturally optimistic; but to get a rise without asking for it, and then a full five shillings! Why, it had taken him three months of hard bargaining with Mrs Skinner to get raised from seventeen and sixpence to nineteen shillings. 'Thank you, madam,' he said hastily; grabbing the money as if at any moment she might change her mind and take it back. Later that same day, she saw that he was wearing a new pair of crimson satin garters, and felt rather annoyed. Surely those five shillings might have been more sensibly spent? What these unfortunate people needed was an education in civilized values— but before she could pursue the thought, Mrs Pond entered, looking aggrieved.

It appeared that Mrs Pond's servant had also demanded a rise, from his nineteen shillings. If Charlie could earn twenty-five shillings, why not he? Marina understood that Mrs Pond was speaking for all the women in the building.

'You shouldn't spoil them,' she said. 'I know you are from England, and all that, but ...'

'It seems to me they are absurdly underpaid,' said Marina.

'Before the war they were lucky to get ten bob.[2] They're never satisfied.'

'Well, according to the cost-of-living index, the value of money has halved,' said Marina. But as even the Government had not come to terms with this official and indisputable fact, Mrs Pond could not be expected to, and she said crossly: 'All you people are the same, you come here with your fancy ideas.'

---

1 A shilling equals 12 pence; one-twentieth of a pound.
2 A bob: one shilling.

Marina was conscious that every time she left her rooms, she was followed by resentful eyes. Besides, she was feeling a little ridiculous. Crimson satin garters, really!

She discussed the thing with Philip, and decided that payment in kind was more practical. She arranged that Charlie should be supplied, in addition to a pound of meat twice a week, with vegetables. Once again Mrs Pond came on a deputation of protest. All the natives in the building were demanding vegetables. 'They aren't used to it,' she complained. 'Their stomachs aren't like ours. They don't need vegetables. You're just putting ideas into their heads.'

'According to the regulations,' Martha pointed out in that high clear voice, 'natives should be supplied with vegetables.'

'Where did you get that from?' said Mrs Pond suspiciously.

Marina produced the regulations, which Mrs Pond read in grim silence. 'The Government doesn't have to pay for it,' she pointed out, very aggrieved. And then, 'They're getting out of hand, that's what it is. There'll be trouble, you mark my words....'

Martha completed her disgrace on the day when she bought a second-hand iron bedstead and installed it in Charlie's room. That her servant should have to sleep on the bare cement floor, wrapped in a blanket, this she could no longer tolerate. As for Charlie, he accepted his good fortune fatalistically. He could not understand Marina. She appeared to feel guilty about telling him to do the simplest thing, such as clearing away cobwebs he had forgotten. Mrs Skinner would have docked his wages, and Mr Skinner cuffed him. This woman presented him with a new bed on the day that he broke her best cut-glass bowl.

He bought himself some new ties, and began swaggering around the back yard among the other servants, whose attitude towards him was as one might expect: one did not expect justice from the white man, whose ways were incomprehensible, but there should be a certain proportion: why should Charlie be the one to chance on an employer who presented him with a fine bed, extra meat, vegetables, and gave him two afternoons off a week instead of one? They looked unkindly at Charlie, as he swanked across the yard in his fine new clothes; they might even shout sarcastic remarks after him. But Charlie was too good-natured and friendly a person to relish such a situation. He made a joke of it, in self-defence, as Marina soon learned.

She had discovered that there was no need to share the complicated social life of the building in order to find out what went on. If, for instance, Mrs Pond had quarrelled with a neighbour over some sugar that had not been returned, so that all the women were taking sides, there was no need to listen to Mrs Pond herself to find the truth. Instead, one went to the kitchen window overlooking the back yard, hid oneself behind the curtain, and peered out at the servants.

There they stood, leaning on their axes, or in the intervals of pegging the washing, a group of laughing and gesticulating men, who were creating the new chapter in that perpetually unrolling saga, the extraordinary life of the white people, their masters, in 138 Cecil John Rhodes Vista....

February, Mrs Pond's servant, stepped forward, while the others fell back in a circle around him, already grinning appreciatively. He thrust out his chest, stuck out his chin, and over a bad-tempered face he stretched his mouth in a smile so poisonously ingratiating that his audience roared and slapped their knees with delight. He was Mrs Pond, one could not mistake it. He minced over to an invisible person, put on an attitude of supplication, held out his hand, received something in it. He returned to the centre of the circle, and looked at what he held with a triumphant smile. In one hand he held an invisible cup, with the other he spooned in invisible sugar. He was Mrs Pond, drinking her tea, with immense satisfaction, in small and dainty sips. Then he belched, rubbed his belly, smacked his lips. Entering into the game another servant came forward, and acted a falsely amiable woman: hands on hips, the jutting elbows, the whole angry body showing indignation, but the face was smiling. February drew himself up, nodded and smiled, turned himself about, lifted something from the air behind him, and began pouring it out: sugar, one could positively hear it trickling. He took the container, and handed it proudly to the waiting visitor. But just as it was taken from him, he changed his mind. A look of agonized greed came over his face, and he withdrew the sugar. Hastily turning himself back, throwing furtive glances over his shoulder, he poured back some of the sugar, then, slowly, as if it hurt to do it, he forced himself round, held out the sugar, and again just as it left his hand, he grabbed it and poured back just a little more. The other servants were rolling with laughter, as the two men faced each other in the centre of the yard, one indignant, but still polite, screwing up his eyes at the returned sugar, as if there were too small a quantity to be seen, while February held it out at arm's length, his face contorted with the agony it caused him to return it at all. Suddenly the two sprang together, faced each other like a pair of angry hens, and began screeching and flailing their arms.

'February!' came a shout from Mrs Pond's flat, in her loud, shrill voice. 'February, I told you to do the ironing!'

'Madam!' said February, in his politest voice. He walked backwards to the steps, his face screwed up in a grimace of martyred suffering; as he reached the steps, his body fell into the pose of a willing servant, and he walked hastily into the kitchen, where Mrs Pond was waiting for him.

But the other servants remained, unwilling to drop the game. There was a moment of indecision. They glanced guiltily at the back of the building: perhaps some of the other women were watching? No, complete silence. It was mid-morning, the sun poured down, the shadows lay deep under the big tree, the sap crystallized into little rivulets like burnt toffee on the wood chips, and sent a warm fragrance mingling into the odours of dust and warmed foliage. For the moment, they could not think of anything to do, they might as well go on with the wood-chopping. One yawned, another lifted his axe and let it fall into a log of wood, where it was held, vibrating. He plucked the handle, and it thrummed like a deep guitar note. At once, delightedly, the men gathered around the embedded axe. One twanged it, and the others began to sing. At first Marina was unable to make out the words. Then she heard.

There's man who comes to our house,
When poppa goes away,
Poppa comes back, and ...

The men were laughing, and looking at No. 4 of the flats, where a certain lady was housed whose husband worked on the railways. They sang it again:

There's a man who comes to this house,
Every single day,
The baas comes back, and
The man goes away....

Marina found that she was angry. Really! The thing had turned into another drama. Charlie, her own servant, was driving an imaginary engine across the yard, chuff chuff, like a child, while two of the others, seated on a log of wood were—really, it was, positively obscene!

Marina came away from the window, and reasoned with herself.

She was using, in her mind, one of the formulae of the country: *What can one expect?*

At this moment, while she was standing beside the kitchen table, arguing with her anger, she heard the shrill cry: 'Peas! Nice potatoes! Cabbage! Ver' chip!'

Yes, she needed vegetables. She went to the back door. There stood a native woman, with a baby on her back, carefully unslinging the sacks of vegetables which she had supported over her shoulder. She opened the mouth of one, displaying the soft mass of green pea-pods.

'How much?'

'Only one sheeling,' said the woman hopefully.

'What!' began Marina, in protest; for this was twice what the shops charged. Then she stopped. Poor woman. No woman should have to carry a heavy child on her back, and great sacks of vegetables from house to house, street to street, all day—'Give me a pound,' she said. Using a tin cup, the woman ladled out a small quantity of peas. Marina nearly insisted on weighing them; then she remembered how Mrs Pond brought her scales out to the back door, on these occasions, shouting abuse at the vendor, if there was short weight. She took in the peas, and brought out a shilling. The woman, who had not expected this, gave Marina a considering look and fell into the pose of a suppliant. She held out her hands, palms upwards, her head bowed, and murmured: 'Present, missus, present for my baby.'

Again Marina hesitated. She looked at the woman, with her whining face and shifty eyes, and disliked her intensely. The phrase: What can one expect? came to the surface of her mind; and she went indoors and returned with sweets. The woman received them in open, humble palms, and promptly popped half into her own mouth. Then she said: 'Dress, missus?'

'No,' said Marina, with energy. Why should she?

Without a sign of disappointment, the woman twisted the necks of the sacks around her hand, and dragged them after her over the dust of the yard, and joined the group of servants who were watching the scene with interest. They exchanged greetings. The woman sat down on a log, easing her strained back, and moved the baby around under her armpit, still in its sling, so it could reach her breast. Charlie, the dandy, bent over her, and they began a flirtation. The others fell back. Who, indeed, could compete with that rainbow tie, the satin garters? Charlie was persuasive and assured, the woman bridling and laughing. It went on for some minutes until the baby let the nipple fall from its mouth. Then the woman got up, still laughing, shrugged the baby back into position in the small of her back, pulled the great sacks over one shoulder, and walked off, calling shrilly back to Charlie, so that all the men laughed. Suddenly they all became silent. The nurse-girl emerged from Mrs Black's flat, and sauntered slowly past them. She was a little creature, a child, in a tight pink cotton dress, her hair braided into a dozen tiny plaits that stuck out all over her head, with a childish face that was usually vivacious and mischievous. But now she looked mournful. She dragged her feet as she walked past Charlie, and gave him a long reproachful look. Jealousy, thought Marina, there was no doubt of that! And Charlie was looking uncomfortable—one could not mistake that either. But surely not! Why, she wasn't old enough for this sort of thing. The phrase, *this sort of thing*, struck Marina herself as a shameful evasion, and she examined it. Then she shrugged and said to herself: All the same, where did the girl sleep? Presumably in one of these rooms, with the men of the place?

Theresa (she had been named after Saint Theresa at the mission school where she had been educated) tossed her head in the direction of the departing seller of vegetables, gave Charlie a final supplicating glance, and disappeared into the sanitary lane.

The men began laughing again, and this time the laughter was directed at Charlie, who received it grinning self-consciously.

Now February, who had finished the ironing, came from Mrs Pond's flat and began hanging clothes over the line to air. The white things dazzled in the sun and made sharp, black shadows across the red dust. He called out to the others—what interesting events had happened since he went indoors? They laughed, shouted back. He finished pegging the clothes and went over to the others. The group stood under the big tree, talking; Marina, still watching, suddenly felt her cheeks grow hot. Charlie had separated himself off and, with a condensing, bowed movement of his body, had become the native woman, the seller of vegetables. Bent sideways with the weight of sacks, his belly thrust out to balance the heavy baby, he approached a log of wood—her own back step. Then he straightened, sprang back, stretched upwards, and pulled from the tree a frond of leaves. These he balanced on his head, and suddenly Marina saw herself. Very straight, precise, finicky, with a prim little face peering this way and that under the broad hat, hands clasped in front of her, she advanced to the log of wood and stood looking downwards.

'Peas, cabbage, potatoes,' said Charlie, in a shrill female voice.

'How much?' he answered himself, in Marina's precise, nervous voice.

'Ten sheelings a pound, missus, only ten sheelings a pound!' said Charlie, suddenly writhing on the log in an ecstasy of humility.

'How ridiculous!' said Marina, in that high, alas, absurdly high voice. Marina watched herself hesitate, her face showing mixed indignation and guilt and, finally, indecision. Charlie nodded twice, said nervously: 'Of course, but certainly.' Then, in a hurried, embarrassed way, he retreated, and came back, his arms full. He opened them and stood aside to avoid a falling shower of money. For a moment he mimed the native woman and, squatting on the ground, hastily raked in the money and stuffed it into his shirt. Then he stood up—Marina again. He bent uncertainly, with a cross, uncomfortable face, looking down. Then he bent stiffly and picked up a leaf—a single pea-pod, Marina realized—and marched off, looking at the leaf, saying: 'Cheap, very cheap!' one hand balancing the leaves on his head, his two feet set prim and precise in front of him.

As the laughter broke out from all the servants, Marina, who was not far from tears, stood by the window and said to herself: Serve you right for eavesdropping.

A clock struck. Various female voices shouted from their respective kitchens:

'February!' 'Noah!' 'Thursday!' 'Sixpence!' 'Blackbird!'

The morning lull was over. Time to prepare the midday meal for the white people. The yard was deserted, save for Theresa the nurse-girl, returning disconsolately from the sanitary lane, dragging her feet through the dust. Among the stiff quills of hair on her head she had perched a half-faded yellow flower that she had found in one of the rubbish cans. She looked hopefully at Marina's flat for a glimpse of Charlie; then slowly entered Mrs Black's.

It happened that Philip was away on one of his trips. Marina ate her lunch by herself, while Charlie, attired in his waiter's outfit, served her food. Not a trace of the cheerful clown remained in his manner. He appeared friendly, though nervous; at any moment, he seemed to be thinking, this strange white woman might revert to type and start scolding and shouting.

As Marina rose from the card-table, being careful not to bump her head on the window, she happened to glance out at the yard and saw Theresa, who was standing under the tree with the youngest of her charges in her arms. The baby was reaching up to play with the leaves. Theresa's eyes were fixed on Charlie's kitchen.

'Charlie,' said Marina, 'where does Theresa sleep?'

Charlie was startled. He avoided her eyes and muttered: 'I don't know, madam.'

'But you must know, surely,' said Marina, and heard her own voice climb to that high, insistent tone which Charlie had so successfully imitated.

He did not answer.

'How old is Theresa?'

'I don't know.' This was true, for he did not even know his own age. As for Theresa, he saw the spindly, little-girl body, with the sharp young breasts pushing out the pink stuff of the dress she wore; he saw the new languor of her walk as she passed him. 'She is nurse for Mrs Black,' he said sullenly, meaning: 'Ask Mrs Black. What's it got to do with me?'

Marina said: 'Very well,' and went out. As she did so she saw Charlie wave to Theresa through the gauze of the porch. Theresa pretended not to see. She was punishing him, because of the vegetable woman.

In the front room the light was falling full on the highland cattle, so that the glass was a square, blinding glitter. Marina shifted her seat, so that her eyes were no longer troubled by it, and contemplated those odious cattle. Why was it that Charlie, who broke a quite fantastic number of cups, saucers and vases, never—as Mrs Skinner said he might—put that vigorously jerking broom-handle through the glass? But it seemed he liked the picture. Marina had seen him standing in front of it, admiring it. Cattle, Marina knew from Philip, played a part in native tribal life that could only be described as religious—might it be that ...

Some letters slapped on to the cement of the veranda, slid over its polished surface, and came to rest in the doorway. Two letters. Marina watched the uniformed postboy cycle slowly down the front of the building, flinging in the letters, eight times, slap, slap, slap, grinning with pleasure at his own skill. There was a shout of rage. One of the women yelled after him: 'You lazy black bastard, can't you even get off your bicycle to deliver the letters?' The postman, without taking any notice, cycled slowly off to the next house.

This was the hour of heat, when all activity faded into somnolence. The servants were away at the back, eating their midday meal. In the eight flats, separated by the flimsy walls which allowed every sound to be heard, the women reclined, sleeping, or lazily gossiping. Marina could hear Mrs Pond, three rooms away, saying: 'The fuss she made over half a pound of sugar, you would think ...'

Marina yawned. What a lazy life this was! She decided, at that moment, that she would put an end to this nonsense of hoping, year after year, for some miracle that would provide her, Marina Giles, with a nice house, a garden, and the other vanishing amenities of life. They would buy one of those suburban houses and she would have a baby. She would have several babies. Why not? Nursemaids cost practically nothing. She would become a domestic creature and learn to discuss servants and children with women like Mrs Black and Mrs Skinner. Why not? What had she expected? Ah, what had she not expected! For a moment she allowed herself to dream of that large house, that fine exotic garden, the free and amiable life released from the tensions and pressures of modern existence. She dreamed quite absurdly—but then, if no one dreamed these dreams, no one would emigrate, continents would remain undeveloped, and then what would happen to Charlie, whose salvation was (so the statesmen and newspapers continually proclaimed) contact with Mrs Pond and Mrs Skinner—white civilization, in short.

But that phrase 'white civilization' was already coming to affect Marina as violently as it affects everyone else in that violent continent. It is a phrase like 'white man's burden,' 'way of life' or 'colour bar'—all of which are certain to touch off emotions better not classified. Marina was alarmed to find that these phrases were beginning to produce in her a feeling of fatigued distaste. For the liberal, so vociferously disapproving in the first six months, is quite certain to turn his back on the whole affair before the end of a year. Marina would soon be finding herself profoundly bored by politics.

But at this moment, having taken the momentous decision, she was quite light hearted. After all, the house next door to this building was an eyesore, with its corrugated iron and brick and wood flung hastily together; and yet it was beautiful, covered with the yellow and purple and crimson creepers. Yes, they would buy a house in the suburbs, shroud it with greenery, and have four children; and Philip would be perfectly happy rushing violently around the country in a permanent state of moral indignation, and thus they would both be usefully occupied.

Marina reached for the two letters, which still lay just inside the door, where they had been so expertly flung, and opened the first. It was from Mrs Skinner, written from Cape Town, where she was, rather uneasily, it seemed, on holiday.

I can't help worrying if everything is all right, and the furniture. Perhaps I ought to have packed away the things, because no stranger understands. I hope Charlie is not getting cheeky, he needs a firm hand, and I forgot to tell you you must deduct one shilling from his wages because he came back late one afternoon, instead of five o'clock as I said, and I had to teach him a lesson.

Yours truly,
Emily Skinner

P.S. I hope the picture is continuing all right.

The second was from Philip.

I'm afraid I shan't be back tomorrow as Smith suggests while we are here we might as well run over to the Nwenze reserve. It's only just across the river, about seventy miles as the crow flies, but the roads are anybody's guess, after the wet season. Spent this morning as planned, trying to persuade these blacks it is better to have one fat ox than ten all skin and bone, never seen such erosion in my life, gullies twenty feet deep, and the whole tribe will starve next dry season, but you can talk till you are blue, they won't kill a beast till they're forced, and that's what it will come to, and then imagine the outcry from the people back home....

At this point Martha remarked to herself: Well, well; and continued:

You can imagine Screech-Jones or one of them shouting in the House: Compulsion of the poor natives. My eye. It's for their own good. Until all this mystical nonsense about cattle is driven out of their fat heads, we might as well save our breath. You should have seen where I was this morning! To get that reserve back in use, alone, would take the entire Vote this year for the whole country, otherwise the whole place will be a desert, it's all perfectly obvious, but you'll never get this damned Government to see that in a hundred years, and it'll be too late in five.

In haste,
Phil.

P.S. I do hope everything is all right, dear, I'll try not to be late.

That night Marina took her evening meal early so that Charlie might finish the washing-up and get off. She was reading in the front room when she understood that her ear was straining through the noise from the wirelesses all around her for a quite different sort of music. Yes, it was a banjo, and loud singing, coming from the servant's rooms, and there was a quality in it that was not to be heard from any wireless set. Marina went through the rooms to the kitchen window. The deserted yard, roofed high with moon and stars, was slatted and barred with light from the eight back doors. The windows of the four servants' rooms gleamed dully; and from the room Charlie shared with February came laughter and singing and the thrumming of the banjo.

There's a man who comes to our house,
When poppa goes away....

Marina smiled. It was a maternal smile. (As Mrs Pond might remark, in a good mood: They are nothing but children.) She liked to think that these men were having a party. And women too: she could hear shrill female voices. How on earth did they all fit into that tiny room? As she returned through the back porch, she heard a man's voice shouting: 'Shut up there! Shut up, I say!' Mr Black from his back porch: 'Don't make so much noise.'

Complete silence. Marina could see Mr Black's long, black shadow poised motionless: he was listening. Marina heard him grumble: 'Can't hear yourself think with these bastards....' He went back into his front room, and the sound of his heavy feet on the wood floor was absorbed by their wireless playing: I love you, Yes I do, I love you.... Slam! Mr Black was in a rage.

Marina continued to read. It was not long before once more her distracted ear warned her that riotous music had begun again. They were singing: Congo Conga Conga, we do it in the Congo....

Steps on the veranda, a loud knock, and Mr Black entered.

'Mrs Giles, your boy's gone haywire. Listen to the din.'

Marina said politely: 'Do sit down Mr Black.'

Mr Black who in England (from whence he had come as a child) would have been a lanky, pallid, genteel clerk, was in this country an assistant in a haberdasher's; but because of his sunfilled and energetic week-ends, he gave the impression, at first glance, of being that burly young Colonial one sees on advertisements for Empire tobacco. He was thin, bony, muscular, sunburnt; he had the free and easy Colonial manner, the back-slapping air that is always just a little too conscious. 'Look,' it seems to say, 'in this country we are all equal (among the whites, that is—that goes without saying) and I'll fight the first person who suggests anything to the contrary.' Democracy, as it were, with one eye on the audience. But alas, he was still a clerk, and felt it; and if there was one class of person he detested it was the civil servant, and if there was another, it was the person new from 'Home.'

Here they were, united in one person, Marina Giles, wife of Philip Giles, soil expert for the Department of Lands and Afforestation, Marina, whose mere appearance acutely irritated him, every time he saw her moving delicately through the red dust, in her straw hat, white gloves and touch-me-not manner.

'I say!' he said aggressively, his face flushed, his eyes hot. 'I say, what are you going to do about it, because if you don't, I shall.'

'I don't doubt it,' said Marina precisely; 'but I really fail to see why these people should not have a party, if they choose, particularly as it is not yet nine o'clock, and as far as I know there is no law to forbid them.'

'Law!' said Mr Black violently. 'Party! They're on our premises, aren't they? It's for us to say. Anyway, if I know anything they're visiting without passes.'

'I feel you are being unreasonable,' said Marina, with the intention of sounding mildly persuasive; but in fact her voice had lifted to that fatally querulous high note, and her face was as angry and flushed as his.

'Unreasonable! My kids can't sleep with that din.'

'It might help if you turned down your own wireless,' said Marina sarcastically.

He lifted his fists, clenching them unconsciously. 'You people ...' he began inarticulately. 'If you were a man, Mrs Giles, I tell you straight ...' He dropped his fists and looked around wildly as Mrs Pond entered, her face animated with delight in the scene.

'I see Mr Black is talking to you about your boy,' she began, sugarily.

'And your boy too,' said Mr Black.

'Oh, if I had a husband,' said Mrs Pond, putting on an appearance of helpless womanhood, 'February would have got what's coming to him long ago.'

'For that matter,' said Marina, speaking with difficulty because of her loathing for the whole thing, 'I don't think you really find a husband necessary for this purpose, since it was only yesterday I saw you hitting February yourself....'

'He was cheeky,' began Mrs Pond indignantly.

Marina found words had failed her; but none were necessary for Mr Black had gone striding out through her own bedroom, followed by Mrs Pond, and she saw the pair of them cross the shadowy yard to Charlie's room, which was still in darkness, though the music was at a crescendo. As Mr Black shouted: 'Come out of there, you black bastards!' the noise stopped, the door swung in, and half a dozen dark forms ducked under Mr Black's extended arm and vanished into the sanitary lane. There was a scuffle, and Mr Black found himself grasping, at arm's length, two people—Charlie and his own nursemaid, Theresa. He let the girl go and she ran after the others. He pushed Charlie against the wall. 'What do you mean by making all that noise when I told you not to?' he shouted.

'That's right, that's right,' gasped Mrs Pond from behind him, running this way and that around the pair so as to get a good view.

Charlie, keeping his elbow lifted to shield his head, said: 'I'm sorry, baas, I'm sorry, I'm sorry....'

'Sorry!' Mr Black, keeping firm grasp of Charlie's shoulder, lifted his other hand to hit him; Charlie jerked his arm up over his face. Mr Black's fist, expecting to encounter a cheek, met instead the rising arm and he was thrown off balance and staggered back. 'How dare you hit me,' he shouted furiously, rushing at Charlie; but Charlie had escaped in a bound over the rubbish-cans and away into the lane.

Mr Black sent angry shouts after him; then turned and said indignantly to Mrs Pond: 'Did you see that? He hit me!'

'He's out of hand,' said Mrs Pond in a melancholy voice. 'What can you expect? He's been spoilt.'

They both turned to look accusingly at Marina.

'As a matter of accuracy,' said Marina breathlessly, 'he did not hit you.'

'What, are you taking that nigger's side?' demanded Mr Black. He was completely taken aback. He looked, amazed, at Mrs Pond, and said: 'She's taking his side!'

'It's not a question of sides,' said Marina in that high, precise voice. 'I was standing here and saw what happened. You know quite well he did not hit you. He wouldn't dare.'

'Yes,' said Mr Black, 'that's what a state things have come to, with the Government spoiling them, they can hit us and get away with it, and if we touch them we get fined.'

'I don't know how many times I've seen the servants hit since I've been here,' said Marina angrily. 'If it is the law, it is a remarkably ineffective one.'

'Well, I'm going to get the police,' shouted Mr Black, running back to his own flat. 'No black bastard is going to hit me and get away with it. Besides, they can all be fined for visiting without passes after nine at night....'

'Don't be childish,' said Marina, and went inside her rooms. She was crying with rage. Happening to catch a glimpse of herself in the mirror as she passed it, she hastily went to splash cold water on her face, for she looked—there was no getting away from it— rather like a particularly genteel school-marm in a temper. When she reached the front room, she found Charlie there throwing terrified glances out into the veranda for fear of Mr Black or Mrs Pond.

'Madam,' he said, 'Madam, I didn't hit him.'

'No, of course not,' said Marina; and she was astonished to find that she was feeling irritated with him, Charlie. 'Really,' she said, 'must you make such a noise and cause all this fuss.'

'But, madam ...'

'Oh, all right,' she said crossly. 'All right. But you aren't supposed to ... Who were all those people?'

'My friends.'

'Where from?' He was silent. 'Did they have passes to be out visiting?' He shifted his eyes uncomfortably. 'Well, really,' she said irritably, 'if the law is that you must have passes, for heaven's sake ...' Charlie's whole appearance had changed; a moment before he had been a helpless small boy; he had become a sullen young man: this white woman was like all the rest.

Marina controlled her irritation and said gently: 'Listen, Charlie, I don't agree with the law and all this nonsense about passes, but I can't change it and it does seem to me ...' Once again her irritation rose, once again she suppressed it, and found herself without words. Which was just as well, for Charlie was gazing at her with puzzled suspicion since he saw all white people as a sort of a homogeneous mass, a white layer, as it were, spread over the mass of blacks, all concerned in making life as difficult as possible for him and his kind; the idea that a white person might not agree with passes, curfew, and so on, was so outrageously new that he could not admit it to his mind at once. Marina said: 'Oh, well, Charlie, I know you didn't mean it, and I think you'd better go quietly to bed and keep out of Mr Black's way, if you can.'

'Yes, madam,' he said submissively. As he went, she asked: 'Does Theresa sleep in the same room as Mr Black's boy?'

He was silent. 'Does she sleep in your room perhaps?' And, as the silence persisted: 'Do you mean to tell me she sleeps with you and February?' No reply. 'But Charlie ...' She was about to protest again: But Theresa's nothing but a child; but this did not appear to be an argument which appealed to him.

There were loud voices outside, and Charlie shrank back: 'The police!' he said, terrified.

'Ridiculous nonsense,' said Marina. But looking out she saw a white policeman; and Charlie fled out through her bedroom and she heard the back door slam. It appeared he had no real confidence in her sympathy.

The policeman entered, alone. 'I understand there's been a spot of trouble,' he said.

'Over nothing,' said Marina.

'A tenant in this building claims he was hit by your servant.'

'It's not true. I saw the whole thing.'

The policeman looked at her doubtfully and said: 'Well, that makes things difficult, doesn't it?' After a moment he said: 'Excuse me a moment,' and went out. Marina saw him talking to Mr Black outside her front steps. Soon the policeman came back. 'In view of your attitude the charge has been dropped,' he said.

'So I should think. I've never heard of anything so silly.'

'Well, Mrs Giles, there was a row going on, and they all ran away, so they must have had guilty consciences about something, probably no passes. And you know they can't have women in their rooms.'

'The woman was Mr Black's own nursemaid.'

'He says the girl is supposed to sleep in the location with her father.'

'It's a pity Mr Black takes so little interest in his servants not to know. She sleeps here. How can a child that age be expected to walk five miles here every morning, to be here at seven, and walk five miles back at seven in the evening?'

The policeman gave her a look: 'Plenty do it,' he said. 'It's not the same for them as it is for us. Besides, it's the law.'

'The law!' said Marina bitterly.

Again the policeman looked uncertain. He was a pleasant young man, he dealt continually with cases of this kind, he always tried to smooth things over, if he could. He decided on his usual course, despite Marina's hostile manner. 'I think the best thing to do,' he said, 'is if we leave the whole thing. We'll never catch them now, anyway—miles away by this time. And Mr Black has dropped the charge. You have a talk to your boy and tell him to be careful. Otherwise he'll be getting himself into trouble.'

'And what are you going to do about the nurse? It amounts to this: It's convenient for the Blacks to have her here, so they can go out at night, and so on, so they ask no questions. It's a damned disgrace, a girl of that age expected to share a room with the men.'

'It's not right, not right at all,' said the policeman. 'I'll have a word with Mr Black.' And he took his leave, politely.

That night Marina relieved her feelings by writing a long letter about the incident to a friend of hers in England, full of phrases such as 'police state,' 'despotism' and 'fascism'; which caused that friend to reply, rather tolerantly, to the effect that she understood these hot climates were rather upsetting and she did so hope Marina was looking after herself, one must have a sense of proportion, after all.

And, in fact, by the morning Marina was wondering why she had allowed herself to be so angry about such an absurd incident. What a country this was! Unless she was very careful she would find herself flying off into hysterical states as easily, for instance as Mr Black. If one was going to make a life here, one should adjust oneself....

Charlie was grateful and apologetic. He repeated: 'Thank you, madam. Thank you.' He brought her a present of some vegetables and said: 'You are my father and my mother.' Marina was deeply touched. He rolled up his eyes and made a half-rueful joke: 'The police are no good, madam.' She discovered that he had spent the night in a friend's room some streets away for fear the police might come and take him to prison. For, in Charlie's mind, the police meant only one thing. Marina tried to explain that one wasn't put in prison without a trial of some sort; but he merely looked at her doubtfully, as if she were making fun of him. So she left it.

And Theresa? She was still working for the Blacks. A few evenings later, when Marina went to turn off the lights before going to bed, she saw Theresa gliding into Charlie's room. She said nothing about it: what could one expect?

Charlie had accepted her as an ally. One day, as he served vegetables, reaching behind her ducked head so that they might be presented, correctly, from the left, he remarked: 'That Theresa, she very nice, madam.'

'Very nice,' said Marina, uncomfortably helping herself to peas from an acute angle, sideways.

'Theresa says, perhaps madam give her a dress?'

'I'll see what I can find,' said Marina, after a pause.

'Thank you very much, thank you madam,' he said. He was grateful; but certainly he had expected just that reply: his thanks were not perfunctory, but he thanked her as one might thank one's parents, for instance, from whom one expects such goodness, even takes it a little for granted.

Next morning, when Marina and Philip lay as usual, trying to sleep through the cheerful din of cleaning from the next room, which included a shrill and sprightly whistling, there was a loud crash.

'Oh, damn the man,' said Philip, turning over and pulling the clothes over his ears.

'With a bit of luck he's broken that picture,' said Marina. She put a dressing-gown on, and went next door. On the floor lay fragments of white porcelain—her favourite vase, which she had brought all the way from England. Charlie was standing over it. 'Sorry, madam,' he said, cheerfully contrite.

Now that vase had stood on a shelf high above Charlie's head— to break it at all was something of an acrobatic feat.... Marina pulled herself together. After all, it was only a vase. But her favourite vase, she had had it ten years: she stood there, tightening her lips over all the angry things she would have liked to say, looking at Charlie, who was carelessly sweeping the pieces together. He glanced up, saw her face, and said hastily, really apologetic: 'Sorry madam, very, very sorry, madam.' Then he added reassuringly: 'But the picture is all right.' He gazed admiringly up at the highland cattle which he clearly considered the main treasure of the room.

'So it is,' said Marina, suppressing the impulse to say: Charlie, if you break that picture I'll give you a present. 'Oh, well,' she said, 'I suppose it doesn't matter. Just sweep the pieces up.'

'Yes, missus, thank you,' said Charlie cheerfully; and she left, wondering how she had put herself in a position where it became impossible to be legitimately cross with her own servant. Coming

back into that room some time later to ask Charlie why the breakfast was so late, she found him still standing under the picture. 'Very
nice picture,' he said, reluctantly leaving the room. 'Six oxes. Six
fine big oxes, in one picture!'

The work in the flat was finished by mid-morning. Marina told
Charlie she wanted to bake; he filled the old-fashioned stove with
wood for her, heated the oven and went off into the yard,
whistling. She stood at the window, mixing her cake, looking out
into the yard.

Charlie came out of his room, sat down on a big log under the
tree, stretched his legs before him and propped a small mirror
between his knees. He took a large metal comb and began to work
on his thick hair, which he endeavoured to make lie flat, white-
man's fashion. He was sitting with his back to the yard.

Soon Theresa came out with a big enamel basin filled with
washing. She wore the dress Marina had given her. It was an old
black cocktail dress which hung loosely around her calves, and she
had tied it at the waist with a big sash of printed cotton. The
sophisticated dress, treated thus, hanging full and shapeless, looked
grandmotherly and old-fashioned, she looked like an impish child
in a matron's garb. She stood beside the washing-line gazing at
Charlie's back; then slowly she began pegging the clothes, with
long intervals to watch him.

It seemed Charlie did not know she was there. Then his pose of
concentrated self-worship froze into a long, close inspection in the
mirror, which he began to rock gently between his knees so that
the sunlight flashed up from it, first into the branches over his head,
then over the dust of the yard to the girl's feet, up her body: the
ray of light hovered like a butterfly around her, then settled on her
face. She remained still, her eyes shut, with the teasing light flick-
ering on her lids. Then she opened them and exclaimed, indignantly: 'Hau!'

Charlie did not move. He held the mirror sideways on his
knees, where he could see Theresa, and pretended to be hard at
work on his parting. For a few seconds they remained thus, Charlie staring into the mirror, Theresa watching him reproachfully.
Then he put the mirror back into his pocket, stretched his arms
back in a magnificent slow yawn, and remained there, rocking back
and forth on his log.

Theresa looked at him thoughtfully; and—since now he
could not see her—darted over to the hedge, plucked a scarlet
hibiscus flower and returned to the washing-line, where she

continued to hang the washing, the flower held lightly between her lips.

Charlie got up, his arms still locked behind his head, and began a sort of shuffle dance in the sunny dust, among the fallen leaves and chips of wood. It was a crisp, bright morning, the sky was as blue and fresh as the sea: this idyllic scene moved Marina deeply, it must be confessed.

Still dancing, Charlie let his arms fall, turned himself round, and his hands began to move in time with his feet. Jerking, lolling, posing, he slowly approached the centre of the yard, apparently oblivious of Theresa's existence.

There was a shout from the back of the building: 'Theresa!' Charlie glanced around, then dived hastily into his room. The girl, left alone, gazed at the dark door into which Charlie had vanished, sighed, and blinked gently at the sunlight. A second shout: 'Theresa, are you going to be all day with that washing?'

She tucked the flower among the stiff quills of hair on her head and bent to the basin that stood in the dust. The washing flapped and billowed all around her, so that the small, wiry form appeared to be wrestling with the big, ungainly sheets. Charlie ducked out of his door and ran quickly up the hedge, out of sight of Mrs Black. He stopped, watching Theresa, who was still fighting with the washing. He whistled, she ignored him. He whistled again, changing key; the long note dissolved into a dance tune, and he sauntered deliberately up the hedge, weight shifting from hip to hip with each step. It was almost a dance: the buttocks sharply protruding and then withdrawn inwards after the prancing, lifting knees. The girl stood motionless, gazing at him, tantalized. She glanced quickly over her shoulder at the building, then ran across the yard to Charlie. The two of them, safe for the moment beside the hedge, looked guiltily for possible spies. They saw Marina behind her curtain—an earnest English face, apparently wrestling: with some severe moral problem. But she was a friend. Had she not saved Charlie from the police? Besides, she immediately vanished.

Hidden behind the curtain, Marina saw the couple face each other, smiling. Then the girl tossed her head and turned away. She picked a second flower from the hedge, held it to her lips, and began swinging lightly from the waist, sending Charlie provocative glances over her shoulder that were half disdain and half invitation. To Marina it was as if a mischievous black urchin was playing the part of a coquette; but Charlie was watching with a broad and appreciative smile. He followed her, strolling in an assured and masterful way, as she went before him into his room. The door closed.

Marina discovered herself to be furious. Really, the whole thing was preposterous!

'Philip,' she said energetically that night, 'we should do something.'

'What?' asked Philip, practically. Marina could not think of a sensible answer. Philip gave a short lecture on the problems of the indigenous African peoples who were half-way between the tribal society and modern industrialization. The thing, of course, should be tackled at its root. Since he was a soil expert, the root, to him, was a sensible organization of the land. (If he had been a churchman, the root would have been a correct attitude to whichever God he happened to represent; if an authority on money, a mere adjustment of currency would have provided the solution—there is very little comfort from experts these days.) To Philip, it was all as clear as daylight. These people had no idea at all how to farm. They must give up this old attitude of theirs, based on the days when a tribe worked out one piece of ground and moved on to the next; they must learn to conserve their soil and, above all, to regard cattle, not as a sort of spiritual currency, but as an organic part of farm-work. (The word *organic* occurred very frequently in these lectures by Philip.) Once these things were done, everything else would follow....

'But in the meantime, Philip, it is quite possible that something may *happen* to Theresa, and she can't be more than fifteen, if that....'

Philip looked a little dazed as he adjusted himself from the level on which he had been thinking to the level of Theresa: women always think so personally! He said, rather stiffly: 'Well, old girl, in periods of transition, what can one expect?'

What one might expect did in fact occur, and quite soon. One of those long ripples of gossip and delighted indignation passed from one end to the other of 138 Cecil John Rhodes Vista. Mrs Black's Theresa had got herself into trouble; these girls had no morals; no better than savages; besides, she was a thief. She was wearing clothes that had not been given to her by Mrs Black. Marina paid a formal visit to Mrs Black in order to say that she had given Theresa various dresses. The air was not at all cleared. No one cared to what degree Theresa had been corrupted, or by whom. The feeling was: if not Theresa, then someone else. Acts of theft, adultery, and so on, were necessary to preserve the proper balance between black and white; the balance was upset, not by Theresa, who played her allotted part, but by Marina, who insisted on introducing these Fabian scruples into a clear-cut situation.

Mrs Black was polite, grudging, distrustful. She said: 'Well, if you've given her the dresses, then it's all right.' She added: 'But it doesn't alter what she's done, does it now?' Marina could make no reply. The white women of the building continued to gossip and pass judgement for some days: one must, after all, talk about something. It was odd, however, that Mrs Black made no move at all to sack Theresa, that immoral person, who continued to look after the children with her usual good-natured efficiency, in order that Mrs Black might have time to gossip and drink tea.

So Marina, who had already made plans to rescue Theresa when she was flung out of her job, found that no rescue was necessary. From time to time Mrs Black overflowed into reproaches, and lectures about sin, Theresa wept like the child she was, her fists stuck into her eyes. Five minutes afterwards she was helping Mrs Black bath the baby, or flirting with Charlie in the yard.

For the principals of this scandal seemed the least concerned about it. The days passed, and at last Marina said to Charlie: 'Well, and what are you going to do now?'

'Madam?' said Charlie. He really did not know what she meant.

'About Theresa,' said Martha sternly.

'Theresa she going to have a baby,' said Charlie, trying to look penitent, but succeeding only in looking proud.

'It's all very well,' said Marina. Charlie continued to sweep the veranda, smiling to himself. 'But Charlie ...' began Marina again.

'Madam?' said Charlie, resting on his broom and waiting for her to go on.

'You can't just let things go on, and what will happen to the child when it is born?'

His face puckered, he sighed, and finally he went on sweeping, rather slower than before.

Suddenly Marina stamped her foot and said: 'Charlie, this really won't do!' She was really furious.

'Madam!' said Charlie reproachfully.

'Everybody has a good time,' said Marina. 'You and Theresa enjoy yourselves, all these females have a lovely time, gossiping, and the only thing no one ever thinks about is the baby.' After a pause, when he did not reply, she went on: 'I suppose you and Theresa think it's quite all right for the baby to be born here, and then you two, and the baby, and February, and all the rest of your friends who have nowhere to go, will all live together in that room. It really is shocking, Charlie.'

Charlie shrugged as if to say: 'Well, what do you suggest?'

'Can't Theresa go and live with her father?'

Charlie's face tightened into a scowl. 'Theresa's father, he no good. Theresa must work, earn money for father.'

'I see.' Charlie waited; he seemed to be waiting for Marina to solve this problem for him; his attitude said: I have unbounded trust and confidence in you.

'Are any of the other men working here married?'

'Yes, madam.'

'Where are their wives?'

'At home.' This meant, in their kraals, in the native reserves. But Marina had not meant the properly married wives, who usually stayed with the clan, and were visited by their men perhaps one month in a year, or in two years. She meant women like Theresa, who lived in town.

'Now listen, Charlie. Do be sensible. What happens to girls like Theresa when they have babies. Where do they live?'

He shrugged again, meaning: They live as they can, and is it my fault the white people don't let us have our families with us when they work? Suddenly he said grudgingly: 'The nannie next door, she has her baby, she works.'

'Where is her baby?'

Charlie jerked his head over at the servant's quarters of the next house.

'Does the baas know she has her baby there?'

He looked away, uncomfortably. 'Well, and what happens when the police find out?'

He gave her a look which she understood. 'Who is the father of that baby?'

He looked away; there was an uncomfortable silence; and then he quickly began sweeping the veranda again.

'Charlie!' said Marina, outraged. His whole body had become defensive, sullen; his face was angry. She said energetically: 'You should marry Theresa. You can't go on doing this sort of thing.'

'I have a wife in my kraal,' he said.

'Well, there's nothing to stop you having two wives, is there?'

Charlie pointed out that he had not yet finished paying for his first wife.

Marina thought for a moment. 'Theresa's a Christian, isn't she?

She was educated at the mission.' Charlie shrugged. 'If you marry Theresa Christian-fashion, you needn't pay lobola, need you?'

Charlie said: 'The Christians only like one wife. And Theresa's father, he wants lobola.'

Marina found herself delighted. At any rate he had tried to marry Theresa, and this was evidence of proper feeling. The fact that whether the position was legalized or not the baby's future was still uncertain, did not at once strike her. She was carried away by moral approval. 'Well, Charlie, that's much better,' she said warmly.

He gave her a rather puzzled look and shrugged again.

'How much lobola does Theresa's father want for her?'

'Plenty. He wants ten cattle.'

'What nonsense!' exclaimed Marina energetically. 'Where does he suppose you are going to find cattle, working in town, and where's he going to keep them?'

This seemed to annoy Charlie. 'In my kraal, I have fine cattle,' he pointed out. 'I have six fine oxes.' He swept, for a while, in silence. 'Theresa's father, he mad, he mad old man. I tell him I must give three oxes this year for my own wife. Where do I find ten oxes for Theresa?'

It appeared that Charlie, no more than Theresa's father, found nothing absurd about this desire for cattle on the part of an old man living in the town location. Involuntarily she looked over her shoulder as if Philip might be listening: this conversation would have plunged him into irritated despair. Luckily he was away on one of his trips, and was at this moment almost certain to be exhorting the natives, in some distant reserve, to abandon this irrational attitude to 'fine oxes' which in fact were bound to be nothing but skin and bone, and churning whole tracts of country to dust.

'Why don't you offer Theresa's father some money?' she suggested, glancing down at Charlie's garters which were, this morning, of cherry-coloured silk.

'He wants cattle, not money. He wants Theresa not to marry, he wants her to work for him.' Charlie rapidly finished sweeping the veranda and moved off, with relief, tucking the broom under his arm, with an apologetic smile which said: I know you mean well, but I'm glad to end this conversation.

But Marina was not at all inclined to drop the thing. She interviewed Theresa who, amid floods of tears, said Yes, she wanted to marry Charlie, but her father wanted too much lobola. The problem was quite simple to her, merely a question of lobola; Charlie's other wife did not concern her; nor did she, apparently, share Charlie's view that a proper wife in the kraal was one thing, while the women of the town were another.

Marina said: 'Shall I come down to the location and talk to your father?'

Theresa hung her head shyly, allowed the last big tears to roll glistening down her cheeks and go splashing to the dust. 'Yes, madam,' she said gratefully.

Marina returned to Charlie and said she would interview the old man. He appeared restive at this suggestion. 'I'll advance you some of your wages and you can pay for Theresa in instalments,' she said. He glanced down at his fine shirt, his gay socks, and sighed. If he were going to spend years of life paying five shillings a month, which was all he could afford, for Theresa, then his life as a dandy was over.

Marina said crossly: 'Yes, it's all very well, but you can't have it both ways.'

He said hastily: 'I'll go down and see the father of Theresa, madam. I go soon.'

'I think you'd better,' she said sternly.

When she told Philip this story he became vigorously indignant. It presented in little, he said, the whole problem of this society. The Government couldn't see an inch in front of its nose. In the first place, by allowing the lobola system to continue, this emotional attitude towards cattle was perpetuated. In the second, by making no proper arrangements for these men to have their families in the towns it made the existence of prostitutes like Theresa inevitable.

'Theresa isn't a prostitute,' said Marina indignantly. 'It isn't her fault.'

'Of course it isn't her fault, that's what I'm saying. But she will be a prostitute, it's inevitable. When Charlie's fed up with her she'll find herself another man and have a child or two by him, and so on....'

'You talk about Theresa as if she were a vital statistic,' said Marina, and Philip shrugged. That shrug expressed an attitude of mind which Marina would very soon find herself sharing, but she did not yet know that. She was still very worried about Theresa, and after some days she asked Charlie: 'Well, and did you see Theresa's father? What did he say?'

'He wants cattle.'

'Well, he can't have cattle.'

'No,' said Charlie, brightening. 'My own wife, she cost six cattles. I paid three last year. I pay three more this year, when I go home.'

'When are you going home?'

'When Mrs Skinner comes back. She no good. Not like you, madam, you are my father and mother,' he said, giving her that touching, grateful smile.

'And what will happen to Theresa?'

'She stay here.' After a long, troubled silence, he said: 'She my town wife. I come back to Theresa.' This idea seemed to cheer him up.

And it seemed he was genuinely fond of the girl. Looking out of the kitchen window, Marina could see the pair of them, during lulls in the work, seated side by side on the big log under the tree—charming! A charming picture! 'It's all very well ...' said Marina to herself, uneasily.

Some mornings later she found Charlie in the front room, under the picture, and looking at it this time, not with reverent admiration, but rather nervously. As she came in he quickly returned to his work, but Marina could see he wanted to say something to her.

'Madam ...'

'Well, what is it?'

'This picture costs plenty money?'

'I suppose it did, once.'

'Cattles cost plenty money, madam.'

'Yes, so they do, Charlie.'

'If you sell this picture, how much?'

'But it is Mrs Skinner's picture.'

His body drooped with disappointment. 'Yes, madam,' he said politely, turning away.

'But wait, Charlie—what do you want the picture for?'

'It's all right, madam.' He was going out of the room.

'Stop a moment—why do you want it? You do want it, don't you?'

'Oh, yes,' he said, his face lit with pleasure. He clasped his hands tight, looking at it. 'Oh, yes, yes, madam!'

'What would you do with it? Keep it in your room?'

'I give it to Theresa's father.'

'Wha-a-a-t?' said Marina. Slowly she absorbed this idea. 'I see,' she said. And then, after a pause: 'I see ...' She looked at his hopeful face, thought of Mrs Skinner, and said suddenly, filled with an undeniably spiteful delight: 'I'll give it to you, Charlie.'

'Madam!' exclaimed Charlie. He even gave a couple of involuntary little steps, like a dance. 'Madam, thank you, thank you.'

She was as pleased as he. For a moment they stood smiling delightedly at each other. 'I'll tell Mrs Skinner that I broke it,' she said. He went to the picture and lifted his hands gently to the great carved frame. 'You must be careful not to break it before you get it to her father.' He was staggering as he lifted it down. 'Wait!' said Marina suddenly. Checking himself, he stood politely: she saw he expected her to change her mind and take back the gift. 'You can't carry that great thing all the way to the location. I'll take it for you in the car!'

'Madam,' he said. 'Madam ...' Then, looking helplessly around him for something, someone he could share his joy with, he said: 'I'll tell Theresa now....' And he ran from the room like a schoolboy.

Marina went to Mrs Black and asked that Theresa might have the afternoon off. 'She had her afternoon off yesterday,' said that lady sharply.

'She's going to marry Charlie,' said Marina.

'She can marry him next Thursday, can't she?'

'No, because I'm taking them both down in the car to the location, to her father, and ...'

Mrs Black said resentfully: 'She should have asked me herself.'

'It seems to me,' said Marina in that high, acid voice, replying not to the words Mrs Black had used, but to what she had meant: 'It seems to me that if one employs a child of fifteen, and under such conditions, the very least one can do is to assume the responsibility for her; and it seems to me quite extraordinary that you never have the slightest idea what she does, where she lives, or even that she is going to get married.'

'You swallowed the dictionary?' said Mrs Black, with an ingratiating smile. 'I'm not saying she shouldn't get married; she should have got married before, that's what I'm saying.'

Marina returned to her flat, feeling Mrs Black's resentful eyes on her back: Who the hell does she think she is, anyway?

When Marina and Philip reached the lorry that afternoon that was waiting outside the gate, Theresa and Charlie were already sitting in the back, carefully balancing the picture on their knees.

The two white people got in the front and Marina glanced anxiously through the window and said to Philip: 'Do drive carefully, dear, Theresa shouldn't be bumped around.'

'I'd be doing her a favour if I did bump her,' said Philip grimly.

He was accompanying Marina unwillingly. 'Well, I don't know what you think you're going to achieve by it ...' he had said. However, here he was, looking rather cross.

They drove down the tree-lined, shady streets, through the business area that was all concrete and modernity, past the slums where the half-caste people lived, past the factory sites, where smoke poured and hung, past the cemetery where angels and crosses gleamed white through the trees—they drove five miles, which was the distance Theresa had been expected to walk every morning and evening to her work. They turned off the main road into the location, and at once everything was quite different. No tarmac road, no avenues of beautiful trees here. Dust roads, dust paths, led from all directions inwards to the centre, where the housing area was. Dust lay thick and brown on the veld trees, the great blue sky was seen through a rust-coloured haze, dust gritted on the lips and tongue, and at once the lorry began to jolt and bounce. Marina looked back and saw Charlie and Theresa jerking and sliding with the lorry, under the great picture, clinging to each other for support, and laughing because of the joy-ride. It was the first time Theresa had ridden in a white man's car; and she was waving and calling shrill greetings to the groups of black children who ran after them.

They drove fast, bumping, so as to escape from the rivers of dust that spurted up from the wheels, making a whirling red cloud behind them, from which crowds of loitering natives ran, cursing and angry. Soon they were in an area that was like a cheap copy of the white man's town; small houses stood in blocks, intersected by dust streets. They were two-roomed shacks with tin roofs, the sun blistering off them; and Marina said angrily: 'Isn't it awful, isn't it terrible?'

Had she known that these same houses represented years of campaigning by the liberals of the city, against white public opinion, which obstinately held that houses for natives were merely another manifestation of that *Fabian* spirit from England which was spoiling the fine and uncorrupted savage, she might have been more respectful. Soon they left this new area and were among the sheds and barns that housed dozens of workers each, a state of affairs which caused Marina the acutest indignation. Another glance over her shoulder showed Theresa and Charlie giggling together like a couple of children as they tried to hold that picture still on their knees, for it slid this way and that as if it had a spiteful life of its own. 'Ask Charlie where we must go' said Philip; and

Marina tapped on the glass till Charlie turned his head and watched her gestures till he understood and pointed onwards with his thumb. More of these brick shacks, with throngs of natives at their doors, who watched the car indifferently until they saw it was a Government car, and then their eyes grew wary, suspicious. And now, blocking their way, was a wire fence, and Martha looked back at Charlie for instructions, and he indicated they should stop. Philip pulled the lorry up against the fence and Charlie and Theresa jumped down from the back, came forwards, and Charlie said apologetically: 'Now we must walk, madam.' The four went through a gap in the fence and saw a slope of soiled and matted grass that ended in a huddle of buildings on the banks of a small river.

Charlie pointed at it, and went ahead with Theresa. He held the picture on his shoulders, walking bent under it. They passed through the grass, which smelled unpleasant and was covered by a haze of flies, and came to another expanse of dust, in which were scattered buildings—no, not buildings, shacks, extraordinary huts thrown together out of every conceivable substance, with walls perhaps of sacking, or of petrol boxes, roofs of beaten tin, or bits of scrap iron.

'And what happens when it rains?' said Marina, as they wound in and out of these dwellings, among scratching chickens and snarling native mongrels. She found herself profoundly dispirited, as if something inside her said: What's the use? For this area, officially, did not exist. The law was that all the workers, the servants, should live inside the location, or in one of the similar townships. But there was never enough room. People overflowed into such makeshift villages everywhere, but as they were not supposed to be there the police might at any moment swoop down and arrest them. Admittedly the police did not often swoop, as the white man must have servants, the servants must live somewhere—and so it all went on, year after year. The Government, from time to time, planned a new housing estate. On paper, all around the white man's city, were fine new townships for the blacks. One had even been built, and to this critical visitors (usually those *Fabians* from overseas) were taken, and came away impressed. They never saw these slums. And so all the time, every day, the black people came from their reserves, their kraals, drawn to the white man's city, to the glitter of money, cinemas, fine clothes; they came in their thousands, no one knew how many, making their own life, as they could, in such hovels. It was all hopeless, as long as Mrs Black, Mr

Black, Mrs Pond were the voters with the power; as long as the experts and administrators such as Philip had to work behind Mrs Pond's back—for nothing is more remarkable than that democratic phenomenon, so clearly shown in this continent, where members of Parliament, civil servants (experts, in short) spend half their time and energy earnestly exhorting Mrs Pond: For heaven's sake have some sense before it is too late; if you don't let us use enough money to house and feed these people, they'll rise and cut your throats. To which reasonable plea for self-preservation, Mrs Pond merely turns a sullen and angry stare, muttering: They're getting out of hand, that's what it is, they're getting spoilt.

In a mood of grim despair, Marina found herself standing with Philip in front of a small shack that consisted of sheets of corrugated iron laid loosely together, resting in the dust, like a child's card castle. It was bound at the corners with string, and big stones held the sheet of iron that served as roof from flying away in the first gust of wind.

'Here, madam,' said Charlie. He thrust Theresa forward. She went shyly to the dark oblong that was the door, leaned inwards, and spoke some words in her own language. After a moment an old man stooped his way out. He was perhaps not so old—impossible to say. He was lean and tall, with a lined and angry face, and eyes that lifted under heavy lids to peer at Marina and Philip. Towards Charlie he directed a long, deadly stare, then turned away. He wore a pair of old khaki trousers, an old, filthy singlet[1] that left his long, sinewed arms bare: all the bones and muscles of his neck and shoulders showed taut and knotted under the skin.

Theresa, smiling bashfully, indicated Philip and Marina; the old man offered some words of greeting; but he was angry, he did not want to see them, so the two white people fell back a little.

Charlie now came forward with the picture and leaned it gently against the iron of the shack in a way which said: 'Here you are, and that's all you are going to get from me.' In these surroundings those fierce Scottish cattle seemed to shrink a little. The picture that had dominated a room with its expanse of shining glass, its heavy carved frame, seemed not so enormous now. The cattle seemed even rather absurd, shaggy creatures standing in their wet sunset, glaring with a false challenge at the group of people. The old man looked at the picture, and then said something angry to

---

1   White cotton sleeveless undershirt.

Theresa. She seemed afraid, and came forward, unknotting a piece of cloth that had lain in the folds at her waist. She handed over some small change—about three shillings in all. The old man took the money, shaking it contemptuously in his hand before he slid it into his pocket. Then he spat, showing contempt. Again he spoke to Theresa, in short, angry sentences, and at the end he flung out his arm, as if throwing something away; and she began to cry and shrank back to Charlie. Charlie laid his hand on her shoulder and pressed it; then left her standing alone and went forward to his father-in-law. He smiled, spoke persuasively, indicated Philip and Marina. The old man listened without speaking, his eyes lowered. Those eyes slid sideways to the big picture, a gleam came into them; Charlie fell silent and they all looked at the picture.

The old man began to speak, in a different voice, sad and hopeless. He was telling how he had wooed his second wife, Theresa's mother. He spoke of the long courting, according to the old customs, how, with many gifts and courtesies between the clans, the marriage had been agreed on, how the cattle had been chosen, ten great cattle, heavy with good grazing; he told how he had driven them to Theresa's mother's family, carefully across the country, so that they might not be tired and thinned by the journey. As he spoke to the two young people he was reminding them, and himself, of that time when every action had its ritual, its meaning; he was asking them to contrast their graceless behaviour with the dignity of his own marriages, symbolized by the cattle, which were not to be thought of in terms of money, of simply buying a woman—not at all. They meant so much: a sign of good feeling, a token of union between the clans, an earnest that the woman would be looked after, an acknowledgment that she was someone very precious, whose departure would impoverish her family—the cattle were all these things, and many more. The old man looked at Charlie and Theresa and seemed to say: 'And what about you? What are you in comparison to what we were then?' finally he spat again, lifted the picture and went into the dark of his hut. They could see him looking at the picture. He liked it: yes, he was pleased, in his way. But soon he left it leaning against the iron and returned to his former pose—he drew a blanket over his head and shoulders and squatted down inside the door, looking out, but not as if he still saw them or intended to make any further sign towards them.

The four were left standing there, in the dust, looking at each other.

Marina was feeling very foolish. Was that all? And Philip answered by saying brusquely, but uncomfortably: 'Well, there's your wedding for you.'

Theresa and Charlie had linked fingers and were together looking rather awkwardly at the white people. It was an awkward moment indeed—this was the end of it, the two were married, and it was Marina who had arranged the thing. What now?

But there was a more immediate problem. It was still early in the afternoon, the sun slanted overhead, with hours of light in it still, and presumably the newly-married couple would want to be together? Marina said: 'Do you want to come back with us in the lorry, or would you rather come later?'

Charlie and Theresa spoke together in their own language, then Charlie said apologetically: 'Thank you, madam, we stay.'

'With Theresa's father?'

Charlie said: 'He won't have Theresa now. He says Theresa can go away. He not want Theresa.'

Philip said: 'Don't worry, Marina, he'll take her back, he'll take her money all right.' He laughed, and Marina was angry with him for laughing.

'He very cross, madam,' said Charlie. He even laughed himself, but in a rather anxious way.

The old man still sat quite motionless, looking past them. There were flies at the corners of his eyes; he did not lift his hand to brush them off.

'Well ...' said Marina. 'We can give you a lift back if you like.' But it was clear that Theresa was afraid of going back now; Mrs Black might assume her afternoon off was over and make her work.

Charlie and Theresa smiled again and said 'Good-bye. Thank you, madam. Thank you, baas.' They went slowly off across the dusty earth, between the hovels, towards the river, where a group of tall brick huts stood like outsize sentry-boxes. There, though neither Marina nor Philip knew it, was sold illicit liquor; there they would find a tinny gramophone playing dance music from America, there would be singing, dancing, a good time. This was the place the police came first if they were in search of criminals. Marina thought the couple were going down to the river, and she said sentimentally: 'Well, they have this afternoon together, that's something.'

'Yes,' said Philip drily. The two were angry with each other, they did not know why. They walked in silence back to the lorry and drove home, making polite, clear sentences about indifferent topics.

Next day everything was as usual, Theresa back at work with Mrs Black, Charlie whistling cheerfully in their own flat.

Almost immediately Marina bought a house that seemed passable, about seven miles from the centre of town, in a new suburb. Mrs Skinner would not be returning for two weeks yet, but it was more convenient for them to move into the new home at once. The problem was Charlie. What would he do during that time? He said he was going home to visit his family. He had heard that his first wife had a new baby and he wanted to see it.

'Then I'll pay you your wages now,' said Marina. She paid him, with ten shillings over. It was an uncomfortable moment. This man had been working for them for over two months, intimately, in their home; they had influenced each other's lives—and now he was off, he disappeared, the thing was finished. 'Perhaps you'll come and work for me when you come back from your family?' said Marina.

Charlie was very pleased. 'Oh, yes, madam,' he said. 'Mrs Skinner very bad, she no good, not like you.' He gave a comical grimace, and laughed.

'I'll give you our address.' Marina wrote it out and saw Charlie fold the piece of paper and place it carefully in an envelope which also held his official pass, a letter from her saying he was travelling to his family, and a further letter, for which he had asked, listing various bits of clothing that Philip had given him, for otherwise, as he explained, the police would catch him and say he had stolen them.

'Well, good-bye, Charlie,' said Marina. 'I do so hope your wife and your new baby are all right.' She thought of Theresa, but did not mention her; she found herself suffering from a curious disinclination to offer further advice or help. What would happen to Theresa? Would she simply move in with the first man who offered her shelter? Almost Marina shrugged.

'Good-bye, madam,' said Charlie. He went off to buy himself a new shirt with the ten shillings, and some sweets for Theresa. He was sad to be leaving Theresa. On the other hand, he was looking forward to seeing his new child and his wife; he expected to be home after about a week's walking, perhaps sooner if he could get a lift.

But things did not turn out like this.

Mrs Skinner returned before she was expected. She found the

flat locked and the key with Mrs Black. Everything was very clean and tidy, but—where was her favourite picture? At first she saw only the lightish square patch on the dimming paint—then she thought of Charlie. Where was he? No sign of him. She came back into the flat and found the letter Marina had left, enclosing eight pounds for the picture 'which she had unfortunately broken.' The thought came to Mrs Skinner that she would not have got ten shillings for that picture if she had tried to sell it; then the phrase 'sentimental value' came to her rescue, and she was furious. Where was Charlie? For, looking about her, she saw various other articles were missing. Where was her yellow earthen vase? Where was the wooden door-knocker that said *Welcome Friend?* Where was ... she went off to talk to Mrs Black, and quite soon all the women dropped in, and she was told many things about Marina. At last she said: 'It serves me right for letting to an immigrant. I should have let it to you, dear.' The dear in question was Mrs Pond. The ladies were again emotionally united; the long hostilities that had led to the flat being let to Marina were forgotten; that they were certain to break out again within a week was not to be admitted in this moment of pure friendship.

Mrs Pond told Mrs Skinner that she had seen the famous picture being loaded on to the lorry. Probably Mrs Giles had sold it—but this thought was checked, for both ladies knew what the picture was worth. No, Marina must have disposed of it in some way connected with her *Fabian* outlook—what could one expect from these white kaffirs?[1]

Fuming, Mrs Skinner went to find Theresa. She saw Charlie, dressed to kill in his new clothes, who had come to say good-bye to Theresa before setting off on his long walk. She flew out, grabbed him by the arm and dragged him into the flat. 'Where's my picture?' she demanded.

At first Charlie denied all knowledge of the picture. Then he said Marina had given it to him. Mrs Skinner dropped his arm and stared: 'But it was my picture ...' She reflected rapidly: that eight pounds was going to be very useful; she had returned from her holiday, as people do, rather short of money. She exclaimed instead: 'What have you done with my yellow vase? Where's my knocker?'

Charlie said he had not seen them. Finally Mrs Skinner fetched the police. The police found the missing articles in Charlie's bun-

---

1 Kaffir: an indigenous African (somewhat derogatory).

dle. Normally Mrs Skinner would have cuffed him and fined him five shillings. But there was this business of the picture—she told the police to take him off.

Now, in this city in the heart of what used to be known as the Dark Continent, at any hour of the day, women shopping, typists glancing up from their work out of the window, or the business men passing in their cars, may see (if they choose to look) a file of handcuffed natives, with two policemen in front and two behind, followed by a straggling group of native women who are accompanying their men to the courts. These are the natives who have been arrested for visiting without passes, or owning bicycles without lights, or being in possession of clothes or articles without being able to say how they came to own them. These natives are being marched off to explain themselves to the magistrates. They are given a small fine with the option of prison. They usually choose prison. After all, to pay a ten shilling fine when one earns perhaps twenty or thirty a month, is no joke, and it is something to be fed and housed, free, for a fortnight. This is an arrangement satisfactory to everyone concerned, for these prisoners mend roads, cut down grass, plant trees: it is as good as having a pool of free labour.

Marina happened to be turning into a shop one morning, where she hoped to buy a table for her new house, and saw, without really seeing them, a file of such handcuffed natives passing her. They were talking and laughing among themselves, and with the black policemen who herded them, and called back loud and jocular remarks at their women. In Marina's mind the vision of that ideal table (for which she had been searching for some days, without success) was rather stronger than what she actually saw; and it was not until the prisoners had passed that she suddenly said to herself: 'Good heavens, that man looks rather like Charlie—and that girl behind there, the plump girl with the spindly legs, there was something about the back view of the girl that was very like Theresa....' The file had in the meantime turned a corner and was out of sight. For a moment Marina thought: Perhaps I should follow and see? Then she thought: Nonsense, I'm seeing things, of course it can't be Charlie, he must have reached home by now.... And she went into the shop to buy her table.

THE ANTHEAP

Beyond the plain rose the mountains, blue and hazy in a strong blue sky. Coming closer they were brown and grey and green, ranged heavily one beside the other. But the sky was still blue. Climbing up through the pass the plain flattened and diminished behind, and the peaks rose sharp and dark grey from lower heights of heaped granite boulder, and the sky overhead was deeply blue and clear and the heat came shimmering off in waves from every surface. 'Through the range, down the pass, and into the plain the other side—let's go quickly, there it will be cooler, the walking easier.' So thinks the traveller. So the traveller has been thinking for many centuries, walking quickly to leave the stifling mountains, to gain the cool plain where the wind moves freely. But there is no plain. Instead, the pass opens into a hollow which is closely surrounded by kopjes: the mountains clench themselves into a fist here, and the palm is a mile-wide reach of thick bush, where the heat gathers and clings, radiating from boulders, rocking off the trees, pouring down from a sky which is not blue, but thick and yellow, because of the smoke that rises, and has been rising so long from this mountain-imprisoned hollow. For though it is hot and close and arid half the year, and then warm and steamy and wet in the rains, there is gold here, so there are always people, and everywhere in the bush are pits and slits where the prospectors have been, or shallow holes, or even deep shafts. They say that the Bushmen were here, seeking gold, hundreds of years ago. Perhaps, it is possible. They say that trains of Arabs came from the coast, with slaves and warriors, looking for gold to enrich the courts of the Queen of Sheba. No one has proved they did not.

But it is at least certain that at the turn of the century there was a big mining company which sunk half a dozen fabulously deep shafts, and found gold going ounces to the ton sometimes, but it is a capricious and chancy piece of ground, with the reefs all broken and unpredictable, and so this company loaded its heavy equipment into lorries and off they went to look for gold somewhere else, and in a place where the reefs lay more evenly.

For a few years the hollow in the mountains was left silent, no smoke rose to dim the sky, except perhaps for an occasional prospector, whose fire was a single column of wavering blue smoke, as from the cigarette of a giant, rising into the blue, hot sky.

Then all at once the hollow was filled with violence and noise and activity and hundreds of people. Mr Macintosh had bought the rights to mine this gold. They told him he was foolish, that no single man, no matter how rich, could afford to take chances in this place.

But they did not reckon with the character of Mr Macintosh, who had already made a fortune and lost it, in Australia, and then made another in New Zealand, which he still had. He proposed to increase it here. Of course, he had no intention of sinking those expensive shafts which might or might not reach gold and hold the dipping, chancy reefs and seams. The right course was quite clear to Mr Macintosh, and this course he followed, though it was against every known rule of proper mining.

He simply hired hundreds of African labourers and set them to shovel up the soil in the centre of that high, enclosed hollow in the mountains, so that there was soon a deeper hollow, then a vast pit, then a gulf like an inverted mountain. Mr Macintosh was taking great swallows of the earth, like a gold-eating monster, with no fancy ideas about digging shafts or spending money on roofing tunnels. The earth was hauled at first, up the shelving sides of the gulf in buckets, and these were suspended by ropes made of twisted bark fibre, for why spend money on steel ropes when this fibre was offered free to mankind on every tree? And if it got brittle and broke and the buckets went plunging into the pit, then they were not harmed by the fall, and there was plenty of fibre left on the trees. Later, when the gulf grew too deep, there were trucks on rails, and it was not unknown for these, too, to go sliding and plunging to the bottom, because in all Mr Macintosh's dealings there was a fine, easy good-humour, which meant he was more likely to laugh at such an accident than grow angry. And if someone's head got in the way of falling buckets or trucks, then there were plenty of black heads and hands for the hiring. And if the loose, sloping bluffs of soil fell in landslides, or if a tunnel, narrow as an ant-bear's hole, that was run off sideways from the main pit like a tentacle exploring for new reefs, caved in suddenly, swallowing half a dozen men—well one can't make an omelette without breaking eggs. This was Mr Macintosh's favourite motto.

The natives who worked this mine called it 'The pit of death', and they called Mr Macintosh 'The Gold Stomach'. Nevertheless, they came in their hundreds to work for him, thus providing free arguments for those who said: 'The native doesn't understand good treatment, he only appreciates the whip, look at Macintosh, he's never short of labour.'

Macintosh's mine, raised high in the mountains, was far from the nearest police station, and he took care that there was always plenty of kaffir beer brewed in the compound, and if the police patrols came searching for criminals, these could count on Mr Macintosh facing the police for them and assuring them that such and such a native, Registration Number Y2345678, had never worked for him. Yes, of course they could see his books.

Mr Macintosh's books and records might appear to the simple-minded as casual and ineffective, but these were not the words used of his methods by those who worked for him, and so Mr Macintosh kept his books himself. He employed no book-keeper, no clerk. In fact, he employed only one white man, an engineer. For the rest, he had six overseers or boss-boys whom he paid good salaries and treated like important people.

The engineer was Mr Clarke and his house and Mr Macintosh's house were on one side of the big pit, and the compound for the natives was on the other side. Mr Clarke earned fifty pounds a month, which was more than he would earn anywhere else. He was a silent, hardworking man, except when he got drunk, which was not often. Three or four times in the year he would be off work for a week, and then Mr Macintosh did his work for him till he recovered, when he greeted him with the good-humoured words: 'Well, laddie, got that off your chest?'

Mr Macintosh did not drink at all. His not drinking was a passionate business, for like many Scots people he ran to extremes. Never a drop of liquor could be found in his house. Also, he was religious, in a reminiscent sort of way, because of his parents, who had been very religious. He lived in a two-roomed shack, with a bare wooden table in it, three wooden chairs, a bed and a wardrobe. The cook boiled beef and carrots and potatoes three days a week, roasted beef three days, and cooked a chicken on Sundays.

Mr Macintosh was one of the richest men in the country, he was more than a millionaire. People used to say of him: But for heaven's sake, he could do anything, go anywhere, what's the point of having so much money if you live in the back of beyond with a parcel of blacks on top of a big hole in the ground?

But to Mr Macintosh it seemed quite natural to live so, and when he went for a holiday to Cape Town, where he lived in the most expensive hotel, he always came back again long before he was expected. He did not like holidays. He liked working.

He wore old, oily khaki trousers, tied at the waist with an old red tie, and he wore a red handkerchief loose around his neck over a white cotton singlet. He was short and broad and strong, with a big square head tilted back on a thick neck. His heavy brown arms and neck sprouted thick black hair around the edges of the singlet. His eyes were small and grey and shrewd. His mouth was thin, pressed tight in the middle. He wore an old felt hat on the back of his head, and carried a stick cut from the bush, and he went strolling around the edge of the pit, slashing the stick at bushes and grass or sometimes at lazy natives, and he shouted orders to his boss-boys, and watched the swarms of workers far below him in the bottom of the pit, and then he would go to his little office and make up his books, and so he spent his day. In the evenings he sometimes asked Mr Clarke to come over and play cards.

Clarke would say to his wife:'Annie, he wants me,' and she nodded and told her cook to make supper early.

Mrs Clarke was the only white woman on the mine. She did not mind this, being a naturally solitary person. Also, she had been profoundly grateful to reach this haven of fifty pounds a month with a man who did not mind her husband's bouts of drinking. She was a woman of early middle age, with a thin, flat body, a thin, colourless face, and quiet blue eyes. Living here, in this destroying heat, year after year, did not make her ill, it sapped her slowly, leaving her rather numbed and silent. She spoke very little, but then she roused herself and said what was necessary.

For instance, when they first arrived at the mine it was to a two-roomed house. She walked over to Mr Macintosh and said:'You are alone, but you have four rooms. There are two of us and the baby, and we have two rooms. There's no sense in it.' Mr Macintosh gave her a quick, hard look, his mouth tightened, and then he began to laugh. 'Well, yes, that is so,' he said laughing, and he made the change at once, chuckling every time he remembered how the quiet Annie Clarke had put him in his place.

Similarly, about once a month Annie Clarke went to his house and said:'Now get out of my way, I'll get things straight for you.' And when she'd finished tidying up she said:'You're nothing but a pig, and that's the truth.' She was referring to his habit of throwing his clothes everywhere, or wearing them for weeks unwashed, and also to other matters which no one else dared to refer to, even as indirectly as this. To this he might reply, chuckling with the pleasure of teasing her:'You're a married woman, Mrs Clarke,' and she said:'Nothing stops you getting married that I can see.' And she walked away very straight, her cheeks burning with indignation.

She was very fond of him, and he of her. And Mr Clarke liked and admired him, and he liked Mr Clarke. And since Mr Clarke and Mrs Clarke lived amiably together in their four-roomed house, sharing bed and board without ever quarrelling, it was to be presumed they liked each other too. But they seldom spoke. What was there to say?

It was to this silence, to these understood truths, that little Tommy had to grow up and adjust himself.

Tommy Clarke was three months when he came to the mine, and day and night his ears were filled with noise, every day and every night for years, so that he did not think of it as noise, rather, it was a different sort of silence. The minestamps thudded *gold*, gold, *gold*, gold, *gold*, gold, on and on, never changing, never stopping. So he did not hear them. But there came a day when the machinery broke, and it was when Tommy was three years old, and the silence was so terrible and so empty that he went screeching to his mother: 'It's stopped, it's stopped,' and he wept, shivering, in a corner until the thudding began again. It was as if the heart of the world had gone silent. But when it started to beat, Tommy heard it, and he knew the difference between silence and sound, and his ears acquired a new sensitivity, like a conscience. He heard the shouting and the singing from the swarms of working natives, reckless, noisy people because of the danger they always must live with. He heard the picks ringing on stone, the softer, deeper thud of picks on thick earth. He heard the clang of the trucks, and the roar of falling earth, and the rumbling of trolleys on rails. And at night the owls hooted and the night-jars screamed and the crickets chirped. And when it stormed it seemed the sky itself was flinging down bolts of noise against the mountains, for the thunder rolled and crashed, and the lightning darted from peak to peak around him. It was never silent, never, save for that awful moment when the big heart stopped beating. Yet later he longed for it to stop again, just for an hour, so that he might hear a true silence. That was when he was a little older, and the quietness of his parents was beginning to trouble him. There they were, always so gentle, saying so little, only: That's how things are; or: You ask so many questions; or: You'll understand when you grow up.

It was a false silence, much worse than that real silence had been.

He would play beside his mother in the kitchen, who never said anything but Yes, and No, and—with a patient, sighing voice, as if even his voice tired her: You talk so much, Tommy!

And he was carried on his father's shoulders around the big, black working machines, and they couldn't speak because of the din the machines made. And Mr Macintosh would say: Well, laddie? and give him sweets from his pocket, which he always kept there, especially for Tommy. And once he saw Mr Macintosh and his father playing cards in the evening, and they didn't talk at all, except for the words that the game needed.

So Tommy escaped to the friendly din of the compound across the great gulf, and played all day with the black children, dancing in their dances, running through the bush after rabbits, or working wet clay into shapes of bird or beast. No silence there, everything noisy and cheerful, and at evening he returned to his equable, silent parents, and after the meal he lay in bed listening to the *thud*, thud, *thud*, thud, *thud*, thud, of the stamps. In the compound across the gulf they were drinking and dancing, the drums made a quick beating against the slow thud of the stamps, and the dancers around the fires yelled, a high, ululating sound like a big wind coming fast and crooked through a gap in the mountains. That was a different world, to which he belonged as much as to this one, where people said: Finish your pudding; or: It's time for bed; and very little else.

When he was five years old he got malaria and was very sick. He recovered, but in the rainy season of the next year he got it again. Both times Mr Macintosh got into his big American car and went streaking across the thirty miles of bush to the nearest hospital for a doctor. The doctor said quinine, and be careful to screen for mosquitoes! It was easy to give quinine, but Mrs Clarke, that tired, easy-going woman, found it hard to say: Don't, and Be in by six; and Don't go near water; and so, when Tommy was seven, he got malaria again. And now Mrs Clarke was worried, because the doctor spoke severely, mentioning blackwater.[1]

Mr Macintosh drove the doctor back to his hospital and then came home, and at once went to see Tommy, for he loved Tommy very deeply.

Mrs Clarke said: 'What do you expect, with all these holes everywhere, they're full of water all the wet season.'

'Well, lassie, I can't fill in all the holes and shafts, people have been digging up here since the Queen of Sheba.'

'Never mind about the Queen of Sheba. At least you could screen our house properly.'

'I pay your husband fifty pounds a month,' said Mr Macintosh, conscious of being in the right.

'Fifty pounds and a proper house,' said Annie Clarke.

---

1 A complication of chronic malaria.

Macintosh gave her that quick, narrow look, and then laughed loudly. A week later the house was encased in fine wire mesh all round from roof-edge to verandah-edge so that it looked like a new meat safe, and Mrs Clarke went over to Mr Macintosh's house and gave it a grand cleaning, and when she left she said: 'You're nothing but a pig, you're as rich as the Oppenheimers, why don't you buy yourself some new vests[1] at least. And you'll be getting malaria, too, the way you go traipsing about at nights.'

She returned to Tommy, who was seated on the verandah behind the grey-glistening wire netting, in a big desk-chair. He was very thin and white after the fever. He was a long child, bony, and his eyes were big and black, and his mouth full and pouting from the petulances of the illness. He had a mass of richly-brown hair, like caramels, on his head. His mother looked at this pale child of hers, who was yet so brightly coloured and full of vitality, and her tired will-power revived enough to determine a new regime for him. He was never to be out after six at night, when the mosquitoes were abroad. He was never to be out before the sun rose.

'You can get up,' she said, and he got up, thankfully throwing aside his covers.

'I'll go over to the compound,' he said at once.

She hesitated, and then said: 'You mustn't play there any more.'

'Why not?' he asked, already fidgeting on the steps outside the wire-netting cage.

Ah, how she hated these Whys, and Why nots! They tired her utterly. 'Because I say so,' she snapped.

But he persisted: 'I always play there.'

'You're getting too big now, and you'll be going to school soon.'

Tommy sank on to the steps and remained there, looking away over the great pit to the busy, sunlit compound. He had known this moment was coming, of course. It was a knowledge that was part of the silence. And yet he had not known it. He said: 'Why, why, why, why?' singing it out in a persistent wail.

'Because I say so.' Then, in tired desperation: 'You get sick from the natives, too.'

At this, he switched his large black eyes from the scenery to his mother, and she flushed a little. For they were derisively scornful. Yet she half-believed it herself, or rather, must believe it, for all through the wet season the bush would lie waterlogged and fester-

---

1 Undershirts.

ing with mosquitoes, and nothing could be done about it, and one has to put the blame on something;

She said: 'Don't argue. You're not to play with them. You're too big now to play with a lot of dirty kaffirs. When you were little it was different, but now you're a big boy.'

Tommy sat on the steps in the sweltering afternoon sun that came thick and yellow through the haze of dust and smoke over the mountains, and he said nothing. He made no attempt to go near the compound, now that his growing manhood depended on his not playing with the black people. So he had been made to feel. Yet he did not believe a word of it, not really.

Some days later, he was kicking a football by himself around the back of the house when a group of black children called to him from the bush, and he turned away as if he had not seen them. They called again and then ran away. And Tommy wept bitterly, for now he was alone.

He went to the edge of the big pit and lay on his stomach looking down. The sun blazed through him so that his bones ached, and he shook his mass of hair forward over his eyes to shield them. Below, the great pit was so deep that the men working on the bottom of it were like ants. The trucks that climbed up the almost vertical sides were like match boxes. The system of ladders and steps cut in the earth, which the workers used to climb up and down, seemed so flimsy across the gulf that a stone might dislodge it. Indeed, falling stones often did. Tommy sprawled, gripping the earth tight with tense belly and flung limbs, and stared down. They were all like ants and flies. Mr Macintosh, too, when he went down, which he did often, for no one could say he was a coward. And his father, and Tommy himself, they were all no bigger than little insects. It was like an enormous ant-working, as brightly tinted as a fresh antheap. The levels of earth around the mouth of the pit were reddish, then lower down grey and gravelly, and lower still clear yellow. Heaps of the inert, heavy yellow soil, brought up from the bottom, lay all around him. He stretched out his hand and took some of it. It was unresponsive, lying lifeless and dense on his fingers, a little damp from the rain. He clenched his fist, and loosened it, and now the mass of yellow earth lay shaped on his palm, showing the marks of his fingers. A shape like—what? A bit of root? A fragment of rock rotted by water? He rolled his palms vigorously around it, and it became smooth like a water-ground stone. Then he sat up and took more earth and formed a pit, and up the sides flying ladders with bits of stick, and little kips of wetted earth for the trucks. Soon the sun dried it, and it all cracked and fell apart. Tommy gave the model a kick and went moodily back to the house. The sun was going down. It seemed that he had left a golden age of freedom behind, and now there was a new country of restrictions and time-tables.

His mother saw how he suffered, but thought: Soon he'll go to school and find companions. But he was only just seven, and very young to go all the way to the city to boarding-school. She sent for school-books, and taught him to read. Yet this was for only two or three hours in the day, and for the rest he mooned about as she complained, gazing away over the gulf to the compound, from where he could hear the noise of the playing children. He was stoical about it, or so it seemed, but underneath he was suffering badly from this new knowledge, which was much more vital than anything he had learned from the school-books. He knew the word loneliness, and lying at the edge of the pit he formed the yellow clay into little figures which he called Betty and Freddy and Dirk. Playmates. Dirk was the name of the boy he liked the best among the children in the compound over the gulf.

One day his mother called him to the back door. There stood Dirk, and he was holding between his hands a tiny duiker,[1] the size of a thin cat. Tommy ran forward, and was about to exclaim with Dirk over the little animal, when he remembered his new status. He stopped, stiffened himself and said: 'How much?'

Dirk, keeping his eyes evasive, said: 'One shilling, Baas.'

Tommy glanced at his mother and then said, proudly, his voice high: 'Damned cheek, too much.'

Annie Clarke flushed. She was ashamed and flustered. She came forward and said quickly: 'It's all right, Tommy, I'll give you the shilling.' She took the coin from the pocket of her apron and gave it to Tommy, who handed it at once to Dirk. Tommy took the little animal gently in his hands, and his tenderness for this frightened and lonely creature rushed up to his eyes and he turned away so that Dirk couldn't see—he would have been bitterly ashamed to show softness in front of Dirk, who was so tough and fearless.

Dirk stood back, watching, unwilling to see the last of the buck. Then he said: 'It's just born, it can die.'

Mrs Clarke said, dismissingly: 'Yes, Tommy will look after it.' Dirk walked away slowly, fingering the shilling in his pocket, but

---

1 A small antelope with horns pointing backward.

looking back at where Tommy and his mother were making a nest for the little buck in a packing-case. Mrs Clarke made a feeding-bottle with some linen stuffed into the neck of a tomato sauce bottle with milk and water and sugar. Tommy knelt by the buck and tried to drip the milk into its mouth.

It lay tremblingly lifting its delicate head from the crumpled, huddled limbs, too weak to move, the big eyes dark and forlorn. Then the trembling became a spasm of weakness and the head collapsed with a soft thud against the side of the box, and then slowly, and with a trembling effort, the neck lifted the head again. Tommy tried to push the wad of linen into the soft mouth, and the milk wetted the fur and ran down over the buck's chest, and he wanted to cry.

'But it'll die, mother, it'll die,' he shouted, angrily.

'You mustn't force it,' said Annie Clarke, and she went away to her household duties. Tommy knelt there with the bottle, stroking the trembling little buck and suffering every time the thin neck collapsed with weakness, and tried again and again to interest it in the milk. But the buck wouldn't drink at all.

'Why?' shouted Tommy, in the anger of his misery. 'Why won't it drink? Why? why?'

'But it's only just born,' said Mrs Clark. The cord was still on the creature's navel, like a shrivelling, dark stick.

That night Tommy took the little buck into his room, and secretly in the dark lifted it, folded in a blanket into his bed. He could feel it trembling fitfully against his chest, and he cried into the dark because he knew it was going to die.

In the morning when he woke, the buck could not lift its head at all, and it was a weak, collapsed weight on Tommy's chest, a chilly weight. The blanket in which it lay was messed with yellow stuff like a scrambled egg. Tommy washed the buck gently, and wrapped it again in new coverings, and laid it on the verandah where the sun could warm it.

Mrs Clarke gently forced the jaws open and poured down milk until the buck choked. Tommy knelt beside it all morning, suffering as he had never suffered before. The tears ran steadily down his face and he wished he could die too, and Mrs Clarke wished very much she could catch Dirk and give him a good beating, which would be unjust, but might do something to relieve her feelings. 'Besides,' she said to her husband, 'it's nothing but cruelty, taking a tiny thing like that from its mother.'

Tommy stood on the verandah, his face tight and angry, and

watched the cookboy shovel his little buck hastily under some bushes, and return whistling.

Then he went into the room where his mother and father were sitting and said: 'Why is Dirk yellow and not dark brown like the other kaffirs?'

Silence. Mr Clarke and Annie Clarke looked at each other. Then Mr Clarke said 'They come different colours.'

'What's a half-caste?'

'You'll understand when you grow up.'

Tommy looked from his father, who was filling a pipe his eyes lowered to the work, then at his mother, whose cheekbones held that proud, bright flush.

'I understand now,' he said, defiantly.

'Then why do you ask?' said Mrs Clarke, with anger. Why, she was saying, do you infringe the rule of silence?

Tommy went out, and to the brink of the great pit. There he lay, wondering why he had said he understood when he did not. Though in a sense he did. He was remembering, though he had not noticed it before, that among the gang of children in the compound were two yellow children. Dirk was one, and Dirk's sister another. She was a tiny child, who came toddling on the fringe of the older children's games. But Dirk's mother was black, or rather, dark-brown like the others. And Dirk was not really yellow, but light copper-colour. The colour of this earth, were it a little darker. Tommy's fingers were fiddling with the damp clay. He looked at the little figures he had made, Betty and Freddy. Idly, he smashed them. Then he picked up Dirk and flung him down. But he must have flung him down too carefully, for he did not break, and so he set the figure against the stalk of a weed. He took up a lump of clay, and as his fingers experimentally pushed and kneaded it, the shape grew into the shape of a little duiker. But not a sick duiker, which had died because it had been taken from its mother. Not at all, it was a fine strong duiker, standing with one hoof raised and its head listening, ears pricked forward.

Tommy knelt on the edge of the great pit, absorbed, while the duiker grew into its proper form. He became dissatisfied—it was too small. He impatiently smashed what he had done, and taking a big heap of the yellowish, dense soil shook water on it from an old rusty railway sleeper that had collected rainwater and made the mass soft and workable. Then he began again. The duiker would be half life-size.

And so his hands worked and his mind worried along its path

of questions: Why? Why? Why? And finally: If Dirk is half black, or rather half white and half dark-brown, then who is his father?

But from time to time he looked across the gulf to where Mr Macintosh was strolling, swinging his big cudgel, and he thought: There are only two white men on this mine.

The buck was now finished, and he wetted his fingers in rusty rainwater, and smoothed down the soft clay to make it glisten like the surfaces of fur, but at once it dried and dulled, and as he knelt there he thought how the sun would crack it and it would fall to pieces, and an angry dissatisfaction filled him and he hung his head and wanted very much to cry. And just as the first tears were coming he heard a soft whistle from behind him, and turned, and there was Dirk, kneeling behind a bush and looking out through the parted leaves.

'Is the buck all right?' asked Dirk.

'It's no good, the sun'll crack it,' said Tommy, and he began to cry, although he was so ashamed to cry in front of Dirk. 'The buck's dead,' he wept, 'it's dead.'

'I can get you another,' said Dirk, looking at Tommy rather surprised. 'I killed its mother with a stone. It's easy.'

Dirk was seven, like Tommy. He was tall and strong, like Tommy. His eyes were dark and full, but his mouth was not full and soft, but long and narrow, clenched in the middle. His hair was very black and soft and long, falling uncut around his face, and his skin was a smooth, yellowish copper. Tommy stopped crying and looked at Dirk. He said: 'It's cruel to kill a buck's mother with a stone.' Dirk's mouth parted in surprised laughter over his big white teeth. Tommy watched him laugh, and he thought: Well, now I know who his father is.

He looked at Mr Macintosh's house, which was a few hundred yards further off. Then he looked at Dirk. He was full of anger, which he did not understand, but he did understand that he was also defiant, and this was a moment of decision. After a long time he said: 'They can see us from here,' and the decision was made.

They got up, but as Dirk rose he saw the little clay figure laid against a stem, and he picked it up. 'This is me,' he said at once. For crude as the thing was, it was unmistakably Dirk, who smiled with pleasure. 'Can I have it?', he asked, and Tommy nodded, equally proud and pleased.

They went off into the bush between the two houses, and then on for perhaps half a mile. This was the deserted part of the hollow in the mountains, no one came here, all the bustle and noise was on the other side. In front of them rose a sharp peak, and low at its foot was a high anthill, draped with Christmas fern and thick with shrub.

The two boys went inside the curtains of fern and sat down. No one could see them here. Dirk carefully put the little clay figure of himself inside a hole in the roots of a tree. Then he said: 'Make the buck again.' Tommy took his knife and knelt beside a fallen tree, and tried to carve the buck from it. The wood was soft and rotten, and was easily carved, and by night there was the clumsy shape of the buck coming out of the trunk. Dirk said: 'Now we've got something.'

The next day the two boys made their way separately to the antheap and played there together, and so it was every day.

Then one evening Mrs Clarke said to Tommy just as he was going to bed: 'I thought I told you not to play with the kaffirs?'

Tommy stood very still. Then he lifted his head and said to her, with a strong look across at his father: 'Why shouldn't I play with Mr Macintosh's son?'

Mrs Clarke stopped breathing for a moment, and closed her eyes. She opened them in appeal at her husband. But Mr Clarke was filling his pipe. Tommy waited and then said good night and went to his room.

There he undressed slowly and climbed into the narrow iron bed and lay quietly, listening to the thud, thud, gold, gold, thud, thud, of the mine-stamps. Over in the compound they were dancing, and the tom-toms were beating fast, like the quick beat of the buck's heart that night as it lay on his chest. They were yelling like the wind coming through gaps in a mountain and through the window he could see the high, flaring light of the fires, and the black figures of the dancing people were wild and active against it.

Mrs Clarke came quickly in. She was crying. 'Tommy,' she said, sitting on the edge of his bed in the dark.

'Yes?' he said, cautiously.

'You mustn't say that again. Not ever.'

He said nothing. His mother's hand was urgently pressing his arm. 'Your father might lose his job,' said Mrs Clarke, wildly. 'We'd never get this money anywhere else. Never. You must understand, Tommy.'

'I do understand,' said Tommy, stiffly, very sorry for his mother, but hating her at the same time. 'Just don't say it Tommy, don't ever say it.' Then she kissed him in a way that was both fond and appealing, and went out, shutting the door. To her husband she said it was time Tommy went to school, the next day she wrote to make the arrangements.

And so now Tommy made the long journey by car and train into the city four times a year, and four times a year he came back for the holidays. Mr Macintosh always drove him to the station and gave him ten shillings pocket money and he came to fetch him in the car with his parents, and he always said: 'Well, laddie, and how's school?' And Tommy said: 'Fine, Mr Macintosh.' And Mr Macintosh said 'We'll make a college man of you yet.'

When he said this, the flush came bright and proud on Annie Clarke's cheeks, and she looked quickly at Mr Clarke, who was smiling and embarrassed. But Mr Macintosh laid his hands on Tommy's shoulders and said: 'There's my laddie, there's my laddie,' and Tommy kept his shoulders stiff and still. Afterwards, Mrs Clarke would say, nervously: 'He's fond of you, Tommy, he'll do right by you.' And once she said: 'It's natural, he's got no children of his own.' But Tommy scowled at her and she flushed and said: 'There's things you don't understand yet, Tommy and you'll regret it if you throw away your chances.' Tommy turned away with an impatient movement. Yet it was not so clear at all, for it was almost as if he were a rich man's son, with all that pocket money, and the parcels of biscuits and sweets that Mr Macintosh sent into school during the term, and being fetched in the great rich car. And underneath it all he felt as if he were dragged along by the nose. He felt as if he were part of a conspiracy of some kind that no one ever spoke about. Silence. His real feelings were growing up slow and complicated and obstinate underneath that silence.

At school it was not at all complicated, it was the other world. There Tommy did his lessons and played with his friends and did not think of Dirk. Or rather, his thoughts of him were proper for that world. A half-caste, ignorant, living in the kaffir location—he felt ashamed that he played with Dirk in the holidays, and he told no one. Even on the train coming home he would think like that of Dirk, but the nearer he reached home the more his thoughts wavered and darkened. On the first evening at home he would speak of the school, and how he was first in the class, and he played with this boy or that, or went to such fine houses in the city as a guest. The very first morning he would be standing on the verandah looking at the big pit and at the compound away beyond it, and his mother watched him, smiling in nervous supplication. And then he walked down the steps, away from the pit, and into the bush to the antheap. There Dirk was waiting for him. So it was every holiday. Neither of the boys spoke, at first, of what divided them. But, on the eve of Tommy's return to school after he had been there a year, Dirk said: 'You're getting educated, but I've nothing to learn.' Tommy said: 'I'll bring back books and teach you.' He said this in a quick voice, as if ashamed, and Dirk's eyes were accusing and angry. He gave his sarcastic laugh and said: 'That's what you say, white boy.'

The two boys were sitting on the antheap under the fine lacy curtains of Christmas fern, looking at the rocky peak soaring into the smoky yellowish sky. There was the most unpleasant sort of annoyance in Tommy, and he felt ashamed of it. And on Dirk's face there was an aggressive but ashamed look. They continued to sit there, a little apart, full of dislike for each other and knowing that the dislike came from the pressure of the outside world. 'I said I'd teach you, didn't I?' said Tommy, grandly, shying a stone at a bush so that leaves flew off in all directions. 'You white bastard,' said Dirk, in a low voice, and he let out that sudden ugly laugh, showing his white teeth. 'What did you say?' said Tommy, going pale and jumping to his feet. 'You heard,' said Dirk, still laughing. He too got up. Then Tommy flung himself on Dirk and they overbalanced and rolled off into the bushes, kicking and scratching. They rolled apart and began fighting properly, with fists. Tommy was better-fed and more healthy. Dirk was tougher. They were a match, and they stopped when they were too tired and battered to go on. They staggered over to the antheap and sat there side by side, panting, wiping the blood off their faces. At last they lay on their backs on the rough slant of the anthill and looked up at the sky. Every trace of dislike had vanished, and they felt easy and quiet. When the sun went down they walked together through the bush to a point where they could not be seen from the houses, and there they said, as always: 'See you tomorrow.'

When Mr Macintosh gave him the usual ten shillings, he put them into his pocket thinking he would buy a football, but he did not. The ten shillings stayed unspent until it was nearly the end of the term, and then he went to the shops and bought a reader and some exercise books and pencils and an arithmetic. He hid these at the bottom of his trunk and whipped them out before his mother could see them.

He took them to the antheap next morning, but before he could reach it he saw there was a little shed built on it, and the Christmas fern had been draped like a veil across the roof of the shed. The bushes had been cut on the top of the anthill, but left on the sides, so that the shed looked as if it rose from the tops of the bushes. The shed was of unbarked poles pushed into the earth, the roof was of thatch, and the upper half of the front was left open. Inside there was a bench of poles and a table of planks on poles. There sat Dirk, waiting hungrily, and Tommy went and sat beside him, putting the books and pencils on the table.

'This shed is fine,' said Tommy, but Dirk was already looking at the books. So he began to teach Dirk how to read. And for all that holiday they were together in the shed while Dirk pored over the books. He found them more difficult than Tommy did, because they were full of words for things Dirk did not know, like curtains or carpet, and teaching Dirk to read the word carpet meant telling him all about carpets and the furnishings of a house. Often Tommy felt bored and restless and said: 'Let's play,' but Dirk said fiercely: 'No, I want to read.' Tommy grew fretful, for after all he had been working in the term and now he felt entitled to play. So there was another fight. Dirk said Tommy was a lazy white bastard, and Tommy said Dirk was a dirty half-caste. They fought as before, evenly matched and to no conclusion, and afterwards felt fine and friendly, and even made jokes about the fighting. It was arranged that they should work in the mornings only and leave the afternoons for play. When Tommy went back home that evening his mother saw the scratches on his face and the swollen nose, and said hopefully: 'Have you and Dirk been fighting?' But Tommy said no, he had hit his face on a tree.

His parents, of course, knew about the shed in the bush, but did not speak of it to Mr Macintosh. No one did. For Dirk's very existence was something to be ignored by everyone, and none of the workers, not even the overseers, would dare to mention Dirk's name. When Mr Macintosh asked Tommy what he had done to his face, he said he had slipped and fallen.

And so their eighth year and their ninth went past. Dirk could read and write and do all the sums that Tommy could do. He was always handicapped by not knowing the different way of living, and soon he said, angrily, it wasn't fair, and there was another fight about it, and then Tommy began another way of teaching. He would tell how it was to go to a cinema in the city, every detail of it, how the seats were arranged in such a way, and one paid so much, and the lights were like this, and the picture on the screen worked like that. Or he would describe how at school they ate such things for breakfast and other things for lunch. Or tell how the man had come with picture slides talking about China. The two boys got out an atlas and found China, and Tommy told Dirk every word of what the lecturer had said. Or it might be Italy or some other country. And they would argue that the lecturer should have said this or that, for Dirk was always hotly scornful of the white man's way of looking at things, so arrogant, he said. Soon Tommy saw things through Dirk; he saw the other life in town clear and brightly-coloured and a little distorted, as Dirk did.

Soon, at school, Tommy would involuntarily think: I must remember this to tell Dirk. It was impossible for him to do anything, say anything, without being very conscious of just how it happened, as if Dirk's black, sarcastic eye had got inside him, Tommy, and never closed. And a feeling of unwillingness grew in Tommy, because of the strain of fitting these two worlds together. He found himself swearing at niggers or kaffirs like the other boys, and more violently than they did, but immediately afterwards he would find himself thinking: I must remember this so as to tell Dirk. Because of all this thinking, and seeing everything clear all the time, he was very bright at school, and found the work easy. He was two classes ahead of his age.

That was the tenth year, and one day Tommy went to the shed in the bush and Dirk was not waiting for him. It was the first day of the holidays. All the term he had been remembering things to tell Dirk, and now Dirk was not there. A dove was sitting on the Christmas fern, cooing lazily in the hot morning, a sleepy, lonely sound. When Tommy came pushing through the bushes it flew away. The mine-stamps thudded heavily, gold, gold, and Tommy saw that the shed was empty even of books, for the case where they were usually kept was hanging open.

He went running to his mother: 'Where's Dirk?' he asked.

'How should I know?' said Annie Clarke, cautiously. She really did not know.

'You do know, you do!' he cried, angrily. And then he went racing off to the big pit. Mr Macintosh was sitting on an upturned truck at the edge, watching the hundreds of workers below him, moving like ants on the yellow bottom. 'Well, laddie?' he asked, amiably, and moved over for Tommy to sit by him.

'Where's Dirk?' asked Tommy, accusingly, standing in front of him.

Mr Macintosh topped his old felt hat even further back and scratched at his front hair and looked at Tommy.

'Dirk's working,' he said, at last.

'Where?'

Mr Macintosh pointed at the bottom of the pit. Then he said again: 'Sit down, laddie, I want to talk to you.'

'I don't want to,' said Tommy, and he turned away and went blundering over the veld to the shed. He sat on the bench and cried, and when dinner-time came he did not go home. All that day he sat in the shed, and when he had finished crying he remained on the bench, leaning his back against the poles of the shed, and stared into the bush. The doves cooed and cooed, kru-kruuuu kru-kruuuuu and a woodpecker tapped, and the mine-stamps thudded. Yet it was very quiet, a hand of silence gripped the bush, and he could hear the borers and the ants at work in the poles of the bench he sat on. He could see that although the anthill seemed dead, a mound of hard, peaked, baked earth, it was very much alive, for there was a fresh outbreak of wet, damp earth in the floor of the shed. There was a fine crust of reddish, lacey earth over the poles of the walls. The shed would have to be built again soon, because the ants and borers would have eaten it through. But what was the use of a shed without Dirk?

All that day he stayed there, and did not return until dark, and when his mother said: 'What's the matter with you, why are you crying?' he said angrily, 'I don't know,' matching her dishonesty with his own. The next day, even before breakfast, he was off to the shed, and did not return until dark, and refused his supper although he had not eaten all day.

And the next day was the same, but now he was bored and lonely. He took his knife from his pocket and whittled at a stick, and it became a boy, bent and straining under the weight of a heavy load, his arms clenched up to support it. He took the figure home at supper-time and ate with it on the table in front of him.

'What's that?' asked Annie Clarke, and Tommy answered: 'Dirk.'

He took it to his bedroom, and sat in the soft lamplight, working away with his knife, and he had it in his hand the following morning when he met Mr Macintosh at the brink of the pit. 'What's that, laddie?' asked Mr Macintosh, and Tommy said: 'Dirk.'

Mr Macintosh's mouth went thin, and then he smiled and said: 'Let me have it.'

'No, it's for Dirk.'

Mr Macintosh took out his wallet and said: 'I'll pay you for it.'

'I don't want any money,' said Tommy, angrily, and Mr Macintosh, greatly disturbed, put back his wallet. Then Tommy, hesitating, said: 'Yes, I do.' Mr Macintosh, his values confirmed, was relieved, and he took out his wallet again and produced a pound note, which seemed to him very generous. 'Five pounds,' said Tommy, promptly. Mr Macintosh first scowled, then laughed. He tipped back his head and roared with laughter. 'Well, laddie, you'll make a business man yet. Five pounds for a little bit of wood!'

'Make it for yourself then, if it's just a bit of wood.'

Mr Macintosh counted out five pounds and handed them over. 'What are you going to do with that money?' he asked, as he watched Tommy buttoning them carefully into his shirt pocket. 'Give them to Dirk,' said Tommy, triumphantly, and Mr Macintosh's heavy old face went purple. He watched while Tommy walked away from him, sitting on the truck, letting the heavy cudgel swing lightly against his shoes. He solved his immediate problem by thinking: He's a good laddie, he's got a good heart.

That night Mrs Clarke came over while he was sitting over his roast beef and cabbage, and said: 'Mr Macintosh, I want a word with you.' He nodded at a chair, but she did not sit. 'Tommy's upset,' she said, delicately, 'he's been used to Dirk, and now he's got no one to play with.'

For a moment Mr Macintosh kept his eyes lowered then he said: 'It's easily fixed, Annie, don't worry yourself.' He spoke heartily, as it was easy for him to do, speaking of a worker, who might be released at his whim for other duties.

That bright protesting flush came on to her cheeks, in spite of herself, and she looked quickly at him, with real indignation. But he ignored it and said: 'I'll fix it in the morning, Annie.'

She thanked him and went back home, suffering because she had not said those words which had always soothed her conscience in the past: You're nothing but a pig, Mr Macintosh....

As for Tommy, he was sitting in the shed, crying his eyes out. And then, when there were no more tears, there came such a storm of anger and pain that he would never forget it as long as he lived. What for? He did not know, and that was the worst of it. It was not simply Mr Macintosh, who loved him, and who thus so blackly betrayed his own flesh and blood, nor the silences of his parents. Something deeper, felt working in the substance of life as he could hear those ants working away with those busy jaws at the roots of the poles he sat on, to make new material for their different forms of life. He was testing those words which were used, or not used—merely suggested—all the time, and for a ten-year-old boy it was almost too hard to bear. A child may say of a companion one day that he hates so and so, and the next: He is my friend. That is how a relationship is, shifting and changing, and children are kept safe in their hates and loves by the fabric of social life their parents make over their heads. And middle-aged people say: This is my friend, this is my enemy, including all the shifts and changes of feeling in one word, for the sake of an easy mind. In between these ages, at about twenty perhaps, there is a time when the young people test everything, and accept many hard and cruel truths about living, and that is because they do not know how hard it is to accept them finally, and for the rest of their lives. It is easy to be truthful at twenty.

But it is not easy at ten, a little boy entirely alone, looking at words like friendship. What, then, was friendship? Dirk was his friend, that he knew, but did he like Dirk? Did he love him? Sometimes not at all. He remembered how Dirk had said: 'I'll get you another baby buck. I'll kill its mother with a stone.' He remembered his feeling of revulsion at the cruelty. Dirk was cruel. But— and here Tommy unexpectedly laughed, and for the first time he understood Dirk's way of laughing. It was really funny to say that Dirk was cruel, when his very existence was a cruelty. Yet Mr Macintosh laughed in exactly the same way, and his skin was white, or rather, white browned over by the sun. Why was Mr Macintosh also entitled to laugh, with that same abrupt ugliness? Perhaps somewhere in the beginnings of the rich Mr Macintosh there had been the same cruelty, and that had worked its way through the life of Mr Macintosh until it turned into the cruelty of Dirk, the coloured boy, the half-caste? If so, it was all much deeper than differently coloured skins, and much harder to understand.

And then Tommy thought how Dirk seemed to wait always, as if he, Tommy, were bound to stand by him, as if this were a justice that was perfectly clear to Dirk; and he, Tommy, did in fact fight with Mr Macintosh for Dirk, and he could behave in no other way. Why? Because Dirk was his friend? Yet there were times when he hated Dirk, and certainly Dirk hated him, and when they fought they could have killed each other easily, and with joy.

Well, then? Well, then? What was friendship, and why were they bound so closely, and by what? Slowly the little boy sitting alone on his antheap came to an understanding which is proper to middle-aged people, that resignation in knowledge which is called irony. Such a person may know, for instance, that he is bound most deeply to another person, although he does not like that person, in the way the word is ordinarily used, or the way he talks, or his politics, or anything else. And yet they are friends and will always be friends, and what happens to this bound couple affects each most deeply, even though they may be in different continents, or may never see each other again. Or after twenty years they may meet, and there is no need to say a word, everything is understood. This is one of the ways of friendship, and just as real as amiability or being alike.

Well, then? For it is a hard and difficult knowledge for any little boy to accept. But he accepted it, and knew that he and Dirk were closer than brothers and always would be so. He grew many years older in that day of painful struggle while he listened to the mine-stamps saying gold, gold, and to the ants working away with their jaws to destroy the bench he sat on, to make food for themselves.

Next morning Dirk came to the shed, and Tommy, looking at him, knew that he, too, had grown years older in the months of working in the great pit. Ten years old—but he had been working with men and he was not a child.

Tommy took out the five pound notes and gave them to Dirk. Dirk pushed them back. 'What for?' he asked.

'I got them from him,' said Tommy, and at once Dirk took them as if they were his right.

And at once, inside Tommy, came indignation, for he felt he was being taken for granted, and he said: 'Why aren't you working?'

'He said I needn't. He means, while you are having your holidays.'

'I got you free,' said Tommy, boasting.

Dirk's eyes narrowed in anger. 'He's my father,' he said, for the first time.

'But he made you work,' said Tommy, taunting him. And then: 'Why do you work? I wouldn't. I should say no.'

'So you would say no?' said Dirk in angry sarcasm.

'There's no law to make you.'

'So there's no law, white boy, no law ...' But Tommy had sprung at him, and they were fighting again, rolling over and over, and this time they fell apart from exhaustion and lay on the ground panting for a long time.

Later Dirk said: 'Why do we fight, it's silly?'

'I don't know,' said Tommy, and he began to laugh, and Dirk laughed too. They were to fight often in the future, but never with such bitterness, because of the way they were laughing now.

It was the following holidays before they fought again. Dirk was waiting for him in the shed.

'Did he let you go?' asked Tommy at once, putting down new books on the table for Dirk.

'I just came,' said Dirk. 'I didn't ask.'

They sat together on the bench, and at once a leg gave way and they rolled off on to the floor laughing. 'We must mend it,' said Tommy. 'Let's build the shed again.'

'No,' said Dirk at once, 'don't let's waste time on the shed. You can teach me while you're here, and I can make the shed when you've gone back to school.'

Tommy slowly got up from the floor, frowning. Again he felt he was being taken for granted. 'Aren't you going to work on the mine during the term?'

'No, I'm not going to work on the mine again. I told him I wouldn't.'

'You've got to work,' said Tommy, grandly.

'So I've got to work' said Dirk, threateningly. 'You can go to school, white boy, but I've got to work, and in the holidays I can't just take time off to please you.'

They fought until they were tired, and five minutes afterwards they were seated on the anthill talking. 'What did you do with the five pounds?' asked Tommy.

'I gave them to my mother.'

'What did she do with them?'

'She bought herself a dress, and then food for us all, and bought me these trousers, and she put the rest away to keep.'

A pause. Then, deeply ashamed, Tommy asked: 'Doesn't *he* give her any money?'

'He doesn't come any more. Not for more than a year.'

'Oh, I thought he did still,' said Tommy casually, whistling.

'No.' Then, fiercely, in a low voice: 'There'll be some more half-castes in the compound soon.'

Dirk sat crouching his fierce black eyes on Tommy, ready to spring at him. But Tommy was sitting with his head bowed, look-ing at the ground. 'It's not fair,' he said. 'It's not fair.'

'So you've discovered that, white boy?' said Dirk. It was said good-naturedly, and there was no need to fight. They went to their books and Tommy taught Dirk some new sums.

But they never spoke of what Dirk would do in the future, how he would use all this schooling. They did not dare.

That was the eleventh year.

When they were twelve, Tommy returned from school to be greeted by the words: 'Have you heard the news?'

'What news?'

They were sitting as usual on the bench. The shed was newly built, with strong thatch, and good walls, plastered this time with mud, so as to make it harder for the ants.

'They are saying you are going to be sent away.'

'Who says so?'

'Oh, everyone,' said Dirk, stirring his feet about vaguely under the table. This was because it was the first few minutes after the return from school, and he was always cautious, until he was sure Tommy had not changed towards him. And that 'everyone' was explosive. Tommy nodded, however, and asked apprehensively: 'Where to?'

'To the sea.'

'How do they know?' Tommy scarcely breathed the word *they*.

'Your cook heard your mother say so ...' And then Dirk added with a grin, forcing the issue: 'Cheek, dirty kaffirs talking about white men.'

Tommy smiled obligingly, and asked: 'How, to the sea, what does it mean?'

'How should we know, dirty kaffirs.'

'Oh, shut up,' said Tommy, angrily. They glared at each other, their muscles tensed. But they sighed and looked away. At twelve it was not easy to fight, it was all too serious. That night Tommy said to his parents: 'They say I'm going to sea. Is it true?'

His mother asked quickly: 'Who said so?'

'But is it true?' Then, derisively: 'Cheeky, dirty kaffirs talking about *us*.'

'Please don't talk like that, Tommy, it's not right.'

'Oh, mother, please, how am I going to sea?'

'But be sensible Tommy, it's not settled, but Mr Macintosh ...'

'So it's Mr Macintosh.'

Mrs Clarke looked at her husband, who came forward and sat down and settled his elbows on the table. A family conference. Tommy also sat down.

'Now listen, son. Mr Macintosh has a soft spot for you. You should be grateful to him. He can do a lot for you.'

'But why should I go to sea?'

'You don't have to. He suggested it—he was in the Merchant Navy himself once.'

'So I've got to go just because he did.'

'He's offered to pay for you to go to college in England, and give you money until you're in the Navy.'

'But I don't want to be a sailor. I've never ever seen the sea.'

'But you're good at your figures, and you have to be, so why not?'

'I won't,' said Tommy, angrily. 'I won't, I won't.' He glared at them through tears. 'You just want to get rid of me, that's all it is. You want me to go away from here, from ...'

The parents looked at each other and sighed.

'Well, if you don't want to, you don't have to. But it's not every boy who has a chance like this.'

'Why doesn't he send Dirk?' asked Tommy, aggressively.

'Tommy,' cried Annie Clarke, in great distress.

'Well, why doesn't he? He's much better than me at figures.'

'Go to bed,' said Mr Clarke suddenly, in a fit of temper. 'Go to bed.'

Tommy went out of the room, slamming the door hard. He must be grown-up. His father had never spoken to him like that. He sat on the edge of the bed in stubborn rebellion, listening to the thudding of the stamps. And down in the compound they were dancing, the lights of the fires flickered red on his window-pane.

He wondered if Dirk were there, leaping around the fires with the others.

Next day he asked him: 'Do you dance with the others?' At once he knew he had blundered. When Dirk was angry, his eyes darkened and narrowed. When he was hurt, his mouth set in a way which made the flesh pinch thinly under his nose. So he looked now.

'Listen, white boy. White people don't like us half-castes. Neither do the blacks like us. No one does. And so I don't dance with them.'

'Let's do some lessons,' said Tommy, quickly. And they went to their books, dropping the subject.

Later Mr Macintosh came to the Clarke's house and asked for Tommy. The parents watched Mr Macintosh and their son walk together along the edge of the great pit. They stood at the window and watched, but they did not speak.

Mr Macintosh was saying easily: 'Well, laddie, and so you don't want to be a sailor.'

'No, Mr Macintosh.'

'I went to sea when I was fifteen. It's hard, but you aren't afraid of that. Besides, you'd be an officer.'

Tommy said nothing.

'You don't like the idea?'

'No.'

Mr Macintosh stopped and looked down into the pit. The earth at the bottom was as yellow as it had been when Tommy was seven, but now it was much deeper. Mr Macintosh did not know how deep, because he had not measured it. Far below, in this man-made valley, the workers were moving and shifting like black seeds tilted on a piece of paper.

'Your father worked on the mines and he became an engineer working at nights, did you know that?'

'Yes.'

'It was very hard for him. He was thirty before he was qualified, and then he earned twenty-five pounds a month until he came to this mine.'

'Yes.'

'You don't want to do that, do you.'

'I will if I have to,' muttered Tommy, defiantly.

Mr Macintosh's face was swelling and purpling. The veins along nose and forehead were black. Mr Macintosh was asking himself why this lad treated him like dirt, when he was offering to do him an immense favour. And yet, in spite of the look of sullen indifference which was so ugly on that young face, he could not help loving him. He was a fine boy, tall, strong, and his hair was soft, bright brown, and his eyes clear and black. A much better man than his own father, who was rough and marked by the long struggle of his youth. He said: 'Well, you don't have to be a sailor, perhaps you'd like to go to university and be a scholar.'

'I don't know,' said Tommy, unwilling, although his heart had moved suddenly. Pleasure—he was weakening. Then he said suddenly: 'Mr Macintosh, why do you want to send me to college?'

And Mr Macintosh fell right into the trap. 'I have no children,' he said, sentimentally. 'I feel for you like my own son.' He stopped. Tommy was looking away towards the compound, and his intention was clear.

'Very well then,' said Mr Macintosh, harshly. 'If you want to be a fool.'

Tommy stood with his eyes lowered and he knew quite well he was a fool. Yet he could not have behaved in any other way.

'Don't be hasty,' said Mr Macintosh, after a pause. 'Don't throw away your chances, laddie. You're nothing but a lad, yet. Take your time.' And with this tone, he changed all the emphasis of the conflict, and made it simply a question of waiting. Tommy did not move, so Mr Macintosh went on quickly: 'Yes, that's right, you just think it over.' He hastily slipped a pound note from his pocket and put it into the boy's hand.

'You know what I'm going to do with it?' said Tommy, laughing suddenly, and not at all pleasantly.

'Do what you like, do just as you like, it's your money,' said Mr Macintosh, turning away so as not to have to understand.

Tommy took the money to Dirk, who received it as if it were his right, a feeling in which Tommy was now an accomplice, and they sat together in the shed. 'I've got to be something,' said Tommy angrily. 'They're going to make me be something.'

'They wouldn't have to make me be anything,' said Dirk sardonically. 'You know what I'd be.'

'What?' asked Tommy, enviously.

'An engineer.'

'How do you know what you've got to do?'

'That's what I want,' said Dirk, stubbornly.

After a while Tommy said: 'If you went to the city, there's a school for coloured children.'

'I wouldn't see my mother again.'

'Why not?'

'There's laws, white boy, laws. Anyone who lives with and after the fashion of the natives is a native.[1] Therefore I'm a native, and I'm not entitled to go to school with the half-castes.'

'If you went to the town, you'd not be living with the natives so you'd be classed as a coloured.'

'But then I couldn't see my mother, because if she came to town she'd still be a native.'

There was a triumphant conclusiveness in this that made Tommy think: He intends to get what he wants another way ... And then: Through me.... But he had accepted that justice a long time ago, and now he looked at his own arm that lay on the rough plank of the table. The outer side was burnt dark and dry with the sun, and the hair glinted on it like fine copper. It was no darker than Dirk's brown arm, and no lighter. He turned it over. Inside, the skin was a smooth, dusky white, the veins running blue and strong across the wrist. He looked at Dirk, grinning, who promptly turned his own arm over, in a challenging way. Tommy said,

---

1 "Statutory Definition of *Native*. Native means any member of the aboriginal tribes or races of Africa or any person having the blood of such tribes or races and living among them and after the manner thereof." *Commission on Coloured Community* 27.

unhappily: 'You can't go to school properly because the inside of your arm is brown. And that's that!' Dirk's tight and bitter mouth expanded into a grin that was also his father's, and he said: 'That is so, white boy, that is so.'

'Well, it's not my fault,' said Tommy, aggressively, closing his fingers and banging the fist down again and again.

'I didn't say it was your fault,' said Dirk at once.

Tommy said, in that uneasy, aggressive tone: 'I've never even seen your mother.'

To this, Dirk merely laughed, as if to say: You have never wanted to.

Tommy said, after a pause: 'Let me come and see her now.'

Then Dirk said in a tone which was uncomfortable, almost like compassion: 'You don't have to.'

'Yes,' insisted Tommy. 'Yes, now.' He got up, and Dirk rose too. 'She won't know what to say,' warned Dirk. 'She doesn't speak English.' He did not really want Tommy to go to the compound; Tommy did not really want to go. Yet they went.

In silence they moved along the path between the trees, in silence skirted the edge of the pit, in silence entered the trees on the other side, and moved along the paths to the compound. It was big, spread over many acres, and the huts were in all stages of growth and decay, some new, with shining thatch, some tumbledown, with dulled and sagging thatch, some in the process of being built, the peeled wands of the roof-frames gleaming like milk in the sun.

Dirk led the way to a big square hut. Tommy could see people watching him walking with the coloured boy, and turning to laugh and whisper. Dirk's face was proud and tight, and he could feel the same look on his own face. Outside the square hut sat a little girl of about ten. She was bronze, Dirk's colour. Another little girl, quite black, perhaps six years old, was squatted on a log, finger in mouth, watching them. A baby, still unsteady on its feet, came staggering out of the doorway and collapsed, chuckling, against Dirk's knees. Its skin was almost white. Then Dirk's mother came out of the hut after the baby, smiled when she saw Dirk, but went anxious and bashful when she saw Tommy. She made a little bobbing curtsey, and took the baby from Dirk, for the sake of something to hold in her awkward and shy hands.

'This is Baas Tommy,' said Dirk. He sounded very embarrassed.

She made another little curtsey and stood smiling.

She was a large woman, round and smooth all over, but her legs were slender, and her arms, wound around the child, thin and knotted. Her round face had a bashful curiosity and her eyes moved quickly from Dirk to Tommy and back while she smiled and smiled, biting her lips with strong teeth, and smiled again.

Tommy said: 'Good morning,' and she laughed and said 'Good morning.'

Then Dirk said: 'Enough now, let's go.' He sounded very angry. Tommy said: 'Good-bye.' Dirk's mother said 'Good-bye,' and made her little bobbing curtsey, and she moved her child from one arm to another and bit her lip anxiously over her gleaming smile.

Tommy and Dirk went away from the square mud hut where the variously-coloured children stood staring after them.

'There now,' said Dirk, angrily. 'You've seen my mother.'

'I'm sorry,' said Tommy uncomfortably, feeling as if the responsibility for the whole thing rested on him. But Dirk laughed suddenly and said: 'Oh, all right, all right, white boy, it's not your fault.'

All the same, he seemed pleased that Tommy was upset.

Later, with an affectation of indifference, Tommy asked, thinking of those new children: 'Does Mr Macintosh come to your mother again now?'

And Dirk answered 'Yes,' just the one word.

In the shed Dirk studied from a geography book, while Tommy sat idle and thought bitterly that they wanted him to be a sailor. Then his idle hands protested, and he took a knife and began slashing at the edge of the table. When the gashes showed a whiteness from the core of the wood, he took a stick lying on the floor and whittled at it, and when it snapped from thinness he went out to the trees, picked up a lump of old wood from the ground, and brought it back to the shed. He worked on it with his knife, not knowing what it was he made, until a curve under his knife reminded him of Dirk's sister squatting at the hut door, and then he directed his knife with a purpose. For several days he fought with the lump of wood, while Dirk studied. Then he brought a tin of boot polish from the house, and worked the bright brown wax into the creamy white wood and soon there was a bronze-coloured figure of the little girl, staring with big, curious eyes while she squatted on spindly legs.

Tommy put it in front of Dirk, who turned it around, grinning a little. 'It's like her,' he said at last. 'You can have it if you like,' said Tommy. Dirk's teeth flashed, he hesitated, and then reached into his pocket and took out a bundle of dirty cloth. He undid it, and Tommy saw the little clay figure he had made of Dirk years ago.

It was crumbling, almost worn to a lump of mud, but in it was still the vigorous challenge of Dirk's body. Tommy's mind signalled recognition—for he had forgotten he had ever made it and he picked it up. 'You kept it?' he asked shyly, and Dirk smiled. They looked at each other, smiling. It was a moment of warm, close feeling, and yet in it was the pain that neither of them understood, and also the cruelty and challenge that made them fight. They lowered their eyes unhappily. 'I'll do your mother,' said Tommy, getting up and running away into the trees, in order to escape from the challenging closeness. He searched until he found a thorn tree, which is so hard it turns the edge of an axe, and then he took an axe and worked at the felling of the tree until the sun went down. A big stone near him was kept wet to sharpen the axe, and next day he worked on until the tree fell. He sharpened the worn axe again, and cut a length of tree about two feet, and split off the tough bark, and brought it back to the shed. Dirk had fitted a shelf against the logs of the wall at the back. On it he had set the tiny, crumbling figure of himself, and the new bronze shape of his little sister. There was a space left for the new statue. Tommy said, shyly: 'I'll do it as quickly as I can so that it will be done before the term starts.' Then, lowering his eyes, which suffered under this new contract of shared feeling, he examined the piece of wood. It was not pale and gleaming like almonds, as was the softer wood. It was a gingery brown, a close-fibred, knotted wood, and down its centre, as he knew, was a hard black spine. He turned it between his hands and thought that this was more difficult than anything he had ever done. For the first time he studied a piece of wood before starting on it, with a desired shape in his mind, trying to see how what he wanted would grow out of the dense mass of material he had.

Then he tried his knife on it and it broke. He asked Dirk for his knife. It was a long piece of metal, taken from a pile of scrap mining machinery, sharpened on stone until it was razor-fine. The handle was cloth wrapped tight around.

With this new and unwieldy tool Tommy fought with the wood for many days. When the holidays were ending, the shape was there, but the face was blank. Dirk's mother was full-bodied, with soft, heavy flesh and full, naked shoulders above a tight, sideways draped cloth. The slender legs were planted firm on naked feet, and the thin arms, knotted with work, were lifted to the weight of a child who, a small, helpless creature swaddled in cloth, looked out with large curious eyes. But the mother's face was not yet there.

'I'll finish it next holidays,' said Tommy and Dirk set it carefully beside the other figures on the shelf. With his back turned he asked cautiously: 'Perhaps you won't be here next holidays?'

'Yes I will,' said Tommy, after a pause. 'Yes I will.'

It was a promise, and they gave each other that small warm, unwilling smile, and turned away, Dirk back to the compound and Tommy to the house, where his trunk was packed for school.

That night Mr Macintosh came over to the Clarke's house and spoke with the parents in the front room. Tommy, who was asleep, woke to find Mr Macintosh beside him. He sat on the foot of the bed and said: 'I want to talk to you, laddie.' Tommy turned the wick of the oillamp, and now he could see in the shadowy light that Mr Macintosh had a look of uneasiness about him. He was sitting with his strong old body balanced behind the big stomach, hands laid on his knees, and his grey Scots eyes were watchful.

'I want you to think about what I said,' said Mr Macintosh, in a quick, bluff good-humour. 'Your mother says in two years' time you will have matriculated, you're doing fine at school. And after that you can go to college.'

Tommy lay on his elbow, and in the silence the drums came tapping from the compound, and he said: 'But Mr Macintosh, I'm not the only one who's good at his books.'

Mr Macintosh stirred, but said bluffly: 'Well, but I'm talking about you.'

Tommy was silent, because as usual these opponents were so much stronger than was reasonable, simply because of their ability to make words mean something else. And then, his heart painfully beating, he said: 'Why don't you send Dirk to college. You're so rich, and Dirk knows everything I know. He's better than me at figures. He's a whole book ahead of me, and he can do sums I can't.'

Mr Macintosh crossed his legs impatiently, uncrossed them, and said: 'Now why should I send Dirk to college?' For now Tommy would have to put into precise words what he meant, and this Mr Macintosh was quite sure he would not do. But to make certain, he lowered his voice and said: 'Think of your mother laddie, she's worrying about you, and you don't want to make her worried, do you?'

Tommy looked towards the door, under it came a thick yellow streak of light: in that room his mother and his father were waiting in silence for Mr Macintosh to emerge with news of Tommy's sure and wonderful future.

'You know why Dirk should go to college,' said Tommy in despair, shifting his body unhappily under the sheets, and Mr Macintosh chose not to hear it. He got up, and said quickly: 'You just think it over, laddie. There's no hurry but by next holidays I want to know.' And he went out of the room. As he opened the door, a brightly-lit, painful scene was presented to Tommy: his father and mother sat, smiling in embarrassed entreaty at Mr Macintosh. The door shut, and Tommy turned down the light, and there was darkness.

He went to school next day. Mrs Clarke, turning out Mr Macintosh's house as usual, said unhappily: 'I think you'll find everything in its proper place,' and slipped away, as if she were ashamed.

As for Mr Macintosh, he was in a mood which made others, besides Annie Clarke, speak to him carefully. His cook-boy, who had worked for him twelve years, gave notice that month. He had been knocked down twice by that powerful, hairy fist, and he was not a slave, after all, to remain bound to a bad-tempered master. And when a load of rock slipped and crushed the skulls of two workers, and the police came out for an investigation, Mr Macintosh met them irritably, and told them to mind their own business. For the first time in that mine's history of scandalous recklessness, after many such accidents, Mr Macintosh heard the indignant words from a police officer: 'You speak as if you were above the law, Mr Macintosh. If this happens again, you'll see ...'

Worst of all, he ordered Dirk to go back to work in the pit, and Dirk refused.

'You can't make me,' said Dirk.

'Who's the boss on this mine?' shouted Mr Macintosh.

'There's no law to make children work,' said the thirteen-year-old, who stood as tall as his father, a straight, lithe youth against the bulky strength of the old man.

The word law whipped the anger in Mr Macintosh to the point where he could feel his eyes go dark, and the blood pounding in that hot darkness in his head. In fact, it was the power of this anger that sobered him, for he had been very young when he had learned to fear his own temper. And above all, he was a shrewd man. He waited until his sight was clear again, and then asked, reasonably: 'Why do you want to loaf around the compound, why not work and earn money?'

Dirk said: 'I can read and write, and I know my figures better than Tommy—Baas Tommy,' he added, in a way which made the anger rise again in Mr Macintosh, so that he had to make a fresh effort to subdue it.

But Tommy was a point of weakness in Mr Macintosh, and it was then that he spoke the words which afterwards made him wonder if he'd gone suddenly crazy. For he said: 'Very well, when you're sixteen you can come and do my books and write the letters for the mine.'

Dirk said: 'All right,' as if this were no more than his due, and walked off, leaving Mr Macintosh impotently furious with himself. For how could anyone but himself see the books? Such a person would be his master. It was impossible, he had no intention of ever letting Dirk, or anyone else, see them. Yet he had made the promise. And so he would have to find another way of using Dirk, or—and the words came involuntarily—getting rid of him.

From a mood of settled bad temper, Mr Macintosh dropped into one of sullen thoughtfulness, which was entirely foreign to his character. Being shrewd is quite different from the processes of thinking. Shrewdness, particularly the money-making shrewdness, is a kind of instinct. While Mr Macintosh had always known what he wanted to do, and how to do it, that did not mean he had known why he wanted so much money, or why he had chosen these ways of making it. Mr Macintosh felt like a cat whose nose has been rubbed into its own dirt, and for many nights he sat in the hot little house, that vibrated continually from the noise of the mine-stamps, most uncomfortably considering himself and his life. He reminded himself, for instance, that he was sixty, and presumably had no more than ten or fifteen years to live. It was not a thought that an unreflective man enjoys, particularly when he had never considered his age at all. He was so healthy, strong, tough. But he was sixty nevertheless, and what would be his monument? An enormous pit in the earth, and a million pounds worth of property. Then how should he spend those ten or fifteen years? Exactly as he had the preceding sixty, for he hated being away from this place, and this gave him a caged and useless sensation, for it had never entered his head before that he was not as free as he felt himself to be.

Well, then—and this thought gnawed most closely to Mr Macintosh's pain—why had he not married? For he considered himself a marrying sort of man, and had always intended to find himself the right sort of woman and marry her. Yet he was already sixty. The truth was that Mr Macintosh had no idea at all why he had not married and got himself sons; and in these slow, uncomfortable ponderings the thought of Dirk's mother intruded itself only to be hastily thrust away. Mr Macintosh, the sensualist, had a taste for dark-skinned women; and now it was certainly too late to admit as a permanent feature of his character something he had always considered as a sort of temporary whim, or makeshift, like someone who learns to enjoy an inferior brand of tobacco when better brands are not available.

He thought of Tommy, of whom he had been used to say: 'I've taken a fancy to the laddie.' Now it was not so much a fancy as a deep, grieving love. And Tommy was the son of his employee, and looked at him with contempt, and he, Mr Macintosh, reacted with angry shame as if he were guilty of something. Of what? It was ridiculous.

The whole situation was ridiculous, and so Mr Macintosh allowed himself to slide back into his usual frame of mind. Tommy's only a boy, he thought, and he'll see reason in a year or so. And as for Dirk, I'll find him some kind of a job when the time comes....

At the end of the term, when Tommy came home. Mr Macintosh asked, as usual, to see the school report, which usually filled him with pride. Instead of heading the class with approbation from the teachers and high marks in all subjects, Tommy was near the bottom, with such remarks as Slovenly, and Lazy, and Bad-mannered. The only subject in which he got any marks at all was that called Art, which Mr Macintosh did not take into account.

When Tommy was asked by his parents why he was not working, he replied, impatiently: 'I don't know,' which was quite true; and at once escaped to the anthill. Dirk was there, waiting for the books Tommy always brought for him. Tommy reached at once up to the shelf where stood the figure of Dirk's mother, lifted it down and examined the unworked space which would be the face. 'I know how to do it,' he said to Dirk, and took out some knives and chisels he had brought from the city.

That was how he spent the three weeks of that holiday, and when he met Mr Macintosh he was sullen and uncomfortable. 'You'll have to be working a bit better,' he said, before Tommy went back, to which he received no answer but an unwilling smile.

During that term Tommy distinguished himself in two ways besides being steadily at the bottom of the class he had so recently led. He made a fiery speech in the debating society on the iniquity of the colour bar, which rather pleased his teachers, since it is a well-known fact that the young must pass through these phases of rebellion before settling down to conformity. In fact, the greater the verbal rebellion, the more settled was the conformity likely to be. In secret Tommy got books from the city library such as are not usually read by boys of his age, on the history of Africa, and on comparative anthropology, and passed from there to the history of the moment—he ordered papers from the Government Stationery Office, the laws of the country. Most particularly those affecting the relations between black and white and coloured. These he bought in order to take back to Dirk. But in addition to all this ferment, there was that subject Art, which in this school meant a drawing lesson twice a week, copying busts of Julius Caesar, or it might be Nelson, or shading in fronds of fern or leaves, or copying a large vase or a table standing diagonally to the class, thus learning what he was told were the laws of Perspective. There was no modelling, nothing approaching sculpture in this school, but this was the nearest thing to it, and that mysterious prohibition which forbade him to distinguish himself in Geometry or English, was silent when it came to using the pencil.

At the end of the term his Report was very bad, but it admitted that he had An Interest in Current Events, and a Talent for Art.

And now this word Art, coming at the end of two successive terms, disturbed his parents and forced itself on Mr Macintosh. He said to Annie Clarke: 'It's a nice thing to make pictures, but the lad won't earn a living by it.' And Mrs Clarke said reproachfully to Tommy: 'It's all very well, Tommy, but you aren't going to earn a living drawing pictures.'

'I didn't say I wanted to earn a living with it,' shouted Tommy, miserably. 'Why have I got to be something, you're always wanting me to be something.'

That holidays Dirk spent studying the Acts of Parliament and the Reports of Commissions and Sub-Committees which Tommy had brought him, while Tommy attempted something new. There was a square piece of soft white wood which Dirk had pilfered from the mine, thinking Tommy might use it. And Tommy set it against the walls of the shed, and knelt before it and attempted a frieze or engraving—he did not know the words for what he was doing. He cut out a great pit, surrounded by mounds of earth and rock, with the peaks of great mountains beyond, and at the edge of the pit stood a big man carrying a stick, and over the edge of the pit wound a file of black figures, tumbling into the gulf. From the pit came flames and smoke. Tommy took green ooze from leaves and mixed clay to colour the mountains and edges of the pit, and he made the little figures black with charcoal, and he made the flames writhing up out of the pit red with the paint used for parts of the mining machinery.

'If you leave it here, the ants'll eat it,' said Dirk, looking with grim pleasure at the crude but effective picture.

To which Tommy shrugged. For while he was always solemnly intent on a piece of work in hand, afraid of anything that might mar it, or even distract his attention from it, once it was finished he cared for it not at all.

It was Dirk who had painted the shelf which held the other figures with a mixture that discouraged ants, and it was now Dirk who set the piece of square wood on a sheet of tin smeared with the same mixture, and balanced it in a way so it should not touch any part of the walls of the shed, where the ants might climb up.

And so Tommy went back to school, still in that mood of obstinate disaffection, to make more copies of Julius Caesar and vases of flowers, and Dirk remained with his books and his Acts of Parliament. They would be fourteen before they met again, and both knew that crises and decisions faced them. Yet they said no more than the usual: Well, so long, before they parted. Nor did they ever write to each other, although this term Tommy had a commission to send certain books and other Acts of Parliament for a purpose which he entirely approved.

Dirk had built himself a new hut in the compound, where he lived alone, in the compound but not of it, affectionate to his mother, but apart from her. And to this hut at night came certain of the workers who forgot their dislike of the half-caste, that cuckoo in their nest, in their common interest in what he told them of the Acts and Reports. What he told them was what he had learnt himself in the proud loneliness of his isolation. 'Education,' he said, 'Education, that's the key'—and Tommy agreed with him, although he had, or so one might suppose from the way he was behaving, abandoned all idea of getting an education for himself. All that term parcels came to 'Dirk, c/o Mr Macintosh,' and Mr Macintosh delivered them to Dirk without any questions.

In the dim and smoky hut every night, half a dozen of the workers laboured with stubs of pencil and the exercise books sent by Tommy, to learn to write and do sums and understand the Laws.

One night Mr Macintosh came rather late out of that other hut, and saw the red light from a fire moving softly on the rough ground outside the door of Dirk's hut. All the others were dark. He moved cautiously among them until he stood in the shadows outside the door, and looked in. Dirk was squatting on the floor, surrounded by half a dozen men, looking at a newspaper.

Mr Macintosh walked thoughtfully home in the starlight. Dirk, had he known what Mr Macintosh was thinking, would have been very angry, for all his flaming rebellion, his words of resentment, were directed against Mr Macintosh and his tyranny. Yet for the first time Mr Macintosh was thinking of Dirk with a certain, rough, amused pride. Perhaps it was because he was a Scot, after all, and in every one of his nation is an instinctive respect for learning and people with the determination to 'get on'. A chip off the old block, thought Mr Macintosh, remembering how he, as a boy, had laboured to get a bit of education. And if the chip was the wrong colour—well, he would do something for Dirk. Something, he would decide when the time came. As for the others who were with Dirk, there was nothing easier than to sack a worker and engage another. Mr Macintosh went to his bed, dressed as usual in vest and pyjama trousers, unwashed and thrifty in candlelight.

In the morning he gave orders to one of the overseers that Dirk should be summoned. His heart was already soft with thinking about the generous scene which would shortly take place. He was going to suggest that Dirk should teach all the overseers to read and write—on a salary from himself, of course—in order that these same overseers should be more useful in the work. They might learn to mark pay-sheets, for instance.

The overseer said that Baas Dirk spent his days studying in Baas Tommy's hut—with the suggestion in his manner that Baas Dirk could not be disturbed while so occupied, and that this was on Tommy's account.

The man, closely studying the effect of his words, saw how Mr Macintosh's big, veiny face swelled, and he stepped back a pace. He was not one of Dirk's admirers.

Mr Macintosh, after some moments of heavy breathing, allowed his shrewdness to direct his anger. He dismissed the man, and turned away.

During that morning he left his great pit and walked off into the bush in the direction of the towering blue peak. He had heard vaguely that Tommy had some kind of a hut, but imagined it as a child's thing. He was still very angry because of that calculated 'Baas Dirk'. He walked for a while along a smooth path through the trees, and came to a clearing. On the other side was an anthill, and on the anthill a well-built hut, draped with Christmas fern around the open front, like curtains. In the opening sat Dirk. He wore a clean white shirt, and long smooth trousers. His head, oiled and brushed close, was bent over books. The hand that turned the pages of the books had a brass ring on the little finger. He was the very image of an aspiring clerk: that form of humanity which Mr Macintosh despised most.

Mr Macintosh remained on the edge of the clearing for some time, vaguely waiting for something to happen, so that he might fling himself, armoured and directed by his contemptuous anger, into a crisis which would destroy Dirk for ever. But nothing did happen. Dirk continued to turn the pages of the book, so Mr Macintosh went back to his house, where he ate boiled beef and carrots for his dinner.

Afterwards he went to a certain drawer in his bedroom, and from it took an object carelessly wrapped in cloth which, exposed, showed itself as that figure of Dirk the boy Tommy had made and sold for five pounds. And Mr Macintosh turned and handled and pored over that crude wooden image of Dirk in a passion of curiosity, just as if the boy did not live on the same square mile of soil with him, fully available to his scrutiny at most hours of the day.

If one imagines a Judgement Day with the graves giving up their dead impartially, black, white, bronze and yellow, to a happy reunion, one of the pleasures of that reunion might well be that people who have lived on the same acre or street all their lives will look at each other with incredulous recognition. 'So that is what you were like,' might be the gathering murmur around God's heaven. For the glass wall between colour and colour is not only a barrier against touch, but has become thick and distorted, so that black men, white men, see each other through it, but see what? Mr Macintosh examined the image of Dirk as if searching for some final revelation, but the thought that came persistently to his mind was that the statue might be of himself as a lad of twelve. So after a few moments he rolled it again in the cloth and tossed it back into the corner of a drawer, out of sight, and with it that unwelcome and tormenting knowledge.

Late that afternoon he left his house again and made his way towards the hut on the antheap. It was empty, and he walked through the knee-high grass and bushes till he could climb up the hard, slippery walls of the antheap and so into the hut.

First he looked at the books in the case. The longer he looked, the faster faded that picture of Dirk as an oiled and mincing clerk, which he had been clinging to ever since he threw the other image into the back of a drawer. Respect for Dirk was reborn. Complicated mathematics, much more advanced than he had ever done. Geography. History. 'The Development of the Slave Trade in the Eighteenth Century.' 'The Growth of Parliamentary Institutions in Great Britain.' This title made Mr Macintosh smile—the free-booting buccaneer examining a coastguard's notice perhaps. Mr Macintosh lifted down one book after another and smiled. Then, beside these books, he saw a pile of slight, blue pamphlets, and he examined them. 'The Natives Employment Act'. 'The Natives Juvenile Employment Act'. 'The Native Passes Act'. And Mr Macintosh flipped over the leaves and laughed, and had Dirk heard that laugh it would have been worse to him than any whip.

For as he patiently explained these laws and others like them to his bitter allies in the hut at night, it seemed to him that every word he spoke was like a stone thrown at Mr Macintosh, his father. Yet Mr Macintosh laughed, since he despised these laws, although in a different way, as much as Dirk did. When Mr Macintosh, on his rare trips to the city, happened to drive past the House of Parliament, he turned on it a tolerant and appreciative gaze. 'Well, why not?' he seemed to be saying. 'It's an occupation, like any other.'

So to Dirk's desperate act of retaliation he responded with a smile, and tossed back the books and pamphlets on the shelf. And then he turned to look at the other things in the shed, and for the first time he saw the high shelf where the statuettes were arranged. He looked, and felt his face swelling with that fatal rage. There was Dirk's mother, peering at him in bashful sensuality from over the baby's head, there the little girl, his daughter, squatting on spindly legs and staring. And there, on the edge of the shelf, a small, worn shape of clay which still held the vigorous strength of Dirk. Mr Macintosh, breathing heavily, holding down his anger, stepped back to gain a clearer view of those figures, and his heel slipped on a slanting piece of wood. He turned to look, and there was the picture Tommy had carved and coloured of his mine. Mr Macintosh saw the great pit, the black little figures tumbling and sprawling over into the flames, and he saw himself, stick in hand, astride on his two legs at the edge of the pit, his hat on the back of his head.

And now Mr Macintosh was so disturbed and angry that he was driven out of the hut and into the clearing, where he walked back and forth through the grass, looking at the hut while his anger growled and moved inside him. After some time he came close to the hut again and peered in. Yes, there was Dirk's mother, peering bashfully from her shelf, as if to say: 'Yes, it's me, remember?' And there on the floor was the square, tinted piece of wood which said what Tommy thought of him and his life. Mr Macintosh took a box of matches from his pocket. He lit a match. He understood he was standing in the hut with a lit match in his hand to no purpose. He dropped the match and ground it out with his foot. Then he put a pipe in his mouth, filled it and lit it, gazing all the time at the shelf and at the square carving. The second match fell to the floor and lay spurting a small white flame. He ground his heel hard on to it. Anger heaved up in him beyond all sanity, and he lit another match, pushed it into the thatch of the hut, and walked out of it and so into the clearing and away into the bush. Without looking behind him he walked back to his house where his supper of boiled beef and carrots was waiting for him. He was amazed, angry, resentful. Finally he felt aggrieved, and wanted to explain to someone what a monstrous injustice was Tommy's view of him. But there was no one to explain it to; and he slowly quietened to a steady, dulled sadness, and for some days remained so, until time restored him to normal. From this condition he looked back at his behaviour and did not like it. Not that he regretted burning the hut, it seemed to him unimportant. He was angry at himself for allowing his anger to dictate his actions. Also he knew that such an act brings its own results.

So he waited, and thought mainly of the cruelty of fate in denying him a son who might carry on his work—for he certainly thought of his work as something to be continued. He thought sadly of Tommy, who denied him. And so, his affection for Tommy was sprung again by thinking of him, and he waited, thinking of reproachful things to say to him.

When Tommy returned from school he went straight to the clearing and found a mound of ash on the antheap that was already sifted and swept by the wind. He found Dirk, sitting on a tree trunk in the bush waiting for him.

'What happened?' asked Tommy. And then, at once: 'Did you save your books?'

Dirk said: 'He burnt it.'

'How do you know?'

'I know.'

Tommy nodded. 'All your books have gone,' he said, very grieved, and as guilty as if he had burnt them himself.

'Your carving and your statues are burnt too.'

But at this Tommy shrugged, since he could not care about his things once they were finished. 'Shall we build the hut again now?' he suggested.

'My books are burnt,' said Dirk, in a low voice, and Tommy, looking at him, saw how his hands were clenched. He instinctively moved a little aside to give his friend's anger space.

'When I grow up I'll clear you all out, all of you, there won't be one white man left in Africa, not one.'

Tommy's face had a small, half-scared smile on it. The hatred Dirk was directing against him was so strong he nearly went away. He sat beside Dirk on the tree trunk and said: 'I'll try and get you more books.'

'And then he'll burn them again.'

'But you've already got what was in them inside your head,' said Tommy, consolingly. Dirk said nothing, but sat like a clenched fist, and so they remained on that tree trunk in the quiet bush while the doves cooed and the mine-stamps thudded, all that hot morning. When they had to separate at midday to return to their different worlds, it was with a deep sadness, knowing that their childhood was finished, and their playing, and something new was ahead.

And at that meal Tommy's mother and father had his school report on the table, and they were reproachful. Tommy was at the foot of his class, and he would not matriculate that year. Or any year if he went on like this.

'You used to be such a clever boy,' mourned his mother, 'and now what's happened to you?'

Tommy, sitting silent at the table, moved his shoulders in a hunched, irritable way, as if to say: Leave me alone. Nor did he feel himself to be stupid and lazy, as the Report said he was.

In his room were drawing blocks and pencils and hammers and chisels. He had never said to himself he had exchanged one purpose for another, for he had no purpose. How could he, when he had never been offered a future he could accept? Now, at this time, in his fifteenth year, with his reproachful parents deepening their reproach, and the knowledge that Mr Macintosh would soon see that Report, all he felt was a locked stubbornness, and a deep strength.

In the afternoon he went back to the clearing, and he took his chisels with him. On the old, soft, rotted tree trunk that he had sat on that morning, he sat again, waiting for Dirk. But Dirk did not come. Putting himself in his friend's place he understood that Dirk could not endure to be with a white-skinned person—a white face, even that of his oldest friend, was too much the enemy. But he waited, sitting on the tree trunk all through the afternoon, with his chisels and hammers in a little box at his feet in the grass, and he fingered the soft, warm wood he sat on, letting the shape and texture of it come into the knowledge of his fingers.

Next day, there was still no Dirk.

Tommy began walking around the fallen tree, studying it. It was very thick, and its roots twisted and slanted into the air to the height of his shoulder. He began to carve the root. It would be Dirk again.

That night Mr Macintosh came to the Clarke's house and read the Report. He went back to his own, and sat wondering why Tommy was set so bitterly against him. The next day he went to the Clarke's house again to find Tommy, but the boy was not there.

He therefore walked through the thick bush to the antheap, and found Tommy kneeling in the grass working on the tree root.

Tommy said: 'Good morning,' and went on working, and Mr Macintosh sat on the trunk and watched.

'What are you making?' asked Mr Macintosh.

'Dirk,' said Tommy, and Mr Macintosh went purple and almost sprang up and away from the tree trunk. But Tommy was not looking at him. So Mr Macintosh remained, in silence. And then the useless vigour of Tommy's concentration on that rotting bit of root goaded him, and his mind moved naturally to a new decision.

'Would you like to be an artist?' he suggested.

Tommy allowed his chisel to rest, and looked at Mr Macintosh as if this were a fresh trap. He shrugged, and with the appearance of anger, went on with his work.

'If you've a real gift, you can earn money by that sort of thing. I had a cousin back in Scotland who did it. He made souvenirs, you know, for travellers.' He spoke in a soothing and jolly way.

Tommy let the souvenirs slide by him, as another of these impositions on his independence. He said: 'Why did you burn Dirk's books?'

But Mr Macintosh laughed in relief. 'Why should I burn his books?' It really seemed ridiculous to him, his rage had been against Tommy's work, not Dirk's.

'I know you did,' said Tommy. 'I know it. And Dirk does too.'

Mr Macintosh lit his pipe in good humour. For now things seemed much easier. Tommy did not know why he had set fire to the hut, and that was the main thing. He puffed smoke for a few moments and said: 'Why should you think I don't want Dirk to study? It's a good thing, a bit of education.'

Tommy stared disbelievingly at him.

'I asked Dirk to use his education, I asked him to teach some of the others. But he wouldn't have any of it. Is that my fault?'

Now Tommy's face was completely incredulous. Then he went scarlet, which Mr Macintosh did not understand. Why should the boy be looking so foolish? But Tommy was thinking: We were on the wrong track.... And then he imagined what this offer must have done to Dirk's angry rebellious pride, and he suddenly understood. His face still crimson, he laughed. It was a bitter, ironical laugh and Mr Macintosh was upset—it was not a boy's laugh at all.

Tommy's face slowly faded from crimson, and he went back to work with his chisel. He said, after a pause. 'Why don't you send Dirk to college instead of me? He's much more clever than me. I'm not clever, look at my Report.'

'Well, laddie ...' began Mr Macintosh reproachfully—he had been going to say: 'Are you being lazy at school simply to force my hand over Dirk?' He wondered at his own impulse to say it; and slid off into the familiar obliqueness which Tommy ignored: 'But you know how things are, or you ought to by now. You talk as if you didn't understand.'

But Tommy was kneeling with his back to Mr Macintosh working at the root, so Mr Macintosh continued to smoke. Next day he returned and sat on the tree trunk and watched. Tommy looked at him as if he considered his presence an unwelcome gift, but he did not say anything.

Slowly, the big fanged root which rose from the trunk was taking Dirk's shape. Mr Macintosh watched with uneasy loathing. He did not like it, but he could not stop watching. Once he said: 'But if there's a veld fire, it'll get burnt. And the ants'll eat it in any case.' Tommy shrugged. It was the making of it that mattered, not what happened to it afterwards, and this attitude was so foreign to Mr Macintosh's accumulating nature that it seemed to him that Tommy was touched in the head. He said: 'Why don't you work on something that'll last? Or even if you studied like Dirk it would be better.'

Tommy said: 'I like doing it.'

'But look, the ants are already at the trunk—by the time you get back from your school next time there'll be nothing left of it.'

'Or someone might set fire to it,' suggested Tommy. He looked steadily at Mr Macintosh's reddening face with triumph. Mr Macintosh found the words too near the truth. For certainly, as the days passed, he was looking at the new work with hatred and fear and dislike. It was nearly finished. Even if nothing were done to it, it could stand as it was, complete.

Dirk's long, powerful body came writhing out of the wood like something struggling free. The head was clenched back, in the agony of the birth, eyes narrowed and desperate, the mouth—Mr Macintosh's mouth—tightened in obstinate purpose. The shoulders were free, but the hands were held; they could not pull themselves out of the dense wood, they were imprisoned. His body was free to the knees, but below them the human limbs were uncreated, the natural shapes of the wood swelled to the perfect muscled knees.

Mr Macintosh did not like it. He did not know what art was, but he knew he did not like this at all, it disturbed him deeply, so that when he looked at it he wanted to take an axe and cut it to pieces. Or burn it, perhaps....

As for Tommy, the uneasiness of this elderly man who watched him all day was a deep triumph. Slowly, and for the first time, he saw that perhaps this was not a sort of game that he played, it might be something else. A weapon—he watched Mr Macintosh's reluctant face, and a new respect for himself and what he was doing grew in him.

At night, Mr Macintosh sat in his candle-lit room and he thought, or rather felt, his way to a decision.

There was no denying the power of Tommy's gift. Therefore, it was a question of finding the way to turn it into money. He knew nothing about these matters, however, and it was Tommy himself who directed him, for towards the end of the holidays he said: 'When you're so rich you can do anything. You could send Dirk to college and not even notice it.'

Mr Macintosh, in the reasonable and persuasive voice he now always used, said: 'But you know these coloured people have nowhere to go.'

Tommy said: 'You could send him to the Cape. There are coloured people in the university there. Or to Johannesburg.' And he insisted against Mr Macintosh's silence: 'You're so rich you can do anything you like.'

But Mr Macintosh, like most rich people, thought not of money as things to buy, things to do, but rather how it was tied up in buildings and land.

'It would cost thousands,' he said. 'Thousands for a coloured boy.'

But Tommy's scornful look silenced him, and he said hastily: 'I'll think about it.' But he was thinking not of Dirk, but of Tommy. Sitting alone in his room he told himself it was simply a question of paying for knowledge.

So next morning he made his preparations for a trip to town. He shaved, and over his cotton singlet he put a striped jacket, which half-concealed his long, stained khaki trousers. This was as far as he ever went in concessions to the city life he despised. He got into his big American car and set off.

In the city he took the simplest route to knowledge.

He went to the Education Department, and said he wanted to see the Minister of Education. 'I'm Macintosh,' he said with perfect confidence; and the pretty secretary who had been patronizing his clothes, went at once to the Minister and said: 'There is a Mr Macintosh to see you.' She described him as an old, fat, dirty man with a large stomach and soon the doors opened, and Mr Macintosh was with the spring of knowledge.

He emerged five minutes later with what he wanted, the name of a certain expert. He drove through the deep green avenues of the city to the house he had been told to go to, which was a large and well-kept one, and comforted Mr Macintosh in his faith that art properly used could make money. He parked his car in the road and walked in.

On the verandah, behind a table heaped with books, sat a middle-aged man with spectacles. Mr Tomlinson was essentially a scholar with working hours he respected, and he lifted his eyes to see a big, dirty man with black hair showing above the dirty whiteness of his vest, and he said sharply: 'What do you want?'

'Wait a minute, laddie,' said Mr Macintosh easily, and he held out a note from the Minister of Education, and Mr Tomlinson took it and read it, feeling reassured. It was worded in such a way that his seeing Mr Macintosh could be felt as a favour he was personally doing the Minister.

'I'll make it worth your while,' said Mr Macintosh, and at once distaste flooded Mr Tomlinson, and he went pink, and said: 'I'm afraid I haven't the time.'

'Damn it, man, it's your job, isn't it? Or so Wentworth said.'

'No,' said Mr Tomlinson, making each word clear, 'I advise on ancient Monuments.'

Mr Macintosh stared, then laughed, and said: 'Wentworth said you'd do, but it doesn't matter, I'll get someone else.' And he left.

Mr Tomlinson watched this hobo go off the verandah and into a magnificent car, and his thought was: 'He must have stolen it.' Then, puzzled and upset, he went to the telephone. But in a few moments he was smiling. Finally he laughed. Mr Macintosh was the Mr Macintosh, a genuine specimen of the old-timer. It was the phrase 'old-timer' that made it possible for Mr Tomlinson to relent. He therefore rang the hotel at which Mr Macintosh, as a rich man, would be bound to be staying, and said he had made an error, he would be free the following day to accompany Mr Macintosh.

And so next morning Mr Macintosh, not at all surprised that the expert was at his service after all, with Mr Tomlinson, who preserved a tolerant smile, drove out to the mine.

They drove very fast in the powerful car, and Mr Tomlinson held himself steady while they jolted and bounced, and listened to Mr Macintosh's tales of Australia and New Zealand, and thought of him rather as he would of an ancient Monument.

At last the long plain ended, and foothills of greenish scrub heaped themselves around the car, and then high mountains piled with granite boulders, and the heat came in thick, slow waves into the car, and Mr Tomlinson thought: I'll be glad when we're through the mountains into the plain. But instead they turned into a high, enclosed place with mountains all around, and suddenly there was an enormous gulf in the ground, and on one side of it were two tiny tin-roofed houses, and on the other acres of kaffir huts. The mine-stamps thudded regularly, like a pulse of the heat, and Mr Tomlinson wondered how anybody, white or black, could bear to live in such a place.

He ate boiled beef and carrots and greasy potatoes with one of the richest men in the sub-continent, and thought how well and intelligently he would use such money if he had it—which is the only consolation left to the cultivated man of moderate income. After lunch, Mr Macintosh said: 'And now, let's get it over.'

Mr Tomlinson expressed his willingness, and smiling to himself, followed Mr Macintosh off into the bush on a kaffir path. He did not know what he was going to see. Mr Macintosh had said: 'Can you tell if a youngster has got any talent just by looking at a piece of wood he has carved?'

Mr Tomlinson had said he would do his best.

Then they were beside a fallen tree trunk and in the grass knelt a big lad with untidy brown hair falling over his face, labouring at the wood with a large chisel.

'This is a friend of mine,' said Mr Macintosh to Tommy, who got to his feet and stood uncomfortably, wondering what was happening. 'Do you mind if Mr Tomlinson sees what you are doing?'

Tommy made that shrugging movement, and felt that things were going beyond his control. He looked in awed amazement at Mr Tomlinson, who seemed to him rather like a teacher or professor, and certainly not at all what he had imagined an artist to be.

'Well?' said Mr Macintosh to Mr Tomlinson, after a space of half a minute.

Mr Tomlinson laughed, in a way which said: 'Now don't be in such a hurry.' He walked around the carved tree root looking at the figure of Dirk from this angle and that.

Then he asked Tommy: 'Why do you make these carvings?'

Tommy very uncomfortably shrugged, as if to say: What a silly question; and Mr Macintosh hastily said: 'He gets high marks for Art at school.'

Mr Tomlinson smiled again, and walked around to the other side of the trunk. From here he could see Dirk's face flattened back on the neck, eyes half-closed and strained, the muscles of the neck shaped from the natural veins of the wood.

'Is this someone you know?' he asked Tommy in an easy intimate way, one artist to another.

'Yes,' said Tommy, briefly; he resented the question.

Mr Tomlinson looked at the face and then at Mr Macintosh. 'It has a look of you,' he observed dispassionately, and coloured himself as he saw Mr Macintosh grow angry. He walked well away from the group, to give Mr Macintosh space to hide his embarrassment. When he returned, he asked Tommy: 'And so you want to be a sculptor?'

'I don't know,' said Tommy, defiantly.

Mr Tomlinson shrugged, rather impatiently, and with a nod at Mr Macintosh suggested it was enough. He said goodbye to Tommy, and went back to the house with Mr Macintosh.

There he was offered tea and biscuits, and Mr Macintosh asked: 'Well, what do you think?'

But by now Mr Tomlinson was certainly offended at this casual cash-on-delivery approach to art, and he said: 'Well, that rather depends, doesn't it?'

'On what?' demanded Mr Macintosh.

'He seems to have talent,' conceded Mr Tomlinson.

'That's all I want to know,' said Mr Macintosh, and suggested that now he could run Mr Tomlinson back to town.

But Mr Tomlinson did not feel it was enough, and he said: 'It's quite interesting, that statue. I suppose he's seen pictures in magazines. It has quite a modern feeling.'

'Modern?' said Mr Macintosh, 'what do you mean?'

Mr Tomlinson shrugged again, giving it up. 'Well,' he said, practically, 'what do you mean to do?'

'If you say he has talent, I'll send him to the university and he can study art.'

After a long pause, Mr Tomlinson murmured: 'What a fortunate boy he is.' He meant to convey depths of disillusionment and irony, but Mr Macintosh said: 'I always did have a fancy for him.'

He took Mr Tomlinson back to the city, and as he dropped him on his verandah, presented him with a cheque for fifty pounds, which Mr Tomlinson most indignantly returned. 'Oh, give it to charity,' said Mr Macintosh impatiently, and went to his car, leaving Mr Tomlinson to heal his susceptibilities in any way he chose.

When Mr Macintosh reached his mine again it was midnight, and there were no lights in the Clarkes' house, and so his need to be generous must be stifled until the morning.

Then he went to Annie Clarke and told her he would send Tommy to university, where he could be an artist, and Mrs Clarke wept gratitude, and said that Mr Macintosh was much kinder than Tommy deserved, and perhaps he would learn sense yet and go back to his books.

As far as Mr Macintosh was concerned it was all settled.

He set off through the trees to find Tommy and announce his future to him.

But when he arrived at seeing distance there were two figures, Dirk and Tommy, seated on the trunk talking, and Mr Macintosh stopped among the trees, filled with such bitter anger at this fresh check to his plans that he could not trust himself to go on. So he returned to his house, and brooded angrily—he knew exactly what was going to happen when he spoke to Tommy, and now he must make up his mind, there was no escape from decision.

And while Mr Macintosh mused bitterly in his house, Tommy and Dirk waited for him; it was now all as clear to them as it was to him.

Dirk had come out of the trees to Tommy the moment the two men left the day before. Tommy was standing by the fanged root, looking at the shape of Dirk in it, trying to understand what was going to be demanded of him. The word 'artist' was on his tongue, and he tasted it, trying to make the strangeness of it fit that powerful shape struggling out of the wood. He did not like it. He did not want—but what did he want? He felt pressure on himself, the faint beginnings of something that would one day be like a tunnel of birth from which he must fight to emerge; he felt the obligations working within himself like a goad which would one day be a whip perpetually falling just behind him so that he must perpetually move onwards.

His sense of fetters and debts was confirmed when Dirk came to stand by him. First he asked: 'What did they want?'

'They want me to be an artist, they always want me to be something,' said Tommy, sullenly. He began throwing stones at the trees, and shying them off along the tops of the grass.

Then one hit the figure of Dirk, and he stopped.

Dirk was looking at himself. 'Why do you make me like that?' he asked. The narrow, strong face expressed nothing but that familiar, sardonic antagonism, as if he said: 'You, too—just like the rest!'

'Why? What's the matter with it?' challenged Tommy at once.

Dirk walked around it, then back. 'You're just like all the rest,' he said.

'Why? Why don't you like it?' Tommy was really distressed. Also, his feeling was: What's it got to do with him? Slowly he understood that his emotion was that belief in his right to freedom which Dirk always felt immediately, and he said in a different voice: 'Tell me what's wrong with it?'

'Why do I have to come out of the wood? Why haven't I any hands or feet?'

'You have, but don't you see ...' But Tommy looked at Dirk standing in front of him and suddenly gave an impatient movement: 'Well, it doesn't matter, it's only a statue.'

He sat on the trunk and Dirk beside him. After a while he said: 'How should you be, then?'

'If you made yourself, would you be half wood?'

Tommy made an effort to feel this, but failed. 'But it's not me, it's you.' He spoke with difficulty, and thought: But it's important, I shall have to think about it later. He almost groaned with the knowledge that here it was, the first debt, presented for payment.

Dirk said suddenly: 'Surely it needn't be wood. You could do the same thing if you put handcuffs on my wrists.' Tommy lifted his head and gave a short, astonished laugh. 'Well, what's funny?' said Dirk, aggressively. 'You can't do it the easy way, you have to make me half wood, as if I was more a tree than a human being.'

Tommy laughed again, but unhappily. 'Oh, I'll do it again,' he acknowledged at last. 'Don't fuss about that one, it's finished. I'll do another.'

There was a silence.

Dirk said: 'What did that man say about you?'

'How do I know?'

'Does he know about art?'

'I suppose so.'

'Perhaps you'll be famous,' said Dirk at last. 'In that book you gave me, it said about painters. Perhaps you'll be like that.'

'Oh, shut up,' said Tommy, roughly. 'You're just as bad as he is.'

'Well, what's the matter with it?'

'Why have I got to *be* something. First it was a sailor, and then it was a scholar, and now it's an artist.'

'They wouldn't *have* to make me be anything,' said Dirk sarcastically.

'I know,' admitted Tommy, grudgingly. And then, passionately: 'I shan't go to university unless he sends you too.'

'I know,' said Dirk at once, 'I know you won't.'

They smiled at each other, that small, shy revealed smile which was so hard for them, because it pledged them to such a struggle in the future.

Then Tommy asked: 'Why didn't you come near me all this time?'

'I get sick of you,' said Dirk. 'I sometimes feel I don't want to see a white face again, not ever. I feel that I hate you all, every one.'

'I know,' said Tommy, grinning. Then they laughed, and the last strain of dislike between them vanished.

They began to talk, for the first time, of what their lives would be.

Tommy said: 'But when you've finished training to be an engineer, what will you do? They don't let coloured people be engineers.'

'Things aren't always going to be like that,' said Dirk.

'It's going to be very hard,' said Tommy, looking at him questioningly, and was at once reassured when Dirk said sarcastically: 'Hard, it's *going* to be hard? Isn't it hard now, white boy?'

Later that day Mr Macintosh came towards them from his house.

He stood in front of them, that big, shrewd, rich man with his small, clever grey eyes, and his narrow, loveless mouth; and he said aggressively to Tommy: 'Do you want to go to the university and be an artist?'

'If Dirk comes too,' said Tommy immediately.

'What do you want to study?' Mr Macintosh asked Dirk, direct.

'I want to be an engineer,' said Dirk at once.

'If I pay your way through the university then at the end of it I'm finished with you. I never want to hear from you and you are never to come back to this mine once you leave it.'

Dirk and Tommy both nodded, and the instinctive agreement

between them fed Mr Macintosh's bitter unwillingness in the choice, so that he ground out viciously: 'Do you think you two can be together in the university? You don't understand. You'll be living separate, and you can't go around together just as you like.'

The boys looked at each other, and then, as if some sort of pact had been made between them, simply nodded.

'You can't go to university, anyway, Tommy, until you've done a bit better at school. If you go back for another year and work you can pass your matric. and go to university, but you can't go now, right at the bottom of the class.'

Tommy said: 'I'll work.' He added at once: 'Dirk'll need more books to study here till we can go.'

The anger was beginning to swell Mr Macintosh's face, but Tommy said: 'It's only fair. You burnt them, and now he hasn't any at all.'

'Well,' said Mr Macintosh heavily. 'Well, so that's how it is!'

He looked at the two boys, seated together on the tree trunk. Tommy was leaning forward, eyes lowered, a troubled but determined look on his face. Dirk was sitting erect, looking straight at his father with eyes filled with hate.

'Well,' said Mr Macintosh, with an effort at raillery which sounded harsh to them all: 'Well, I send you both to university and you don't give me so much as a thank you!'

At this, both faced towards him, with such bitter astonishment that he flushed.

'Well, well,' he said. 'Well, well ...' And then he turned to leave the clearing, and cried out as he went, so as to give the appearance of dominance: 'Remember, laddie, I'm not sending you unless you do well at school this year.'

And so he left them and went back to his house, an angry old man, defeated by something he did not begin to understand.

As for the boys, they were silent when he had gone.

The victory was entirely theirs, but now they had to begin again, in the long and difficult struggle to understand what they had won and how they would use it.

Appendix A: Interviews

1. Roy Newquist, "Interview with Doris Lessing," *Counterpoint* (Rand McNally, 1964): 413-24.

...

Newquist: When did you start writing?

Lessing: I think I've always been a writer by temperament. I wrote some bad novels in my teens. I always knew I would be a writer, but not until I was quite old—twenty-six or -seven—did I realize that I'd better stop saying I was going to be one and get down to business. I was working in a lawyer's office at the time, and I remember walking in and saying to my boss, "I'm giving up my job because I'm going to write a novel." He very properly laughed, and I indignantly walked home and wrote *The Grass Is Singing*. I'm oversimplifying; I didn't write it as simply as that because I was clumsy at writing and it was much too long, but I did learn by writing it. It focused upon white people in Southern Rhodesia, but it could have been about white people anywhere south of the Zambezi, white people who were not up to what is expected of them in a society where there is very heavy competition from the black people coming up.

Then I wrote short stories set in the district I was brought up in, where very isolated white farmers lived immense distances from each other. You see, in this background, people can spread themselves out. People who might be extremely ordinary in a society like England's, where people are pressed into conformity, can become wild eccentrics in all kinds of ways they wouldn't dare try elsewhere. This is one of the things I miss, of course, by living in England. I don't think my memory deceives me, but I think there were more colorful people back in Southern Rhodesia because of the space they had to move in. I gather, from reading American literature, that this is the kind of space you have in America in the Midwest and West.

I left Rhodesia and my second marriage to come to England, bringing a son with me. I had very little money, but I've made my living as a professional writer ever since, which is really very hard to do. I had rather hard going, to begin with, which is not a complaint; I gather from my American writer-friends that it is easier to be a writer in England than in America because there is much less pressure put on us. We are not expected to be successful, and it is no sin to be poor.

...

Newquist: Right now a great many criticisms are leveled against bored Americans who have a surfeit of what they want. Is this true of England?

Lessing: I think that England is much more of a class society than America. This street I live on is full of very poor people who are totally different from my literary friends. They, in turn, are different from the family I come from, which is ordinary middle class. It isn't simple to describe life in England. For instance, in any given day I can move in five, six different strata or groups. None of them know how other people live, people different from themselves. All these groups and layers and classes have unwritten rules. There are rigid rules for every layer, but they are quite different from the rules in the other groups.

...

Newquist: [W]hat are you working at now?

Lessing: I'm writing volumes four and five of a series I'm calling *Children of Violence*. I planned this out twelve years ago, and I've finished the first three. The idea is to write about people like myself, people my age who are born out of wars and who have lived through them, the framework of lives in conflict. I think the title explains what I essentially want to say. I want to explain what it is like to be a human being in a century when you open your eyes on war and on human beings disliking other human beings. I was brought up in Central Africa, which means that I was a member of the white minority pitted against a black majority that was abominably treated and still is. I was the daughter of a white farmer who, although he was a very poor man in terms of what he was brought up to expect, could always get loans from the Land Bank which kept him going. (I won't say that my father liked what was going on; he didn't.) But he employed anywhere from fifty to one hundred working blacks. An adult black earned twelve shillings a month, rather less than two dollars, and his food was rationed to corn meal and beans and peanuts and a pound of meat per week. It was all grossly unfair, and it's only part of a larger picture of inequity.

...

2. Eve Bertelsen, "An Interview with Doris Lessing," *Journal of Commonwealth Literature* 21 (1986): 134–61.

...

Bertelsen: Can I move on to ask about the degrees of generalization that occur when you're writing a fiction about Africa? You've said in several places that your stories were "not about the color problem, but about the atrophy of the imagination," or "the lack of feeling for all creatures that live under the sun." And elsewhere you've said "the states of Southern Africa in their political economy are all one." I wonder whether when you ask the reader to take a general meaning out of the stories you are downplaying the historical particulars—the fact that there were specific policies that caused the suffering and problems in Rhodesia at that historical time?

Lessing: Well, I've written so much about that I can hardly be accused of playing it down! About this color-bar thing: the point I was making was that it's not just the white man's attitude towards the black, but people's attitudes to each other in general—all over the world you'll have a dominant group despising the rest. This is the pattern. This is what interests me more and more. I've found it very limiting when people say, "You are a writer about color-bar problems." I wasn't writing only about color-bar problems. Not even my first volume was only about color-bar problems; there were a lot of other themes in it. I used the background as something to take off from. About the historic thing: South Africa and Rhodesia had a great deal in common, you see, because, as you know, Rhodesia usually passed laws that had been passed in South Africa, shortly afterwards. The whole legal structure of Rhodesia was patterned on South Africa. That became very clear over the Federation business. There was this brilliant idea to federate Rhodesia, Northern Rhodesia and Nyasaland against the will of the Africans. What they were overlooking was that the Africans in Rhodesia were very much more enslaved on the South African pattern than the Africans in Nyasaland and what was then Northern Rhodesia. And the Africans up north certainly did not want to come under the umbrella of Rhodesia, the stronger economically, because they knew that they would become enslaved to the same extent. And the interesting thing was that in this country absolutely not one of the big newspapers noticed this, including *The Guardian* which campaigned for federation (because *The Guardian* is a paper that tends to fall in love with grandiose ideas). And practically nobody in this country—excepting the left, the left of the Labour Party and some Communists and some people who knew Africa—pointed out that this was absolutely unworkable. And of course the thing didn't work. This demonstrated, as seen by the Africans, how similar to South Africa Rhodesia was and is in some ways still.

3. Thomas Frick, "The Art of Fiction: Doris Lessing" (interview), *The Paris Review* 106 (1988): 80-106.

...

Frick: You were born in Persia, now Iran. How did your parents come to be there?

Lessing: My father was in the First World War. He couldn't stick England afterwards. He found it extremely narrow. The soldiers had these vast experiences in the trenches and found they couldn't tolerate it at home. So he asked his bank to send him somewhere else. And they sent him to Persia, where we were given a very big house, large rooms and space, and horses to ride on. Very outdoors, very beautiful. I've just been told this town is now rubble. It's a sign of the times, because it was a very ancient market town with beautiful buildings. No one's noticed. So much is destroyed, we can't be bothered. And then they sent him to Teheran, which is a very ugly city.... Then in 1924, we came back to England where something called the Empire Exhibition (which turns up from time to time in literature) was going on and which must have had an enormous influence. The Southern Rhodesian stand had enormous maize cobs, corn cobs, slogans saying "Make your fortune in five years" and that sort of nonsense. So my father, typically for his romantic temperament, packed up everything. He had this pension because of his leg, his war wounds—minuscule, about five thousand pounds—and he just set off into a totally unknown setup to be a farmer. His childhood had been spent near Colchester, which was then a rather small town, and he had actually lived the life of a farmer's child and had a country childhood. And that's how he found himself in the veld of Rhodesia. His story is not atypical of that lot. It took me some time, but it struck me quite forcibly when I was writing *Shikasta* how many wounded ex-servicemen there were out there, both English and German. All of them had been wounded, all of them were extremely lucky not to be dead, like their mates were. It didn't strike me at the time, but it's struck me since.

...

Appendix B: Reviews

1. J.D. Scott, "Man Is the Story," *New York Times Book Review*, 7 November 1965: 4. Review of *African Stories*. New York: Simon & Schuster, 1965.

In reissuing in a single volume all short stories that she has written about Africa, Doris Lessing, who was brought up in Rhodesia and is now a British-based writer, will give a new circle of admirers a clearer view of her talent, a view over a wide, diverse and magnificently populated landscape.

...

The characters in Mrs. Lessing's stories are very often middle-class white farmers and their families, some prosperous, some hard-up, living on isolated farms but with bursts of intense social life. They have ample opportunity for visiting, for drinking, for adultery, for opening the eyes of their children to their neuroses, loneliness and hysteria, and also to their limitations—their complacent exile from thought and feeling; These children, or adolescents, play an important role in Mrs. Lessing's stories; their role is to perceive the truth and reveal it to the reader, and they play it with perspicacity and, although often themselves troubled, yet with a certain cool grace.

When the characters are neither farmers nor children they are Africans: "kaffirs," or "natives." In some of the stories there are indeed no, or only unimportant, identifiable white characters....Yet in this black world, the whites, if not always present, are always a presence—and vice versa. It is only the presence of African laborers and servants that subtracts enough work from daily life to permit the full seedy ripening of colonial complacency and colonial *cafard*.[1]

Those of Mrs. Lessing's characters who are psychically capable of it thus have time for a full savoring of odd relationships.... In "The Antheap," a boy educates a half-caste boy whom he both detests and loves.... In "A Home for the Highland Cattle," an educated, sophisticated girl from England is drawn into a relationship of almost manic intensity with her tragi-comic primitive white neighbors.

---

1 "The blues," melancholia.

After a time, in reading these stories, one has a curious feeling of having been here before: the sense of isolation and forged intimacy; of limitless space and provincial fatuity; of great innocence; of exact, ironic perceptiveness; of outbreaks of violence and of basic social injustice as pervasive as the smell of trash. Where has one found so much of this before? Of course, it is in the Russian novelists, and Mrs. Lessing has acknowledged this influence in her preface, where she expresses the hope of seeing from Africa a comic novel of the order of *Dead Souls*.

Let us hope that she writes it herself. She has great gifts, the first of them being creative authority. Her stories almost always open mildly; during the first paragraph or so they would be easy to put down. They have no tricks. The hold they establish is not merely a grip on the attention; it is a direct grasp of the reader's moral sensibility. As the author points out in her preface (which offers some perceptive remarks upon her own work and its development), her stories are not really "about" relations between the white and black races. It is rather that in Africa, in the years when she was being formed as a writer, the color line was the volcanic fault along which the flames of drama and the lava of passion erupted. It was along this line that human beings, being under most stress, revealed themselves most fully. And it is with this revelation itself, and not with its circumstances, that Mrs. Lessing is fundamentally concerned.

2. Mary Ellman, "Stitches in a Wound," *The Nation*, 17 January 1966: 78–79. Review of *African Stories*.

As political and social evidence, Doris Lessing's *African Stories* confirm in precise and painful detail, like stitches in a wound, the abuse of the native population of Southern Rhodesia by the white settlers of British descent. To bring these stories together for the first time, when they have been dispersed over many years of writing, has a retrospective effect, summing up Mrs. Lessing's permanent image of the colonials: as fat, white, motionless grubs absorbing nourishment from an immense and ceaseless black exertion beneath them. Helpless without African labor in every corner of their lives, the colonials, in managing to extort that labor, experience sensations of independence and power. They grow as reluctant to leave as to stay in Rhodesia. Their vanity and complacence are marred only by their terror of rebellion.

Yet to the American reader, even this explicit statement of racial injustice in the stories seems a fantastic version of the familiar. The defensive sophistries ("Their stomachs aren't like ours"), the repressive pseudo-legalities, the passive contempt ("What can you expect?") of the Rhodesian settler are those of the American segregationist. We recognize, as in the semantic shifts of a nightmare, that the *cheeky native* is the *uppity nigger*, the *white kaffir* is the *nigger lover*, the Afrikaaners are, for the British, the poor whites. And there are further reaches of similarity in the stories: it is as though our own national guilts had swirled, in erosive release, half around the world, to settle again in new but still too recognizable patterns. As the *natives*, those from whom the country has been taken, the Rhodesians (in "The Old Chief Mshlanga") are like the American Indians, while as the blacks, from whom labor has been taken, they reflect the American Negroes.

In describing the first, the taking of the country, the stories are disturbing for an American too in their evocation of a second pioneer period. Doris Lessing's work is an uninterrupted study of loneliness, but here it is particularly the isolation of a few white exiles, claiming vast strange land. By daylight the men hope to exploit its fertility, the women to remake tiny plots into nostalgic, postcard pictures of Home. But at night both are intimidated by the same country they may eventually subdue. So, almost comically, in all the stories, the whites, who think of themselves as warders, live like prisoners. Huddled, nervous, wary of an alien vegetation and an alien skin, they are deprived, as they would be in jail, of the privacies and subtleties they enjoyed in tiny, crowded England.... The more widely their control spreads, the more tightly the masters restrict their own freedom. Mrs. Lessing dwells—as she says in her preface, with "bile" upon their self-encasements: their tworoomed, tin-roofed brick house (fending off all seasons), their barred windows (fending off robbery and murder by those whom they have robbed and beaten), their screens (fending off exotic diseases) and, always, outdoors, their hats (fending off that most unEnglish sun). Even the eyes of the men, the last aperture through which the black might approach the white, are squinted almost shut. The women nurse headaches in darkened rooms or take solitary, endless walks. Relieved by Africans of all the household chores except introspection, they circumnavigate their geranium beds, asking themselves, "Who am I?"

...

The better stories are not those of the native, but those of the outsider, whose perceptions of the country, however sharp, are also oblique. The better subjects are two varieties of spectator: the resident, even from birth, of a country which never becomes quite his, and the new arrival. A paradigm of the second is "A Home for the Highland Cattle" in which an Englishwoman stands behind her curtains to overhear, with shock and envy and amusement the houseboys' talk in the yard. The social, the *placed*, are outdoors, and indoors the individual longing to know and listening to understand.

For her first thirty years, while she thought of going to England, Doris Lessing seems to have listened to Southern Rhodesia as no other writer has been able to do. It remained, even after she had left it, all nature to her. As one associates her English work with flats and offices, one associates the African stories with swollen suns and moons, head-tall grass, and the secret constant stirring of animal life.... Africa is for her not only a society in which the white people use their exile like a weapon against the black; but also a place, supporting both white and black, which endlessly enacts the conflict of forms, the effort of every living thing, at the cost of other living things, to achieve what is right for itself, its sustenance and continuation....

...The settler's error ... is the failure to honor the illusion of distinction between natural and human life. Irony lies in the simultaneous sense of illusion and the determination to maintain it. The settler who turns his gold mine into an ant heap, his African laborers into its scurrying ants, imitates a nature which, even without imitation, must always encroach upon human settlements and must always, with each new season and new birth, be pressed back by the makeshift and surprisingly fragile devices of justice.

...

3. Edward Hickman Brown, "The Eternal Moment," *Saturday Review*, 24 September 1966: 4. Review of *African Stories*.

Opinions on the essential responsibility of the serious writer will vary with the individual. Were one to attempt to isolate it—particularly in this age when most of us are almost solely concerned with the material and the superficial, and our outlooks are clouded and colored by the constant tensions and confusions of the endless power struggle—he might venture to suggest that it is the duty of the writer to knife through the illusion and the falsity cloaking our lives and reveal, through the medium of his art, the verities. After reading this comprehensive collection of Doris Lessing's shorter fiction, it becomes clear that from the very beginning she has attempted to discharge that exacting, fundamental obligation, and has largely succeeded.

Spanning her entire career, this volume includes every story she has written about Africa, from her earliest collection to the most recent. Two of them have never previously appeared in the States. Even in her first, *This Was the Old Chief's Country*, the stories are astonishingly mature and consistent, three among them having an enduring, diamond-hard quality.

"The Old Chief Mshlanga" hinges on the awakening of responsibility in a sensitive, adolescent girl when her attention is abrupt ly focused on the human realities beyond the traditional race attitudes that she'd previously adopted so casually. "Little Tembi" deals with the complex and bewildering relationship between a white farmer's wife and, as he grows to manhood, the African whose life she saved as a baby. In "Old John's Place" Mrs. Lessing brings a quality of freshness to the old tale of the maverick versus the remainder of the herd. The action is seen through the eyes of the teen-age girl who is the central character or narrator of a number of these stories. While she is possessed of a well-formed sense of irony and an understanding terribly beyond her years, the latter is never carried as a burden, and she is thoroughly credible. As with all fine stories, in these three there is far more to them than appears on the surface. "Little Tembi," for example, is perfect testimony to the groping need of black and white for one another, and the misunderstanding by each not merely of the other's intentions but also of his own.

The reader unfamiliar with Mrs. Lessing's work might well wonder if this early standard can be sustained. Of course, it improves. And the growth in the later stories is marked by an exceptional ability to capture the attention and set the mood instantly, to say so much more in fewer words. Happily, she does it in the same limpid and unmannered prose, maintaining the while an easy control. In the stories that are concerned with the Rhodesian farming country and bushveld the author's love of that land and yearning for it are manifest; her descriptions bring it to life with rare brilliance.

Yes, this is the Africa she knew, all right; it's the Africa we all knew. But one need have no knowledge of the locale to be struck by the intrinsic truth of these tales. And this is what I believe to be the mark of her artistry: this ability repeatedly to strike—suddenly, deeply, and unerringly—into the tenuous vein that is verity. Mrs. Lessing's precision can be disconcerting. One stops reading, and thinks, "But I've known these people" or "I've witnessed just such a scene."

And, indeed, one has....

This volume contains a wide variety of beautifully-wrought stories by a sensitive and thoughtful but fiercely honest writer whose humanity soon becomes as patent as her love of the sun-washed land where she spent her formative years. These are stories to be savored.

4. **Gabriel Pearson, "Africa—the Grandeur and the Hurt," *The Guardian Weekly*, 14 April 1973: 25. Review of *Inklings* by Dan Jacobson, London: Weidenfeld, 1973 and *This Was the Old Chief's Country* and *The Sun Between Their Feet*, Volumes One and Two of *Collected African Stories*, by Doris Lessing, London: Michael Joseph, 1973.**

Almost simultaneous publication of these collections of short stories tempts one to suspect a providential intelligence beneath the random workings of the book trade. These volumes mutually illuminate and interestingly contrast and finally endorse each other. For their writers are very different with different styles. Doris Lessing has a boundless fecundity and flow which these two massive volumes illustrate. Jacobson is fastidious and tentative as the title *Inklings* suggests, though the word is perhaps a little too preciously mean. Yet through these quite different refractions looms the oneness of their subject matter, the vast irresolvable grandeur and hurt of Southern Africa which the short story with its own compressions and retractions and brokenness seems more ideally suited to express than the novel.

Here, in both volumes, the sheer racial rifts of almost geological proportion, the unassuageable guilt and the implacable wrong may all be registered, as much by the scars they leave, the connections they fail to make, as by any direct report. The shortness of the story seems to point to a true honest abbreviation of understanding.

Jacobson is essentially a moralist, Doris Lessing a visionary. She speaks characteristically of opening "a gate into a landscape which is always there. Time has nothing to do with it." And her stories are oddly timeless, as though heat and wilderness and vast space took the place of time. Some stories are set in the twenties, others in the war, others thereafter, but all draw with unhampered directness upon childhood sensation undiminished by distance and memory. This, given her kind of writing, is not surprising, but it is illuminating to find a more moderated vivid infection of the senses in Jacobson, a writer whose stories—even when they are anecdotes—are much more carefully, almost diagramatically, plotted than Mrs Lessing's, who proceeds by great, natural curves and wheelings. Both writers are in fact highly autobiographical yet in a way which is uninsistent and unindulgent.

This must be because the barriers and removes of subsequent exile give these earlier selves a kind of objectivity, a sharply alien salience of identities which have had to be known all over again, when prised out of the native matrix. Both writers are unblinkingly aware of how tortuous and intricate the whole question of identity is in Southern Africa and how fiercely it has to be extricated before it can be examined at all.

What have they become, who are they, these Jews and Englishmen, settlers, and farmers among fellow humans perpetually beyond reach by virtue of race and servitude? One senses in both writers the enormous cultural emptiness, where such questions cannot get formulated and where the human facts have an explosiveness and immediacy that there are no traditions to muffle.

And the absence of native tradition forces them back, as writers, upon variations of old fashioned realism which they handle with none of that anxiety about the status of fictions which few contemporary novelists fail to cultivate. And surprisingly, it does convince, and devices and cadences that derive from Chekhov and Gorky and Kipling and even Henry James seem right.

The reason for success here may be paradoxical. Traditional realism seems in its deepest assumptions about human nature recalcitrantly European and constitutes precisely the literary equivalent of the settler and suburban culture which at once occupies and refuses the land. Mrs Lessing, it should be added, has an extraordinarily generous and uncontemptuous feeling for the values of settler life style without ever condoning its fundamental injustices.

The black presence is everywhere, determining the shapes of feeling as much between whites as between white and black. A Rhodesian farmer, in one Doris Lessing short story, is torn with anxiety and guilt about employing a poor Boer assistant with nine children because of the hostility between Boer and native workers. Tension between Boer and Jew explodes, in a Jacobson story, at the sight of a Boer family apparently ill-treating a black child.

The very nouns which stud impeccable stretches of English prose disturb it with unassimilable presences: veld, stoep, vlei, kopje, piccanin, Kaffir.

Finally, one brings away from both writers a deeply unsettling sense of the sheer human impossibility of Southern Africa, as a place only fit for habitation, by the imagination of exiles and of children. All else seems lost, betrayed and spoiled, except the glare of sun, the dust, the boulders. Jacobson beautifully suspends "A Way of Life" about an African servant of a poorish, decent liberal couple who cannot afford to keep her when she falls ill but cannot abandon her either at that point of chronic impossibility, dropping the quandary into the reader's lap. In story after story Doris Lessing portrays the helpless collisions and alienations of children and sexes of the races.

Appendix C: Contemporary Literary Writing

1. Mabel Dove Danquah, "Anticipation," 1947; rprt. *Unwinding Threads: Writing by Women in Africa*, ed. Charlotte H. Bruner (Exeter, NH: Heinemann, 1983), 3-7.

Nana Adaku II, Omanhene[1] Akwasin,[2] was celebrating the twentieth anniversary of his accession to the stool of Akwasin. The capital, Nkwabi, was thronged with people from the outlying towns and villages.

It was in the height of the cocoa season, money was circulating freely and farmers were spending to their hearts' content. Friends who had not seen one another for a long time were renewing their friendship. They called with gifts of gin, champagne or whisky, recalled old days with gusto and before departing imbibed most of the drinks they brought as gifts. No one cared, everyone was happy. Few could be seen in European attire; nearly all were in Gold Coast costume. The men had tokota sandals on their feet, and rich multi-coloured velvet and gorgeous, hand woven kente cloths nicely wrapped round their bodies. The women, with golden earrings dangling, with golden chains and bracelets, looked dignified in their colourful native attire.

The state drums were beating paeans of joy.

It was four o'clock in the afternoon and people were walking to the state park where the Odwira[3] was to be staged. Enclosures of palm leaves decorated the grounds.

The Omanhene arrived in a palanquin under a brightly-patterned state umbrella, a golden crown on his head, his kente studded with tiny golden beads, rows upon rows of golden necklaces piled high on his chest. He wore bracelets of gold from the wrists

---

1 Male ruler appointed by the Queen Mother. (Footnotes 1–4 adapted from those by Austin J. Shelton.)
2 This main character represents the author's brother-in-law, Nana Ofori Atta I of Kibi, King of Abuakwa, elder brother to Joseph Baokye Danquah.
3 Purification festival at end of Akan year.

right up to the elbows. He held in his right hand a decorated elephant tail which he waved to his enthusiastic, cheering people. In front of him sat his 'soul[bearer]' a young boy of twelve, holding the sword of office.

After the Omanhene came the Adontehene,[1] the next in importance. He was resplendent in rich green and red velvet cloth; his head band was studded with golden bars. Other chiefs came one after the other under their brightly-coloured state umbrellas. The procession was long. The crowd raised cheers as each palanquin was lowered, and the drums went on beating resounding joys of jubilation. The Omanhene took his seat on the dais with the Elders. The District Commissioner, Captain Hobbs, was near him. Sasa, the jester, looked ludicrous in his motley pair of trousers and his cap of monkey skin. He made faces at the Omanhene, he leered, did acrobatic stunts; the Omanhene could not laugh; it was against custom for the great Chief to be moved to laughter in public.

The state park presented a scene of barbaric splendour. Chiefs and their retinue sat on native stools under state umbrellas of diverse colours. The golden linguist staves of office gleamed in the sunlight. The women, like tropical butterflies, looked charming in their multi-coloured brocaded silk, kente and velvet, and the Oduku headdress, black and shiny, studded with long golden pins and slides.[2] Young men paraded the grounds, their flowing cloths trailing behind them, their silken plaited headbands glittering in the sun.

The drums beat on.

The women are going to perform the celebrated Adowa dance. The decorated calabashes make rhythm. The women run a few steps, move slowly sideways and sway their shoulders. One dancer looks particularly enchanting in her green, blue and red square kente, moving with the simple, charming grace of a wild woodland creature; the Chief is stirred, and throws a handful of loose cash into the crowd of dancers. She smiles as the coins fall on her and tinkle to the ground. There is a rush. She makes no sign but keeps on dancing.

The Omanhene turns to his trusted linguist:

"Who is that beautiful dancer?"

---

1 The commander of the main body of the army.
2 Barrettes.

"I am sorry, I do not know her."

"I must have her as a wife."

Nana Adaku II was fifty-five and he had already forty wives, but a new beauty gave him the same new thrill as it did the man who is blessed—or cursed—with only one better half. Desire again burned fiercely in his veins; he was bored with his forty wives. He usually got so mixed up among them that lately he kept calling them by the wrong names. His new wife cried bitterly when he called her Oda, the name of an old, ugly wife.

"This dancer is totally different," thought the Chief; "she will be a joy to the palace." He turned round to the linguist:

"I will pay one hundred pounds for her."

"She might already be married, Nana."

"I shall pay the husband any moneys he demands."

The linguist knew his Omanhene: when he desired a woman he usually had his way.

"Get fifty pounds from the chief treasurer, find the relatives, give them the money and when she is in my palace tonight I shall give her the balance of fifty pounds. Give the linguist staff to Kojo and begin your investigations now."

Nana Adaku II was a fast worker. He was like men all over the world when they are stirred by feminine charm: a shapely leg, the flash of an eye, the quiver of a nostril, the timbre of a voice, and the male species becomes frenzy personified. Many men go through this sort of mania until they reach their dotage. The cynics among them treat women with a little flattery, bland tolerance, and take fine care not to become seriously entangled for life. Women, on the other hand, use quite a lot of common sense: they are not particularly thrilled by the physical charms of a man; if his pockets are heavy and his income sure, he is a good matrimonial risk. But there is evolving a new type of hardheaded modern woman who insists on the perfect lover as well as an income and other necessaries, or stays forever from the unbliss of marriage.

By 6 p.m. Nana Adaku II was getting bored with the whole assembly and very glad to get into his palanquin. The state umbrellas danced, the chiefs sat again in their palanquins, the crowd cheered wildly, the drums beat. Soon the shadows of evening fell and the enclosures of palm leaves in the state park stood empty and deserted.

The Omanhene had taken his bath after dusk and changed into a gold and green brocaded cloth. Two male servants stood on either side and fanned him with large ostrich feathers as he reclined on a velvet-cushioned settee in his private sitting room. An envelope containing fifty golden sovereigns was near him. He knew his linguist as a man of tact and diplomacy and he was sure that night would bring him a wife to help him celebrate the anniversary of his accession to the Akwasin Stool.

He must have dozed. When he woke up the young woman was kneeling by his feet. He raised her onto the settee.

"Were you pleased to come?"

"I was pleased to do Nana's bidding."

"Good girl. What is your name?"

"Effua, my lord and master."

"It is a beautiful name, and you are a beautiful woman, too. Here are fifty gold sovereigns, the balance of the marriage dowry. We will marry privately tonight and do the necessary custom afterward." Nana Adaku II is not the first man to use this technique. Civilized, semi-civilized, and primitive men all over the world have said the very same thing in nearly the same words.

"I shall give the money to my mother," said the sensible girl. "She is in the corridor. May I?" The Chief nodded assent.

Effua returned.

"Nana, my mother and other relatives want to thank you for the hundred pounds."

"There is no need, my beauty," and he played with the ivory beads lying so snugly on her bosom.

"They think you must have noticed some extraordinary charm in me for you to have spent so much money," she smiled shyly at the Omanhene.

"But, my dear, you are charming. Haven't they eyes?"

"But, Nana, I cannot understand it myself."

"You cannot, you modest woman? Look at yourself in that long mirror over there."

The girl smiled mischievously, went to the mirror, looked at herself. She came back and sat on the settee and leaned her head on his bosom.

"You are a lovely girl, Effua." He caressed her shiny black hair, so artistically plaited.

"But, my master, I have always been like this, haven't I?"

"I suppose so, beautiful, but I only saw you today."

"You only saw me today?"

"Today."

"Have you forgotten?"

"Forgotten what, my love?"
"You paid fifty pounds ... and married me two years ago."

2. Efua Sutherland, "New Life at Kyerefaso" 1957; rprt. *Unwinding Threads: Writing by Women in Africa*, ed. Charlotte H. Bruner (Exeter, NH: Heinemann, 1983).

Shall we say
Shall we put it this way
Shall we say that the maid of Kyerefaso, Foruwa, daughter of the Queen Mother, was as a young deer, graceful in limb? Such was she, with head held high, eyes soft and wide with wonder. And she was light of foot, light in all her moving.

Stepping springily along the water path like a deer that had strayed from the thicket, springily stepping along the water path, she was a picture to give the eye a feast. And nobody passed her by but turned to look at her again.

Those of her village said that her voice in speech was like the murmur of a river quietly flowing beneath shadows of bamboo leaves. They said her smile would sometimes blossom like a lily on her lips and sometimes rise like sunrise.

The butterflies do not fly away from the flowers, they draw near. Foruwa was the flower of her village.

So shall we say,

Shall we put it this way, that all the village butterflies, the men, tried to draw near her at every turn, crossed and crossed her path? Men said of her, "She shall be my wife, and mine, and mine and mine."

But suns rose and set, moons silvered and died and as the days passed Foruwa grew more lovesome, yet she became no one's wife. She smiled at the butterflies and waved her hand lightly to greet them as she went swiftly about her daily work:

"Morning, Kweku
Morning, Kwesi
Morning, Kodwo" but that was all.

And so they said, even while their hearts thumped for her:
"Proud!

Foruwa is proud ... and very strange." And so the men when they gathered would say:

"There goes a strange girl. She is not just the stiff-in-the-neck proud, not just breasts-stuck-out I-am-the-only-girl-in-the-village proud. What kind of pride is hers?"

The end of the year came round again, bringing the season of festivals. For the gathering in of corn, yams and cocoa there were harvest celebrations. There were bride-meetings too. And it came to the time when the Asafo companies should hold their festival. The village was full of manly sounds, loud musketry and swelling choruses.

The pathfinding, path-clearing ceremony came to an end. The Asafo marched on toward the Queen Mother's house, the women fussing round them, prancing round them, spreading their cloths in their way.

"Osee!" rang the cry. "Osee!" to the manly men of old. They crouched like leopards upon the branches.

Before the drums beat

Before the danger drums beat, beware!

Before the horns moaned

Before the wailing horns moaned, beware!

They were upright, they sprang. They sprang. They sprang upon the enemy. But now, blood no more! No more thundershot on thundershot.

But still we are the leopards on the branches. We are those who roar and cannot be answered back. Beware, we are they who cannot be answered back.

There was excitement outside the Queen Mother's courtyard gate.

"Gently, gently," warned the Asafo leader. "Here comes the Queen Mother.

Spread skins of the gentle sheep in her way.

Lightly, lightly walks our Mother Queen.

Shower her with silver,

Shower her with silver for she is peace."

And the Queen Mother stood there, tall, beautiful, before the men and there was silence.

"What news, what news do you bring?" she quietly asked.

"We come with dusty brows from our pathfinding, Mother. We come with tired, thorn-pricked feet. We come to bathe in the coolness of your peaceful stream. We come to offer our manliness to new life."

The Queen Mother stood there, tall and beautiful and quiet. Her fanbearers stood by her and all the women clustered near. One by one the men laid their guns at her feet and then she said:

"It is well. The gun is laid aside. The gun's rage is silenced in the stream. Let your weapons from now on be your minds and your hands' toil.

"Come maidens, women all, join the men in dance for they offer themselves to new life."

There was one girl who did not dance.

"What, Foruwa!" urged the Queen Mother, "Will you not dance? The men are tired of parading in the ashes of their grandfathers' glorious deeds. That should make you smile. They are tired of the empty croak: 'We are men, we are men.'—

"They are tired of sitting like vultures upon the rubbish heaps they have piled upon the half-built walls of their grandfathers. Smile, then, Foruwa, smile.

"Their brows shall now indeed be dusty, their feet thorn-picked, and 'I love my land' shall cease to be the empty croaking of a vulture upon the rubbish heap. Dance, Foruwa, dance!"

Foruwa opened her lips and this was all she said: "Mother, I do not find him here."

"Who? Who do you not find here?"

"He with whom this new life shall be built. He is not here, Mother. These men's faces are empty; there is nothing in them, nothing at all."

"Alas, Foruwa, alas, alas! What will become of you, my daughter?"

"The day I find him, Mother, the day I find the man, I shall come running to you, and your worries will come to an end."

"But, Foruwa, Foruwa," argued the Queen Mother, although in her heart she understood her daughter, "five years ago your rites were fulfilled. Where is the child of your womb? Your friend Maanan married. Your friend Esi married. Both had their rites with you."

"Yes, Mother, they married and see how their steps once lively now drag in the dust. The sparkle has died out of their eyes. Their husbands drink palm wine the day long under the mango trees, drink palm wine and push counters across the draughtboards all the day, and are they not already looking for other wives? Mother, the man I say is not here."

This conversation had been overheard by one of the men and soon others heard what Foruwa had said. That evening there was heard a new song in the village.

There was a woman long ago,
Tell that maid, tell that maid,

There was a woman long ago,
She would not marry Kwesi,
She would not marry Kwaw,
She would not, would not, would not.
One day she came home with hurrying feet,
I've found the man, the man, the man,
Tell that maid, tell that maid,
Her man looked like a chief,
Tell that maid, tell that maid,
Her man looked like a chief,
Most splendid to see,
But he turned into a python,
He turned into a python
And swallowed her up.

From that time onward there were some in the village who turned their backs on Foruwa when she passed.

Shall we say

Shall we put it this way

Shall we say that a day came when Foruwa with hurrying feet came running to her mother? She burst through the courtyard gate; and there she stood in the courtyard, joy all over. And a stranger walked in after her and stood in the courtyard beside her, stood tall and strong as a pillar. Foruwa said to the astonished Queen Mother:

"Here he is, Mother, here is the man."

The Queen Mother took a slow look at the stranger standing there strong as a forest tree, and she said:

"You carry the light of wisdom on your face, my son. Greetings, you are welcome. But who are you, my son?"

"Greetings, Mother," replied the stranger quietly, "I am a worker. My hands are all I have to offer your daughter, for they are all my riches. I have travelled to see how men work in other lands. I have that knowledge and my strength. That is all my story."

Shall we say,

Shall we put it this way,

strange as the story is, that Foruwa was given in marriage to the stranger.

There was a rage in the village and many openly mocked saying, "Now the proud ones eat the dust."

Shall we say,

Shall we put it this way

that soon, quite soon, the people of Kyerefaso began to take notice of the stranger in quite a different way.

"Who," some said, "is this who has come among us? He who mingles sweat and song, he for whom toil is joy and life is full and abundant?"

"See," said others, "what a harvest the land yields under his ceaseless care."

"He has taken the earth and moulded it into bricks. See what a home he has built, how it graces the village where it stands."

"Look at the craft of his fingers, baskets or kente, stool or mat, the man makes them all."

"And our children swarm about him, gazing at him with wonder and delight."

Then it did not satisfy them any more to sit all day at their draughtboards under the mango trees.

"See what Foruwa's husband has done," they declared; "shall the sons of the land not do the same?"

And soon they began to seek out the stranger to talk with him. Soon they too were toiling, their fields began to yield as never before, and the women laboured joyfully to bring in the harvest. A new spirit stirred the village. As the carelessly built houses disappeared one by one, and new homes built after the fashion of the stranger's grew up, it seemed as if the village of Kyerefaso had been born afresh.

The people themselves became more alive and a new pride possessed them. They were no longer just grabbing from the land what they desired for their stomachs' present hunger and for their present comfort. They were looking at the land with new eyes, feeling it in their blood, and thoughtfully building a permanent and beautiful place for themselves and their children.

"Osee!" It was festival-time again. "Osee!" Blood no more. Our fathers found for us the paths. We are the roadmakers. They bought for us the land with their blood. We shall build it with our strength. We shall create it with our minds.

Following the men were the women and children. On their heads they carried every kind of produce that the land had yielded and crafts that their fingers had created. Green plantains and yellow bananas were carried by the bunch in large white wooden trays. Garden eggs, tomatoes, red oilpalm nuts warmed by the sun were piled high in black earthen vessels. Oranges, yams, maize filled shining brass trays and golden calabashes. Here and there were children proudly carrying colourful mats, baskets and toys which they themselves had made.

The Queen Mother watched the procession gathering on the new village playground now richly green from recent rains. She watched the people palpitating in a massive dance toward her where she stood with her fanbearers outside the royal house. She caught sight of Foruwa. Her load of charcoal in a large brass tray which she had adorned with red hibiscus danced with her body. Happiness filled the Queen Mother when she saw her daughter thus.

Then she caught sight of Foruwa's husband. He was carrying a white lamb in his arms, and he was singing happily with the men. She looked on him with pride. The procession had approached the royal house.

"See!" rang the cry of the Asafo leader. "See how the best in all the land stands. See how she stands waiting, our Queen Mother. Waiting to wash the dust from our brow in the coolness of her peaceful stream. Spread skins of the gentle sheep in her way, gently. Spread the yield of the land before her. Spread the craft of your hands before her, gently, gently. Lightly, lightly walks our Queen Mother, for she is peace."

Appendix D: Historical Documents

1. Three Miners' Letters from Charles van Onselen's *Chibaro*, London: Pluto Press, 1976, 252-54.

Gwelo,
Rhodesia,
21st, 1920

To the
Native Affair,
Zomba,
Nyasaland

Dear's Sir,
We have the honour to acknowledge you that the time we left Blantyre and we arrived at Rezende G. Mine the Compound Manager of the place he treat us as he treat pigs and he often gives us good shambok (along) even with his native Police boys. We was working as Hammer boys he did not know that we are Education boys. Even education boys he do treat them the same and the General Manager he doesn't know all this we wish you to write the General Manager Mr. Rome that he must put another man, on that place. And the General Manager is a new man on that Mine; and also he doesn't feed the boys, and he take care for his Police boys in every thing and if you will write him he will double his bad character and but better write General Manager on otherwise all Compound boys and they never get good meat nor Vegetables, Beans, and Monkey nuts we saw only meat ¼ lb per head but other mine they use to get 1 lb meat per head twice a week including Vegetables, Monkey nuts and Beans but on that Mine at Resende Gold Mine only once a week to get meat no beans no monkey nuts.

We have the honour to be,
Dear Sir,
We are Your most humble and obedient Servants,
(Signed) KNIGHT and WALTER & etc.,

P.S. Now we are work here, They treat us all right. Nyasaland

Source: National Archives of Rhodesia, File N3/22/5

24/1/25
Eldorado Mine,
Station,
Sinoia

Dear Sir,

But I am asking you Sir. I left there Nyasaland to seek work here, I left with my wife; I have been here 5 years with her. The reason why I am asking you, Sir, is because my wife refused me here. I went to the Boma[1] that the Boma might judge this case. The woman had been married to another husband. The Boma asked the woman that 'do you want your new husband?' she said 'yes,' and the Boma said 'alright, take your child.' Therefore I, your slave, beg to ask you whether it is right for the woman to bring the child and not for me the husband. The Boma of here dislike to properly judge us, your slaves. I, your servant, beg you, Sir, to help me; I got no other father or mother than you. I want you, Sir, to call altogether with my wife and hear this case, because the Boma of here dislike to help us, the people of Nyasaland.

Because we are living as if there is no Europeans of the Boma here, therefore I thought it is right to put my complaint before you. I don't wish to leave my wife. If I am not your slave tell me.

Sir,
I am,
Your servant,
(Sgd) Simon Banda

Source: National Archives of Rhodesia, File S138/31

---

1 Administrative Centre; headquarters.

QUE QUE LOCATION
6th July, 1926

To Government Chief Secretary,
Zomba,
Nyasaland Protectorate

Sir,
I have the honour to be to lay down my report to you that on May last I had reported to you my report in connection with my injure while working in the Gaika Gold Mining Company that I may be compensated by that Mine and also that I may be issued with a Railway Warrant to take me to my home to the fact that I am unable to travel by land, and there is no reply since now. I shall be glad if you will have kindly communicate with the Compound Manager of that Mine in respect with my being injured while serving in that Mine please.

May I mention that I have already been discharged from that Mine, and has no any money to enable me to get my living or to enable me to go back to my born country under these circumstances I draw your attention and beg you most humble to that you may deal with the matter accordingly. Hope that this letter will meet with your kind consideration and that you will do according to what I have asked you about. Thanking you with anticipation.

I have the honour to be,
Sir,
Your obedient Servant,
(Sgd) YORAM WANCHA GULU

Source: National Archives of Rhodesia, File S138/41 (1926–1931)

2. The Empire Settlement Act, 1922 (12 & 13 Geo. 5 ch. 13) An Act to make better provision for furthering British settlement in His Majesty's Oversea Dominions.

Be it enacted by the King's most Excellent Majesty, by and with the advice and consent of the Lords Spiritual and Temporal, and Commons, in this present Parliament assembled, and by the authority of the same, as follows:

1. (1) It shall be lawful for the Secretary of State, in association with the government of any part of His Majesty's Dominions, or with public authorities or public or private organisations either in the United Kingdom or in any part of such Dominions, to formulate and co-operate in carrying out agreed schemes for affording joint assistance to suitable persons in the United Kingdom who intend to settle in any part of His Majesty's Oversea Dominions.

1. (2) An agreed scheme under this Act may be either:

(a) a development or a land settlement scheme; or

(b) a scheme for facilitating settlement in or migration to any part of His Majesty's Oversea Dominions by assistance with passages, initial allowances, training or otherwise; and shall make provision with respect to the contributions to be made, either by way of grant or by way of loan or otherwise, by the parties to the agreed scheme towards the expenses of the scheme.

1. (3) The Secretary of State shall have all such powers as may be necessary for carrying out his obligations under any scheme made in pursuance of this Act:

Provided that:

(a) the Secretary of State shall not agree to any scheme without the consent of the Treasury, who shall be satisfied that the contributions of the government, authority, or organisation with whom the scheme is agreed towards the expenses of the scheme bear a proper relation to the contribution of the Secretary of State; and

(b) the contribution of the Secretary of State shall not in any case exceed the expenses of the scheme; and

(c) the liability of the Secretary of State to make contributions under the scheme shall not extend beyond a period of fifteen years after the passing of this Act.

1. (4) Any expenses of the Secretary of State under this Act shall be paid out of moneys provided by Parliament:

Provided that the aggregate amount expended by the Secretary of State under any scheme or schemes under this Act shall not exceed one million five hundred thousand pounds in the financial year current at the date of the passing of this Act, or three million pounds in any subsequent financial year, exclusive of the amount of any sums received by way of interest on or repayment of advances previously made.

2. His Majesty may by Order in Council direct that this Act shall apply to any territory which is under His Majesty's protection, or in respect of which a mandate is being exercised by the government of any part of His Majesty's Dominions as if that territory were a part of His Majesty's Dominions, and, on the making of any such Order, this Act shall, subject to the provision of the Order, have effect accordingly.

This Act may be cited as the Empire Settlement Act, 1922.

3. From Ethel Tawse Jollie, *The Real Rhodesia*, London: Hutcheson & Co.: 1924; rprt. Bulawayo: Books of Rhodesia, 1971, 269–82.

...

A perception of the limitations of Native education as carried on by mission bodies led, in 1920, to the initiation of a Government Scheme, which owed its inception to the interest of the Resident Commissioner, Mr. C. Douglas Jones, C.M.G., and one of the Native Commissioners, Mr. H.S. Keigwin. A Department of Native Industries was formed, with the main idea of providing for natives, preferably from the various mission schools, an industrial continuation school, where simple handicrafts could be mastered which would send them back to their reserves, rather than out into the labour market, and make them the apostles of sweetness and light to their own people. They were to learn how to build better houses with the materials available, and how to make doors and windows from packing cases and native timber, also simple furniture. Improved methods of agriculture, the care of animals and the training and driving of oxen form part of the curriculum, which at first included no formal attempt at ordinary book teaching or religious instruction. The scheme included the development and marketing of native handicrafts such as basket making, mats, pottery, brooms and weaving, all of which are now being taught in one or other of the mission schools, but this part of the development of native industries has so far made little progress. Two schools are now open and a third is in contemplation, the work done consisting of building (all the school buildings and furniture being made by the pupils under supervision), gardening and agriculture, with special attention to crop rotation and methods which should enable the native to make a better use of his reserves. From the beginning, however, the boys desired literary education. In the mission schools they regard all their manual work, not as education, but as the return they have to make for their book lessons. The passion of the native for book learning is one of the remarkable features of his present condition. Somehow he has the idea that the secret of the white man's superiority is bound up with that power to read and write—it is to be found in those books of which he has such a number. The mere possession of books has a fascination, and one notices that even old catalogues which are thrown away will be picked up and preserved. An old boy is in charge of the place where this is written. He has just told the N'kosikas who is writing a book that he, too, has books in his kraal although he cannot read them. This morning he brought a treasured volume which he said he had bought in Salisbury. It turned out surprisingly to be a midget collection of "Gems from Ella Wheeler Wilcox!" With such a profound belief in the printed word as the Open Sesame to civilization it is not surprising to find that the natives are opening schools of their own, studying by themselves, and that every houseboy has his much-thumbed exercise books and native primers, while the farm and the mine have their group of students by every fire in the evenings....

The Government native training school has, therefore, modified its scheme to the extent of having definite hours for book lessons, and has also appointed a clergyman as principal of each of the schools, though no denominational teaching is given unless some particular church desires to have its members visited. The full course lasts for three years, and a fee is charged, but the boys are provided with clothes, food and all necessaries. It is obviously too soon to judge of the results, but very encouraging opinions have been expressed by experts on native affairs. It is argued by some that the training now given does not differ in essentials from that which is given, or could with Government assistance be given, in some of the mission schools. The missionaries are quite alive to the need for industrial training, and many of them are doing their best to carry it on, and it is claimed that the £8,000 spent on the Government schools, of which a certain amount necessarily goes in overhead charges, could be used to more advantage if divided among the missions.

...

The strongest brake on native progress is undoubtedly the position of their women. Sexual interests play the greatest part in the mental development of the average native, and often account for his apparent stagnation, and as has been shown already, he is dependent on his women for the performance of many essential tasks. The payment of *lobola*, the sum paid to the wife's father, is not so much objectionable in itself (since it certainly adds to the value of a wife that she cannot be had for nothing) as in the financial obligations and complications which it creates, which form a sort of net from which a man can often only escape by a clean cut with his family. Attempts to place marriage on a Christian basis have not been successful. Polygamy is deeply rooted in native life, and without it the problem of widows and other unprotected females would have to be met. At present a native who has married by Christian rites is liable to prosecution if he takes a second wife by native rites, but he has discovered that the law cannot touch him if he takes them merely by native custom on terms which are valid in native eyes but really amount to concubinage, and that, moreover, he can escape paying the hut tax for the second and subsequent wives by the simple expedient of having one "Christian wife" and placing the other women of his household on an unofficial basis. The native draws quite as strong a distinction between marriage and concubinage as the white man, but there is no public opinion against the latter, so that the opportunity for evading the tax is too good to be lost. One thing is certain, the ideal of making the native a better man and citizen without divorcing him altogether from his family can never be attained so long as the only wives available for him are still dominated by superstition of the grossest kind, and content to live on the low plane set by the traditions of their race. It appears essential that far more should be done to train and raise the women, who at present get comparatively little attention, and have not the educative influences which their brothers get in working for white masters. Most of the missions run girls' schools, but the work is far less developed and systematic than that done for boys, and so far prejudice, both on the part of parents and employers, prevents girls from entering the only occupation suitable for them, domestic service. Missions almost always employ their girl pupils, and many of them become most efficient, while it is now customary in the district where the writer lives to have a native maid in the house, usually for the children, but she is probably the only woman, outside a mission, who has a whole staff of girls in the house, and her experience convinces her that the little extra trouble involved in making suitable provision for them is amply repaid by the comfort and security they give to a woman who may have to be left by herself.

...

Despite certain drawbacks most women in Rhodesia are prepared to give thanks to providence for their native servants. They are cheap, teachable and amenable, easy to feed and, as a rule, cheerful and not quarrelsome. Their efficiency depends upon their mistress or master, for unless one is prepared to give the very highest rate of wages one cannot expect to get the really well-trained ones, but once trained they may stay for years, and many women have family treasures who have been with them ever since they started housekeeping. Northern boys are considered the best servants....

...

Farmers, too, when they compare their lives with that of their brothers in Canada or Australia, must give thanks for their labour supply, and almost every man one meets has some paragon of a boy who has become his right hand on the farm. And yet, if one were asked what is one of the greatest hindrances to Rhodesia, one would feel inclined to find it in this very supply of cheap labour, which has led to a lot of bad and careless work, and is apt to de-energize the white settler. The effect on immigration has been well stated by one who is himself a negro, Professor Kelly Miller [:]

> The white man avoids competition with the black workman and will hardly condescend to compete with him on equal terms. Wherever white men and women have to work for their living they arrogantly avoid those sections where they are placed on a par with negro competitors, and if indigenous to those regions they frequently migrate to others where the black man and rival is less numerous. For this reason white immigration avoids the black belts as an infected region. Among South African politicians there are those who compare the stream of home-seekers who enter the other great self-governing dominions with the almost imperceptible trickle that comes to the Union of South Africa. They point to our vast open spaces and sunlit skies and ask: how is it we cannot attract them.... [Jollie's ellipsis] They blame the Government for apathy, or worse, a deliberate attempt to discourage any increase of our population from the surplus of Europe. They fail to see that sun and space are not all the immigrant seeks. The vast majority hope to live

first by manual toil, and they consciously or semi-consciously pass by any country where they must compete with a backward race or live as they do.

Rhodesia is a difficult country to populate with white people for these reasons. She is not a plantation country, where the white man is only a supervisor, but at the same time the white artisan must demand a standard of living which places him far above what Kelly calls "his negro competitor." Fortunately there is not, so far, in Rhodesia that Poor White class which is so serious a problem in the Union [of South Africa], and the Rhodesians are determined that it shall never be created. It is realized that the only cure in the Union is to educate the children, who will then rise out of the slough of unemployables of which the poor whites are largely composed. If the white man is to retain his position in Rhodesia it must be by the superiority of his attainments, but that cannot be achieved merely by keeping the natives at a low level, rather by directing them into useful channels and giving them inducements to improve along the lines of their own tribal and family existence. The present necessity seems to be to provide incentives for this sort of progress rather than for that which brings the black man into competition with the white.

The Chief Native Commissioner, in his report for 1923, suggests that the first step should be to encourage a better use of the land already set aside as native reserves, which is for the most part cultivated on the well-known wasteful native lines, and this appears to be of such paramount importance that one would like to see a larger vote for Agricultural education not only given in Government schools but also given to the missions, to encourage the employment of men qualified to teach improved methods. Only one mission, so far, employs such an expert, and a good deal of his time is taken up with other work. As a corollary there should be a beginning made in the direction of marking out areas in which the native could acquire individual tenure of land, possibly contiguous to the existing reserves. A great deal of nonsense is talked about the necessity of preserving land for European occupation, for there are many regions where white settlement will never take place, and there is plenty of land for both black and white if it is properly utilized. At present many white farmers would be better off with less land and more improvements. At the same time, one cannot contemplate mixing white and black settlers in the same district, so that segregation is absolutely necessary, but should not be incompatible with the object lesson provided by a man who has been able to buy a bit of land, build a decent house, and live comfortably, which will be of more value than many lectures on the dignity of labour.

The next problem is what market can be found for the labour or the products of the trained native. As to labour the difficulty does not yet arise, and at present he has the same market for maize, wheat or other agricultural products as his white brother, but fewer facilities for storing or transporting them. He sells a great deal in small quantities to the storekeeper, by way of barter, which is not a sound economic basis for him, whatever it may be for the storekeeper. He is also a buyer of grain at times, and the writer has seen natives from the same kraal buying and selling on the same day, and paying more than they got.

It appears that no real improvement in this respect can be made so long as every member of the family has their own bit of ground and deals with its products individually, and here one comes up against the woman question. When a man starts in to cultivate scientifically with the aid of his family, and the crop is properly reaped and stored and sold as a whole, after deducting the family's needs, there will be some chance of system, and also of preventing the alternate feasts and famines that now rule the native commissariat, but this involves a re-arrangement of family finances. Nothing but education can do this, but the missions should not be the sole agencies for this sort of education. In another part of this book reference is made to the work done by Native Administrators in other parts of the world, and the writer believes that a good deal more might be done in these ways in Rhodesia by men who regarded themselves as something more than tax gatherers. Here and there one finds men who do take the view that they are responsible for the subject race in more than one way, and who give time and thought to their welfare, but the tendency (noticed by the Civil Service Commission which reported in 1907) to become "office wallahs" is even more evident to-day, and while, in some cases, it is due to pressure of red tape work, in others it resolves itself into a question of atmosphere. English born people are usually curious about native life and customs, and inclined to be sympathetic, whereas most South[ern] African born men and women regard the native as a necessary evil, and have absorbed all sorts of stereotyped ideas about him. It appears to the writer that a very important sphere of usefulness is reserved for the native administrators who will take something of the same view of their functions that used to animate the Commissioners of Native Districts in India, and resulted in lives of patient, unselfish, disinterested devotion, often unrewarded save by the consciousness of work well done. The importance and value of such work among South[ern] African natives ought to be more generally acknowledged.

The Rhodesian system recognizes the chiefs and indunas, and imposes on them certain responsibilities in return for small subsidies, but the power of these chiefs is rapidly decreasing, and the old men of all tribes are shaking their heads over the decay of authority. It is obvious that something must be put in the place of these old-time checks and controls, but the native as a whole is not ready yet to be handed over altogether to the cold processes of the law. The Native Commissioner must supply the gap, and he can only do so if he is a student of native life and languages, and knows his own district thoroughly....

...

The importance of the native question to the future of Rhodesia cannot be exaggerated. The presence of this reservoir of labour differentiates Rhodesia from all other white man's colonies, if we except the highlands of Kenya, and at the same time the presence of this backward race imposes obligations and responsibilities which are a heavy burden. Although the direction of native policy is nominally under the control of the Imperial Government it must receive all its vital impulses from the people of the country and their Government, and in this connection it is satisfactory to be able to bear witness to the satisfactory relations which, on the whole, prevail between the settlers and the natives with whom they are brought into contact in so many departments of life.

4. "The Colour Bar": [Letter] to the Editor of *The Manchester Guardian*, 17 May 1928.

Sir,—Dr. Leyes's letter, in its theoretical consideration of the Rhodesian native problem, is an admirable example of the attitude of the detached observer in this country. His letter and that of Mr. Ginders contain obvious misstatements of fact that must be corrected before a broad view of the subject can be got.

"Alienation of native land rights" and "steady retrogression of the country into slavery" are excellent as catch-phrases; but the Rhodesian native has never been so well cared for as since the British control of the country—cared for to an extent that has sapped his moral strength. We have given him security from starvation in the event of the failure of his crops, and security of life—a most precarious thing in the days of the murderous annual forays of Lobengula's impis, days when slavery *was* slavery. What work does he do in return that is not voluntary? Furthermore, huge tracts of land in various parts of the country have been set aside as native reserves, where he may pursue his occupations and live his own life according to his own standards without being forced to work. With a native population of nearly 1,000,000 the shortage of land is acute and agricultural labour is at a premium: of the available supply a great part is made up of alien natives passing through Rhodesia to the Transvaal gold reef and working a single season in transit.

Dr. Leyes writes in a pleasantly Utopian strain, but much of it is impracticable. Before considering a big question of this nature you must know the man you are dealing with—the African native,—and know him as he is, not as you would like to think of him. The Rhodesian native is not yet equipped, mentally or morally, for the franchise or political authority according to our standards. Whether he ever will be is a moot question: the essential qualities of honesty, truthfulness, industry, and sobriety are absent from his character, and, what is probably the greatest obstacle of all, the Bantu tongues hold no word for gratitude. That is what you are up against: if you propose raising the Bantu tribes to anything approaching the white man's standard you have to undertake the gigantic task of completely altering their nature, and that is not the work of one generation but of many, with very doubtful prospects of success. These are basic facts, and to anyone who doubts them I would recommend residence, if only for a month, and close observation in any native compound.

M. Amery is rightly against intervention: the best interests of the native rest securely in the hands of the Rhodesian Government, who, we must remember, have a duty equally to the white community as to the black.—Your, &c.,

F.L. Barratt.
7, Station Road, Cheadle Hulme [U.K.]
May 15

5. "Report on Urban Conditions in Southern Rhodesia," *African Studies* (vol. 4, 1945): 9-22.

This contribution is the full text of the Report of an official committee of inquiry that in 1943 investigated the economic, social and health conditions of Africans employed in urban areas in Southern Rhodesia.

In kindly giving us permission to publish this Report, the Minister asks us to say that his permission to do so should not be taken to imply that the Government of Southern Rhodesia is in agreement with the conclusions and recommendations of the Committee in their entirety.

The Report is prefaced by a letter to the Minister for Native Africa, dated 27 January 1944, from the Committee, which consisted of E.G. Howman (chairman) and W.A. Carnegie and Henry W. Watt.

The letter says:—

1. We took evidence at Bulawayo, Gatooma, Gwelo, Que, Salisbury, Selukwe and Umtali.
2. Over one hundred and twenty witnesses—Europeans and Africans—came forward and we desire to place on record our thanks to them. A most friendly atmosphere was noticeable at every centre and the willingness to assist displayed by every witness was very pleasing. This demonstrated to a marked degree the great interest shown in our investigations.
3. A large number of memoranda was submitted and these showed that a vast amount of time and work had been spent on their preparation. We are most grateful for these invaluable documents.
4. We realise that our main recommendations are identical with those put forward by the Reverend Percy Ibbotson in his admirable "Report on a Survey of Urban African Conditions in Southern Rhodesia." As our conclusions were reached independently they are strengthened by the fact that they coincide with those of so well-known and capable an investigator as Mr. Ibbotson.

E.G. Howman Chairman
W.A. Carnegie [and] Henry W. Watt, Members of Committee
...

Wages

The question of a minimum wage excited more public interest than any other aspect of the Committee's enquiry. The conclusion was reached that to recommend an indiscriminate minimum wage based on an arbitrary calculation of a minimum standard of living would not only be disastrous to the economic structure of the country but would have the worst possible influence on an African population ill-equipped morally, socially, physically and in health to justify such a wage. There must be a relationship between wages and productive efficiency, which includes both the capacity and the willingness to be efficient.

2. The Committee has the utmost sympathy with African claims to higher wages, and so had the industrialists who gave evidence, but it feels that any imposition of such wages must be the last step in the series of steps it has tried to bring out in the course of this report, otherwise there will be more exciting gambling, more flourishing prostitutes, and aggravated malnutrition and inefficiency.

3. The Committee has enjoyed the enormous advantage of having at its disposal the Report on a Survey, recently made by the Reverend Percy Ibbotson, of Urban African Conditions in Southern Rhodesia and gladly pays tribute to his painstaking work. From this exhaustive study much valuable information was drawn. Mr. Ibbotson also gave considerable evidence orally.

4. Mr. Ibbotson examined the position of 26,494 Africans in the seven larger towns of the Colony and found that—

5744 or 21.7 per cent received cash wages only.
1335 or 5.0 per cent received cash wages and food only.
1973 or 7.4 per cent received cash wages and accommodation only.
17442 or 65.9 per cent received cash wages, accommodation and food.

These figures represent a sample survey most carefully selected and may be taken as characteristic of the whole urban situation.

It is revealing to find that of the total of 26,494 which includes neither juveniles nor women, that 4,154 Africans, or 15.7 per cent were being paid less than £1 per month and 5 per cent of them were not receiving food and accommodation.

5. In the building industry in Salisbury, the Midlands and

Umtali under the Industrial Conciliation Act the minimum rate for Africans is 26s. a month (1½d. an hour)[1] and food and accommodation are supposed to be provided, but as no scale of rations has been laid down it is improbable that they are fed properly; 8s. a month may be deducted from their wages for the rations issued. In Bulawayo the minimum wage is 47s. 8d. per month (2¾d. an hour) but neither food nor accommodation is provided. An extra 4s. a month as a cost of living allowance is made. Few builders who appeared before the Committee appeared to realise the economic importance of well-nourished labourers.

6. *The committee is most unfavourably impressed by the conditions imposed on Africans under the Industrial Conciliation Act and recommends that before the scope of the Act is extended to other Africans, or present agreements reversed, an Adviser should be appointed to represent their interests.*[2]

7. It appears clearly that the bachelor African is financially far better off than the married man. In fact, if Mr. Ibbotson's calculation of £4 15s. 0d. as the average minimum monthly requirements of a man and his wife and two children is accepted then very large numbers of families must be perilously near starvation point. It has been emphasized that married men are not as liable to deficiency diseases as are bachelors. The interrelationships between wages earned and standards of living maintained, between income and habits of spending, are much more complicated than sets of figures imply.

...

10. Employers were almost unanimous in their replies to questions on this subject: "We pay a man for the value of the work he does, we are not concerned with his wife and family". This is of course a typical employer-like answer but an unwise view to take when skill, efficiency and reliability are important, as they are becoming in secondary industries. It was the manager of one of these new industries who replied: "We encourage married men. In industry we must have continuity of service. There is such a lot of training involved that we cannot afford to lose a Native if he is good". It is certain that the married man living with his family is the steady, long-time worker; the bachelor is always irresponsible,

---

1 £(pound) s.(shillings) d.(pence).
2 This paragraph, and others italicised, are emphasized in the original document.—Editors [of *African Studies*].

here today and gone tomorrow, attracted to the "shebeen", and the bane of the employer's life with his absenteeism. It will be impossible to build up an efficient, reliable, first-class labour force out of the vagrant bachelor. In the absence of the married man, industry cannot expect to compete with the products of other countries.

11. *The Committee feels that it can only recommend to the Government that it make enquiries into the subject of marriage allowances being paid from Public Revenue to African workers in Urban Areas when the whole system of social security is under consideration.*

...

13. One important fact does emerge from Mr. Ibbotson's figures—that 15.7 per cent of those in his sample survey are drawing less than £1 per month and we feel that this is exploitation of labour by a certain class of employer, European, Asiatic and African. It can only be possible where the job involves so little work that it is sheer waste of labour and inefficiency in the town, or where the ignorance of some raw recruit leads him to accept, or where a visitor from the reserve is anxious to earn some specific sum such as his tax and then return home. This last possibility, of the rural dweller being able to accept a less wage and so depress urban wage rates, must be faced. The same consideration applies to the juveniles who wander about accepting wages of 5s. to 12s. 6d. a month and learning all the wrong ideas about what good service means.

14. *The Committee therefore recommends that a minimum wage of 20s. per month should be imposed, which will apply to all African workers, men, women and juveniles, in the Urban and Commonage Areas, with food (to be laid down) and accommodation supplied by the employer.*

...

16. The Committee considers that the time has arrived when a Wage Act on the lines of that already in force in the Union of South Africa and Northern Rhodesia should be enacted in this Colony. Enactment of such legislation is a matter of urgency and importance.

Social Conditions

Urban Native Policy

17. The Land Apportionment Act of 1931, which was later redesigned in 1941, introduced a policy of semi-segregation which at the time appeared to be most just and reasonable but economic pressures both in the Native Areas and in the urban cut across

Native Policy, with the result that male African labourers have thronged to the urban areas in their thousands.

18. Segregation has assigned to these labourers a purely temporary, make-shift existence in the urban area; the very words "Location" and "Compound" are expressive of the theory which visualizes "homes" and "communities" as something to be associated only with the Native Reserves to which the labourer was expected to return. As the years have passed experience has increasingly overridden this relief, but the failure to adapt to changed conditions is manifested in the serious inadequacy of governmental and municipal services and administration in urban areas.

...

20. African life in the urban areas can be characterised as casual and precarious and nourished by roots that go no deeper than the daily contingencies of living; community life has been shattered; the family suppressed. Men have left their villages and failed to return over long periods, deterioration of the natural resources of the reserves has inevitably led to an exodus to labour centres and vast numbers of labourers from beyond our borders have been attracted here. As a result, an abnormal social structure has been erected in which there is an overwhelming preponderance of men, an almost complete absence of old age and the moderation and guidance old age provides, and a coming and going which cuts away the roots of every association, society and personal leadership that might crystallise out of the fluid mass of the irresponsible 18-35 age group. Visualising this induces the reflection that the African has been remarkably law-abiding and well-behaved.

21. A principal feature of urban life over the past few years has been the startling increase in the number of women flocking to the towns. Wives, deserted by their husbands, follow them up; young wives, presented with an easy way of escape from the traditional authority of husbands, run off to town without hesitation; girls in great numbers break away from their families to sample the glitter of the urban areas. Inevitably innumerable domestic arrangements of varying degrees of permanency are set up in addition to commercialised vice centres, prostitution and illicit beer brewing.

22. Into this social chaos and conflict of many different tribal customs, children, legitimate and illegitimate, are being reared; others, hasty of discipline, run away from homes to the freedom of the

towns and others are permitted by wearied parents to live and earn as they please.

23. In this general disintegration of all traditional controls the urban African has gained a freedom indistinguishable from licence, freedom for almost every momentary impulse, but has lost all direction save the external control of law and regulation.

24. Segregation has not only tended to suppress family life, but to place most strenuous obstacles in the way of those who have sought to set up homes in the urban areas and the consequences ramify into every field of the economic, industrial, moral and social order. Perhaps such unnatural conditions are an inevitable phase in the quick transition from a simple peasantry to an urban proletariate but the tragedy lies in the failure to appreciate the grave need to provide the fullest possible community facilities, housing and educational machinery that would make possible the growth of a natural family, community and social urban life. Evidence is not lacking that given such facilities and control the African does respond and there is no reason whatever why in time an urban culture with its own standards, civic consciousness, leadership and spontaneous controls should not emerge.

25. It is against this background, so briefly sketched above, that the Committee desire its recommendations to be placed and to urge the serious necessity for co-ordinated planning and deliberate control of urban life. The European, by his demands for labour, is responsible for the uprooting of the old traditional standards of African life; on him, therefore, devolves the responsibility of re-creating new standards in the hearts, minds and actions of the people; he cannot expect such standards to materialise from a policy of laissez faire, nor from the narrow confines of a classroom, courthouse, or gaol.

26. *The Committee therefore feels that it cannot over-emphasise the paramount importance of focusing urban Native policy on the provision and maintenance of homes.*

This means the acquisition and setting aside of adequate Urban Native Areas and Village Settlements wherever urban conditions develop; the planning and design of villages or town with adequate houses, allotment areas and all the apparatus necessary for the achievement of health, education and civic consciousness. It also means the recognition of the importance of groups of families cohering into community wholes and so avoiding an indiscriminate and unwieldy mass of population unresponsive to the processes of social self-control.

Hostels for Women

27. *The Committee recommends the erection of hostels for African women in all Urban Areas.*

Their numbers are already considerable and many are visiting town for legitimate purposes. The absence of accommodation save where employers provide a room must drive those without relatives to lead an immoral life and thereby secure accommodation. The only method whereby they may be safe-guarded to some extent is the provision of hostels. Certain rules and regulations would have to be imposed on them and the direct supervision of a European Woman Superintendent, most carefully selected, would be imperative, but the greatest care would be necessary to avoid regimentation and the routine of a concentration camp. Such a hostel might advisably be associated with an employment bureau and the provision of academic and domestic education as well as recreation.

Juveniles

28. Africans are unanimous in the opinion that juveniles should not be allowed to work or wander freely in towns, and this view is supported by almost all European witnesses. Senior Officers of the Police are most emphatic that nothing could be worse for juveniles, morally, mentally and physically, than the undisciplined life of a town and that the future criminals of the Colony are emerging from such juveniles.

29. Juvenile delinquency, the "broken home" and lack of parental discipline have been proved to be inter-related in other countries. We dare not ignore their experience.

30. *The Committee recommends that additional undenominational schools be established at the earliest possible date; that these schools and their equipment be free and that education for all juveniles of ages eight to fifteen within the Urban Areas, including the commonages, be made compulsory.*

Where evidence of age cannot be procured the opinion of the Native Commissioner shall be accepted as final.

31. It would be advisable to consider the possibility of linking this compulsory education with the development of a probationary service attached to the Courts, for the number of Africans being sentenced to imprisonment is a problem of grave concern.

Health

Family Life

32. The fundamental failure to plan for family life is again evident in our consideration of the health of urban Africans. Venereal diseases are rife and whatever medical inspection and treatment may be imposed they cannot be expected to cope with a situation in which stable family life is almost impossible. Malnutrition and deficiency diseases are particularly evident amongst the industrialised bachelor labourers, who are the worst sufferers. They have never been taught to cook, they tend to skimp the preparation of properly cooked food and after the day's work lack the time and energy necessary in the preparation of all those extras with which a wife makes her meals appetizing and nutritive. Family life also implies separate living establishments, not to mention the care and cleanliness devoted to their homes by most women whose "house pride" stands out in remarkable contrast to the unhygienic filth of single quarters. The present over-crowding of single men and women into confined quarters is a prime factor in the spread of tuberculosis.

Over-crowding

33. Africans employed in the urban areas are very largely dependent on the action of the local authorities for their health. When the local authorities neglect their elementary duties, ill health inevitably increases. The danger of overcrowding in the Locations, in the rooms provided for domestic servants, or in private compounds, is a very real one. Lack of accommodation is not a sudden growth but has been steadily increasing over many years. Conditions are particularly bad where congestion is greatest and the local authorities are responsible. Industries are encouraged to start and are springing up in the areas set aside for them, but no thought and no provision is made for the African workers employed there. The scarcity of houses is not due to the war but arises out of a shortsighted and unsocial view of industrial progress extending over many years.

Malnutrition

34. Medical evidence given to the Committee is almost unan-

imous in stating that malnutrition is seriously prevalent everywhere in the urban areas, particularly amongst the factory (labourer) class. Domestic servants are generally well fed because the
nature of their duties does not make the same physical demands on
them, and the kitchen, legitimately and illegitimately, provides a
variety of foodstuffs. This widespread malnutrition is due to inadequate rations, to ignorance of what constitutes proper nutrition
and tribal prejudices, to the intestinal parasites of bilharzia, hook-
worm, etc., and the general absence of any facilities, for the urban
dweller to acquire cheap, properly cooked meals and those foods
whose fresh greenness are so essential to health. Scurvy has
appeared in Bulawayo during the dry season and pellagra has
increased in Umtali.

...

Food

45. The Committee has been particularly struck by the complete ignorance and lack of interest displayed by so many employers as to the manner in which their workers feed themselves; they
appeared to be unconscious of the fact that an under-fed, mal-
nourished man is quite incapable of performing a good day's work
and that the African does not know how to feed himself up to
European standards of energy. When asked what rations they issued
the reply was, "Oh, the usual ration", and when questioned further
added, "some meal, salt and 6d. a week for meat"—and then they
hold forth on "the damned lazy [native] who won't work"!
46. This attitude of the man-in-the-street is due to unthinking
ignorance. To combat it, propaganda by pamphlets, lectures and
wireless talks to the public is essential.
47. On the other hand the Committee has been equally struck
by the study which some employers have given to improving the
efficiency of their labourers and the extraordinary results which
proper feeding has achieved. One witness stated that having insisted on a breakfast and a scientifically prepared lunch eaten on the
premises he had been able to dispense with half his labour force and
maintain the same output as he did when no rations were supplied.

...

49. *The Committee strongly recommends that a balanced minimum scale
of rations be laid down and that it be made obligatory on all employers in urban
and commonage areas to provide their African employees with such rations.*

...

Housing

64. There is a great shortage of accommodation for Africans in the locations, in all the towns and also in the Village Settlements of Highfield and Luveve. Overcrowding is met with everywhere and householders are constantly in difficulty trying to find somewhere for their servants to live. The result is that Africans squeeze into what rooms they can find, seek out all kinds of shelters about the towns and "married" couples share rooms with bachelors.

65. The Municipal heath authorities would willingly condemn certain places if other accommodation were available but under present conditions this is impossible. Location Superintendents have waiting lists that include hundreds of applicants and it takes sometimes many months' waiting before a man can procure accommodation.

...

Economic

Social Attitudes as they influence Economic Status.

...

73. Only in exceptional cases has the African attained any consciousness of efficiency and the need for it, any sense of censure for idleness and of "the dignity of labour", any appreciation of the monetary value of time, and the binding moral nature of a contract of service is something alien to his whole background. But apart from these deficiencies in his traditional attitudes, whose design was naturally never evolved to meet urban industrial conditions, there has emerged a generation of Africans confused by contradictory behaviour patterns, deprived of the self-control which deeply laid family discipline and standards bequeath, moving uneasily and suspiciously in a business world that is ruled over by a sense of urgency, productive efficiency, *quid pro quo* and punctuality demanded by intertwined time engagements. As a result of the strain imposed on them a spirit of irresponsibility, mistrust and misunderstanding is growing; household relationships are often corroded by worry, bitterness and disillusionment; industry by malingering, unreliability and the need for vigilant supervision.

74. The transition from one type of life to another so different must inevitably give rise to this state of affairs but what is culpable is our failure to recognise it as a transitional phase which deserves

all the social or educational machinery we can bring to bear on it. Instead our segregation policy prolongs it by endeavouring to keep the African a tribal peasant, in a peasant's home with haphazard peasant standards and attitudes, with an occasional spell in industry: a chameleon-like change to meet the regime of town life and efficiency. The change is impossible and industry is loud in its complaints about the service rendered by the African—not only Europeans but even responsible old Africans of many years' service in the towns gave evidence as to the refractory character of so many employees.

75. The root of the situation lies in our failure to appreciate the importance of the family, and it is certain that until we cater for family and community life in an urban environment we cannot expect industrial and urban standards to emerge.

...

Conclusion

96. To some it may appear that the Committee has overportrayed a disordered and confused world in which there is a constant struggle with disease, poverty, industrial difficulties and social disorganization. The realities of what is so unconcernedly called "the Native problem" require to be faced not only by those who give hardly a thought to the problem and react with prejudice, but also by those whose humanitarian assumptions lead them astray into wishful thinking.

The sudden transmutation of a simple tribal people into a modern industrialised community is full of complexities and ugly currents of change; it cannot take place without an abnormal degree of social and personal demoralization; the disruption of the old is a necessary preliminary to the emergence of the new, but if we see in it the opportunity to stimulate, mould and discipline the slow processes of reorganization and renewal which are already in action, there is no reason whatever why sound, healthy, efficient and prosperous urban African communities should not be built up.

6. *Report of the Commission of Enquiry regarding the Social Welfare of the Coloured Community of Southern Rhodesia* (Salisbury: [1946] TS on microfilm). 196–214.

ChapterVI: The Suitability and Adequacy of the Present Arrangements for the Education of Coloured Children in Southern

Rhodesia, with Special Reference to Post Primary Education and Future Employment

General

407) In 1933 the Government appointed a Committee, now known as the Foggin Committee, to enquire into and report upon the educational facilities for Coloured children in the Colony. This report has been of much assistance to the Commission. In general the evidence given before the Commission substantiates the findings of the Foggin Committee, with the exception of that section of the Committee's Report dealing with first generation Coloured children, or half-caste children as they are referred to in the Foggin Committee's report, with which section of that report your Commission does not agree.

408) The general educational policy during the past ten years has undoubtedly been sound and the Coloured community has on the whole been well served. With the growth of the Coloured population in the Colony certain extensions of the system have become necessary. An alteration in the policy regarding the education of the first generation of Coloured children is also desirable. Apart from this, however, no radical alteration in the present policy appears necessary or desirable.

...

(D) Post-School Education

428) Most Coloured children leave school at about the age of 15 years and there are no facilities in the Colony for any post-school or adult education for Coloured adolescents in the Colony to-day. It was suggested by many witnesses that some provision for such education should be made, and in particular that facilities should be provided for vocational training.

429) Many of the Coloured children leaving school do not obtain employment immediately; there is then often nothing for them to do to bridge the gap between leaving school and obtaining employment. If some form of post-school education were provided these children might well take advantage of it with great benefit to themselves.

430) It is considered, therefore that some form of post-school education should be provided for Coloured persons. This might take the form of continuation classes in such subjects as, for example, English, book keeping, woodwork, practical mathematics and mechanics, domestic science and dressmaking. Only Bulawayo and Salisbury have a population large enough to warrant such classes. The numbers of Coloured pupils would hardly warrant the establishment of special establishments, but no doubt accommodation for these classes could be made available at the local Coloured schools.

(E) Education of First Generation Coloured Children

431) This section deals only with those children who are the children of Native mothers and European fathers and who are living after the manner of natives. The expression "first generation" Coloured children used in this section includes a number of children living after the manner of natives who are not first generation Coloured children but are the progeny of such children, so they are really second generation.
...
433) The Foggin Committee [1933] considered this subject with great thoroughness and ultimately came to the conclusion that these children should not be removed from their Native environment and educated in Coloured schools, but should be left in their Native environment and educated at Native schools in the hope that they might become absorbed in the Native race....

434) Broadly the reasons given for this recommendation were:—

(i) The administrative difficulty of collecting these children and accommodating them satisfactorily at Coloured Schools.
(ii) The possible opposition on the part of the Native mother to have her child removed from her, a removal which incidentally, if due consideration is given to "mother love", might to many appear inhuman, and contrary to nature.
(iii) The fact that Coloured persons already found it hard to obtain employment and if these children were brought up as Coloured persons this difficulty would be accentuated.
(iv) That with their European blood these children, if absorbed into Native life, were likely to become leaders in the native community, and it was better that their energies should be guid-

ed in that direction.

435) The principle of the Foggin Committee's recommendation is enshrined in the present Education Act. Under that Act a person who has Native blood in his veins and who lives after the manner of a Native does not come under the Act and is not eligible for admission to a Government Coloured School, nor entitled to a Government boarding grant at an Aided School.

436) Before dealing with the detailed reasons of the Foggin Committee's recommendation it would be as well to deal with the principle. There are three possible positions which these unfortunate children can be brought up to occupy in the society of this Colony:—

(i) They can be permanently identified with their Native mother and relegated to a Native society.
(ii) They can be treated in the same manner as other persons of mixed blood and brought up in Coloured society.
(iii) They can be identified with their European fathers and raised to the level of European society.

437) From a purely human and moral point of view these children should be uplifted and brought up as Europeans, but as has so frequently been pointed out in this Report, a very definite "color prejudice" exists to-day and this prejudice would effectively prevent these children being raised as Europeans. To suggest for example that these children should be educated at European schools would under conditions existing today be unthinkable. It is, therefore, quite impracticable to suggest that such a child should be brought up to occupy the position in society enjoyed by his European father.

438) It by no means follows, however, that because it is impracticable to absorb these children in European society it is unnecessary to relegate them to Native society; the least that can be done for them is to endeavour to bring them up so as to be able to maintain a position in that society to which other persons of mixed blood belong. This view is stressed by the Native Department. In reply to a letter on this subject the Chief Native Commissioner observed:—

The "hybrid" child is a misfit in either the European or Native Social system, and I consider that he or she should be brought up as a "Coloured child" and that generally every effort should be made to give him or her the higher standard of education and living which the Coloured community enjoy.

It seems clear, therefore, that the principle underlying the Foggin Committee's recommendation is difficult to uphold today.

439) To deal now with the detailed reasons given by the Foggin Committee:—

(i) Administrative Difficulties

The administrative difficulties of educating these children as Coloured are considerable and it appears to the Commission that it was probably the magnitude of these difficulties which was the main factor in influencing the Foggin Committee. In giving evidence to the Commission the then Chief Education Officer, with the permanent official's eye on administration, though he freely admitted to the soundness of the principle, greeted the suggestion of educating all these children at Coloured schools without any marked enthusiasm. But administrative problems, however great, should not be allowed to cloud principle.

440) The first administrative difficulty is the question of accommodation; the number of these children is likely to be so large as to swamp existing Coloured schools. Furthermore, most of these children are rural dwellers and even where they are not they obviously could not continue to live in a Native environment when being educated in a Coloured school. Hostel accommodation for them is, therefore, essential and as will appear later in this Chapter the hostel accommodation for other Coloured children is at the moment inadequate. There may also be some opposition on the part of the other Coloured parents to permitting these children to enter existing Coloured schools. This administrative difficulty can be overcome by establishing a special boarding school for these children at least for primary education. Broadly the education they receive should be the same as given in other Coloured primary schools and those pupils who show promise might then go to the proposed Coloured secondary schools. The establishment of such a school may take time but it should be at least a long term policy.

441) The second administrative difficulty is that of collecting the children. All the officials of the Native Department and the Native witnesses were emphatic that if the Native mothers were informed that their half-caste children could be educated at Coloured schools at State expense they would be anxious in the interests of the children to bring them to the school. The Native Department officials consider that their Department could easily be responsible for the necessary propaganda which would ensure that most of these children would be brought quite voluntarily to the school. The difficulties of collecting these children are, therefore, not as great as would appear.

(ii) Opposition of Native Mother

442) As pointed out in the previous paragraph all the evidence given before the Commission supports the view that far from opposing any scheme of having their children educated away from the Native area as Coloured children, the Native would welcome it as they appreciate it is in the interests of the children. Native Department officials stated that such Native mothers often approach them and ask them whether some provision such as that suggested in the previous paragraph could be made for the education of their children. There is evidence also that Native mothers often approach the authorities and ask to have these children committed so that they can be educated out of a Native environment....

443) There is thus not likely to be much opposition from the Native mothers. Since educating such children as Coloured children must ultimately mean the removal of the child from its mother it is not suggested that at this stage any element of compulsion should be used. The mother would have to be a consenting party. As regards payment hardly any Native mother could afford to pay for the child's education, so the education of these children would have to be at state expense. The school holidays will present a problem. When the child has just recently left the mother it might be advisable to allow it to return to its mother for a portion of the longer holidays. It is obvious, however, that a long residence in a native environment would undo much of the good of education at a Coloured school. These visits home during the holidays should, therefore, gradually become less and less frequent until finally they cease altogether. Facilities should, however, always be provided to enable the mother to visit the child at school.

...

Conclusion

447) The Commission is, therefore, perfectly satisfied that the recommendation of the Foggin Committee so far as the first generation Coloured children are concerned was not sound and the policy founded on that recommendation should be altered. The long term policy should be the setting up of a special Coloured Primary School, with adequate hostel accommodation, preferably in the country but outside the Native area, where facilities should be provided for educating every first generation Coloured child and for giving that child a start in life equivalent to that given other Coloured children. The education provided should have a bias in favor of subjects which would assist these children to follow rural pursuits. If the numbers of these children are as great as estimated there will probably have to be more than one school. In the meantime where such schools as Embakwe and St. John's are prepared to accept these children every encouragement should be given them to do so and adequate grants should be paid by the State to assist them. This may involve a[n] amendment to the Education Act but this should be no insuperable obstacle.

7. Godfrey Huggins [Lord Malvern], "Southern Rhodesia," *African Affairs: Journal of the Royal African Society* (vol. 51, 1952): 143–49.

At a Joint Meeting of the Royal Empire Society and the Royal African Society on Thursday, January 24th, an address was given by the Prime Minister of Southern Rhodesia [The Rt. Hon. Sir Godfrey Huggins, C.H., K.C.M.G], in London for talks on Central Africa. The Chair was taken by the High Commissioner, Mr. K.M. Goodenough, C.M.G., M.C.

Mr. Chairman and Members of the Royal Empire Society and Royal African Society, I thank you for inviting me to address you on this occasion when I am in London trying to negotiate a Federal Constitution for Northern and Southern Rhodesia and Nyasaland. This matter is not so easy as some people think, seeing that the Constitution has to be accepted by four countries. Trying to obtain something that will satisfy the House of Commons and the people of Southern Rhodesia is rather like trying to diminish the distance between the North and South Poles, but, on the other hand, I do not think it is entirely impossible. It entails a good deal of hard thinking on practical common-sense lines in this country and in the Colonies, an acceptance of something unpalatable now, with a view to the building up of a strong, self-reliant, self-supporting State owing allegiance to the Crown; an inland State in Central Africa where British influence can be maintained, and where a multi-racial society can live in peace and friendship.

There are roughly three patterns that State might follow; one is to hand the country over willy-nilly to the Bantu people who arrived there a few years before we did (I need not go into the pros and cons of this argument with my present audience, though with some it would be quite necessary); the second would be to hold the country by European dominance and the possession of arms. Such a State with a minority holding the majority down would have to be a police State in perpetuity—I do not think that we can seriously countenance that solution; the third pattern would be one like Southern Rhodesia, where an attempt is being made to improve the lot of the Bantu people and, as they advance, increase their opportunities so that the races can live side by side in complete amity, each with its own social life, but working together in a common cause—the improvement in the lot of all the people.

This policy has been called partnership and is exemplified by our sharing our political institutions. The common voters roll was enshrined in the Constitution that was granted to Southern Rhodesia nearly thirty years ago, and the Southern Rhodesian Parliament confirmed this policy about a year ago. It is true that the property qualification was raised at the same time, but this rise merely balanced the fall in the value of the pound. There has always been a property qualification because whatever the value of having a vote based on the attainment of a certain age may have in this country, something more than that is required in a multi-racial society so that a certain standard of ability, although a fairly low one, may be maintained.

I might for a moment digress to discuss this blessed word "partnership" which has supplanted paramountcy in Whitehall. I find I first used the word in an address to a Rotary Club at the end of 1950 and this is roughly what I meant by the expression—"partnership in a multi-racial society means the co-operation of all races to the full extent of their capacity in developing a country in the best interests of all its inhabitants".

It may be said that that sounds quite a fair and reasonable proposition—what is the difficulty in devising a Federal Constitution on such a basis? Strange to say, the policy in the countries for which the House of Commons is responsible does not practice partnership, and I will indicate to you what I mean by comparison. Our native Africans take part in our elections and vote on the policy of the party or the opinion of the particular candidate. There are not many on the voters' roll at present but there could be several thousand if they wished to register. These people are not hard up; if we have time I will give you some particulars of the earnings of these people. But for the most part they are not interested; they are satisfied to leave it to the Europeans, whom they realise know more about it and with whom they are for the most part on very good terms. Those that have registered, however, appreciate the vote and working in this European institution; candidates have to meet their African constituents, who influence elections.

In most of the countries for which you are responsible you have instituted nominated native African members. These so-called nominated members are chosen by an attempt at an electoral system, the best that can be done in their present state of development, but they are chosen on colour not on policy. Having special members to represent Africans and chosen in a different way from the Europeans immediately suggests that their interests are not the same, and it creates a gulf between them that can only increase with time. The introduction of the so-called nominated African members should never have been allowed in view of the Bledisloe Report on amalgamation of Northern and Southern Rhodesia and the formation of the Central African Council. You may ask me why we did not protest at the time. The reason was we had hoped for amalgamation of the countries concerned, which would have entailed a bi-cameral Parliament, and we considered the proper place for the African at this stage was the Upper House or Senate, where nominated members are not unusual; the switch from amalgamation to Federation makes these nominated members an embarrassment which may have to be accepted for a time, but the worst feature is that it starts the Federal Parliament off with a membership divided by colour and not by policy. There is another feature in your system that is even worse. You have nominated European members to represent African interests. This suggests that the ordinary member of the House is incapable of representing the interests of the African or unwilling to do so. I cannot think of a better way of inducing into the mind of the ordinary member that he can shirk his responsibility, seeing that there is someone else especially elected to relieve him of his duty. In our House of some thirty members, I think every one of them has, on some occasion or other, championed the cause of the native African. What we in Southern Rhodesia require for the African is more and better housing in the native urban areas, more water conservation schemes, more schools, more hospitals and other social amenities. More politics can come later when he is a better and more self-respecting citizen. To provide his requirements, we require a larger national income so that we can have more money to spend on him, and this provision should be obtained earlier if we can bring about Federation, which will improve and hasten the development of all three countries.

I know that in a limited circle in this country it is considered that those of us who have migrated have become brutalised in the process. It was not long ago that Mr. Driberg stated that "talking to Huggins about the natives is like talking to Streicher about the Jews".

There are others who regard us as "nitwits", who have learnt nothing from your industrial disturbances caused by the industrial era of the Victorian age when the country went to town, and who are incapable of drawing conclusions from countries such as Malaya. I mention this because Southern Rhodesia would be like the senior partner in a Federation if it came to pass. These same people to whom I have referred seem to ignore the fact that the average Southern Rhodesian regards Rhodesia as his home and his children's home and he knows that if he wishes to stay in Africa he must carry the African with him. A hostile majority would make the situation quite impossible. He further knows that, for economic reasons, even if there were not others, he must raise the African from the ignorance and sloth and the chronic maladies which in fact create the sloth. Who is more likely to do what is best for the African than the people whose future depends on good race relations or a body of officials who live a long way away, who know little or nothing of the psychology of the people and who, I think, judging from their remarks, find the burden of responsibility for trusteeship almost overwhelming—so much so that (although no doubt acting in good faith) there are examples of their acting from our point of view in a very irresponsible manner, by treating the Africans as children and not adults, and trying to teach them to perform in a play which is beyond their ability in their present stage of development.

I would like at this stage to say that I know there are a few African natives who have risen out of their environment in one generation and they have become knowledgeable, highly civilised beings. These are the people whom you see over here and they are the people who can lead their community to a higher standard, and they are, from the European point of view, a problem because they are so different from most of their fellow-men. These are the people we have to encourage and to create opportunities for them to meet our better people on the level, so that they do not develop an inferiority complex.

The problem of race relations is a human problem. The matters to be resolved change from year to year. In 1929 we never visualised a permanent native urban population. At that time every native African working in the European area was a bird of passage. He worked for a short time and then returned to his home in the country where he had left his wife and children to carry on some very indifferent agricultural pursuit. Now we have more and more of them wanting security of tenure near their work and it will be a great test of the European's sincerity when they are asked to find land which the native can have on a long lease where he can run his own home somewhere near his work. I believe they will rise to the occasion when this new problem for settlement is put before them.

I would like to tell you how some of your ideas are not altogether appreciated by the natives. In the course of a survey of native opinion in Southern Rhodesia in regard to Federation, some of the town workers stated that they would much prefer to join the Union of South Africa. They were not worried by the obscure word "apartheid" as so many people here seem to be. All they knew was that cash wages—not real wages—were higher in the Union, but they did not know that real wages were about the same.

I feel that probably I have said enough about the Federal problem from our point of view, and I would pass on to something else after reminding you that this Federation is much more important to you even than it is to us, because you are counted in millions and we are only a small community. Great Britain in recent years has lost many spheres of influence; everything is turning against her. She will be left with nothing but this little island eventually, if she is not careful. You have to import all your raw materials for your factories and to find a home for your surplus population. Now you have an opportunity of being a reasonable people, by trusting your kith and kin on the spot, and by staking a claim in South Central Africa where your ideas of the British way of life can prevail.

There is no more loyal part of the world to the King and Crown than Southern Rhodesia. Therefore I would like to ask you to wake up and not let this matter fail on a lot of academic things, like the right of Governors General and so on. You can trust us; we have got a fine record. We have no trouble with our African people; they trust us. All we have to do is to carry our beliefs to our British neighbours.

I think perhaps I had better go on to one or two general points. We are extremely optimistic in regard to the development of our Colony. We have made tremendous strides since the war. We have a number of large schemes for development which are being investigated, but there are certain priorities to which we have to attend. Another railway link to the Portuguese East African coast is absolutely essential, a link to reduce the distance from the Northern Rhodesian copper belt and to relieve the strain on the existing system is another urgent necessity. The long time it takes and has taken ever since the war to get delivery of locomotives and rolling stock for the railway system is the greatest bottleneck holding up the development of the Colony.

Then, on the other hand, we have proved a very large body of iron ore. We have a small pilot steelworks, and when the capital can be found to turn those steelworks into a really large undertaking we shall be able to produce the cheapest steel in the world, and, incidentally, by throwing the plant out of balance, we could sell you 100,000 tons of pig-iron a year at a price below anything you can obtain from any other source.

We are not a wheat-growing country, which is unfortunate in these days when balance payments loom so large, but we have established a pilot scheme to try out various crops. An irrigation scheme has been recommended in the Sabi valley by the British firm of Alexander Gibb & Co. If this is successful we hope to produce most of our wheat requirements and a considerable amount of sugar. A scheme for producing cheap electricity from the great Zambesi has been favourably reported on by British engineers, and is almost ready for starting, with the same proviso "if only the very large capital required can be found". A pilot plant is nearly ready for producing ferro-chrome, and we hope to turn some of our chrome ore, of which we have vast deposits, into ferro-chrome.

It is essential that some of our raw products should be processed or semiprocessed in the Colony. The export of ore does not leave enough money behind to pay for the education and public health requirements of the people who produce it, and a manufacturing industry is essential if the ordinary people are not to remain in poverty. It is the failure to recognise this in the past that has caused poverty and unrest in some parts of the Colonial Empire. I think the lesson has been learnt and you will not expect only the raw products for your factories in the future. Recently, when discussing our steelworks with a British industrialist who visited the Colony, we mentioned that we could let them have extremely cheap pig-iron for their steel industry, and he said, "Why not the ore ?" I replied, "Because we have grown out of that." That is the one and only thing that can be counted against Great Britain, whose capitalists failed to leave enough behind for the people actually producing the wealth; otherwise the imperialism of Great Britain was a great thing and a benefit for the undeveloped part of the world. They made that one slip-up, they took out the raw products and carried out no manufacture in the country of origin.

Discussion

Mr. Howes: Would Sir Godfrey Huggins explain the principles of the intended Federation between Southern Rhodesia and Northern Rhodesia and Nyasaland?

Sir Godfrey Huggins: I do not think I could explain that; it is under negotiation at the present time. The original proposals can be obtained in a cheap form from H.M. Stationery Office. They are now, as I say, under discussion. As I pointed out in my opening remarks, the difficulty is to reconcile certain very divergent points of view on this matter.

Dr. Olumbe Bassir: May I ask the speaker if he could say a few further words about this proposed Federation? First of all, he talks about the European population. Is he a democrat? If so, does he believe that a very small group of people should continue to rule over the vast majority for ever? In his speech he made it clear that it is not the intention of Southern Rhodesia to allow Africans to come into central policies for a very long time yet. What method does he propose to use to see that they do come in? If they do come in, on what democratic basis will they come?

Sir Godfrey Huggins: I cannot answer the question with regard to the time factor; it would depend on circumstances. A great many more Africans could take part in the elections than do at present. That number must increase very rapidly with education and improved economic conditions. Perhaps I had better answer another question which has not been asked here, and that is how it is proposed to prevent the Europeans from being swamped by the natives when the latter have all got the vote. My answer to that is this and I will be perfectly frank—that I believe that if they enter into our political institution we shall go along together and shape our party politics, which will not be colour politics. I believe my grandchildren, if partnership does not eventuate, will at a certain stage have to call a halt.

Dr. Bassir: May I ask exactly what the speaker means by that last sentence?

Sir Godfrey Huggins: I believe if partnership does not materialise, that it will be the duty of my grandchildren to make an agreement and alter the Constitution. There should be no super senior partner in this firm. They would merely get to the equality stage and no further.

...

Mr. Hood: Could Sir Godfrey tell us how many British immigrants of the right type Southern Rhodesia can take per annum at present?

Sir Godfrey Huggins: The number at present is very limited by reason of housing and general shortage of materials such as you also suffer from here, as does the whole of the sterling group. The number we are taking at present from this country is in the neighbourhood of 500 a month. We have cut them down considerably. We are all going to be desperately short of steel, and this is not a period in which we can hope to speed up immigration, unless the people are prepared to live as the pioneers did, which the public health laws and town-planners will not allow them to do now.

...

A Member: Would Sir Godfrey Huggins give us some idea of the wage level of Africans?

Sir Godfrey Huggins: Out of curiosity, when I was told that the increased property qualifications would make it so difficult for the African, I got out a list of some of the wages that are being earned to-day by Africans in Salisbury. A taxi-driver, getting 15 per cent. of each £ in fares, receives from £40 to £50 a month. Heavy truck drivers average about £28 a month. A tailor, self-employed, earns £35 to £40 a month. Those employed in clothing factories earn £30 a month. A clerk on African newspapers earns £30 a month. Panel beaters and card trimmers earn from £25 to £35 a month. Semi-skilled mechanics earn £5 a week. Carpenters and joiners, not mechanised, working on their own, earn from £30 to £50 a month. Greengrocers, self-employed, earn £20 to £25 a month.

Joiners and cabinet makers, employing machines, make about £70 a month. Owners of buses and stores to £100 a month. It will be seen that the property qualification is not going to keep the enterprising African off the voters' roll.

...

Select Bibliography

Non-Fiction by Lessing

Prisons We Choose to Live Inside. London: Jonathan Cape; New
   York: Knopf, 1985.
"Impertinent Daughters." Granta 14 (Winter 1984):51-68.
"Autobiography (Part Two): My Mother's Life." Granta 17
   (Autumn 1985):225-38.
The Wind Blows Away Our Words. London: Picador; New York:
   Random House: 1987.

Website

http://lessing.redmood.com/

Critical Works on Lessing

Books

Fahim, Shadia S. *Doris Lessing: Sufi equilibrium and the Form of the
   Novel*. New York: St. Martin's Press, 1994.
Greene, Gayle. *Doris Lessing: The Poetics of Change*. Ann Arbor:
   University of Michigan Press, 1994.
Kaplan, Carey, and Ellen Cronan Rose. *Doris Lessing: The Alchemy
   of Survival*. Athens: Ohio University Press, 1988.
Knapp, Mona. *Doris Lessing*. New York: Ungar, 1984.
Pickering, Jean. *Understanding Doris Lessing*. Columbia, SC: Uni-
   versity of South Carolina Press, 1990.
Rowe, Margaret Moan. *Doris Lessing*. New York: St. Martin's
   Press, 1994.
Sage, Lorna. *Doris Lessing*. New York: Methuen, 1983.
Singleton, Mary Ann. *The City and the Veld: The Fiction of Doris
   Lessing*. Lewisburg, PA: Bucknell University Press, 1977.
Thorpe, Michael. *Doris Lessing's Africa*. London: Evans Brothers,
   1978.
Yelin, Louise. *From the Margins of Empire: Christina Stead, Doris
   Lessing, Nadine Gordimer*. Ithaca, NY: Cornell University Press,
   1998.

Special Journal Issues

Contemporary Fiction Studies 14 (Autumn 1973), ed. Annis Pratt and L.S. Dembo.

Modern Fiction Studies 26 (Spring 1980), ed. Annis Pratt and William T. Stafford.

Related Reading

Abrahams, Peter. *Tell Freedom: Memories of Africa*. New York: Knopf, 1954.

Bhebe, Ngwabi. B. *Burombo: African Politics in Zimbabwe 1947-1958*. Harare, Zimbabwe: The College Press, 1989.

Bourdillon, M.F.C. *The Shona Peoples*. Gwelo, Rhodesia: Mambo Press, 1976.

Gordimer, Nadine. "The Train from Rhodesia" (1947). In Jean Marquand, ed., *A Century of South African Stories*. Johannesburg: Donker, 1978: 170-74.

Hare, William Francis, Fifth Earl of Listowel. *Memoirs* (http://redrice.com/listowel).

Hartly, Jenny, ed. *Hearts Undefeated*. London: Virago Press, 1994.

Hensman, Howard. *A History of Rhodesia*. London: Blackwood, 1900. Rpt. New York: Negro Universities Press, 1970.

Macdonald, Sheila. *Sally in Rhodesia*. 1927, rprt. Bulawayo, Rhodesia: Books of Rhodesia Publishing, 1970.

Ranger, Terence. *Peasant Consciousness and Guerrilla War in Zimbabwe*. London: James Currey, 1985.

Reeves, Frank. *British racial discourse: A study of British political discourse about race and race-related matters*. London: Cambridge University Press, 1983.

Schmidt, Elizabeth. *Peasants, Traders, and Wives*. Portsmouth, NH: Heinemann, 1992.

Wallis, J.P.R., ed. *The Northern Goldfield Diaries of Thomas Baines*. 3 vols. London: Chatto and Windus, 1946.

Vambe, Lawrence. *An Ill-Fated People: Zimbabwe before and after Rhodes*. Foreword by Doris Lessing. London: Heinemann; Pittsburgh, PA: University of Pittsburgh Press, 1972.

"Vindex" (F. Verschoyle), ed. *Cecil Rhodes: His Political Life and Speeches*. London: Chapman and Hall, 1900.

Sources

Lessing, Doris. "A Home for the Highland Cattle" and "The Antheap." *Five*. London: Michael Joseph, 1953. Copyright © 1953 by Doris Lessing. (First available in the United States in *African Stories*. New York: Simon and Schuster, 1965. Copyright © 1951, 1953, 1954, 1957, 1958, 1962, 1963, 1964, 1965, 1972, 1981 by Doris Lessing.) Reprinted by kind permission of Jonathan Clowes Ltd., London, on behalf of Doris Lessing, and by kind permission of Simon and Schuster.

Bertelsen, Eve. "An Interview with Doris Lessing." *Journal of Commonwealth Literature* Vol. 21 (1986): 134-61. Reproduced with the kind permission of Cambridge Scientific Abstracts and of the author.

Brown, Hickman Edward. "The Eternal Moment." (Review of Doris Lessing's *African Stories*.) *Saturday Review* (September 24, 1966): 4.

Danquah, Mabel Dove. "Anticipation." 1947. Reprinted in *Unwinding Threads: Writing by Women in Africa*, ed. Charlotte H. Bruner. Exeter, NH: Heinemann, 1983. pp. 3-7. (Previously published in *The African Assertion*, ed. Austin J. Shelton. New York: The Odyssey Press, 1968.)

Ellman, Mary. "Stitches in a Wound." (Review of Doris Lessing's *African Stories*.) *The Nation* (January 17, 1966): 78. Reprinted with permission.

Frick, Thomas. "The Art of Fiction ...: Doris Lessing." (Interview.) *The Paris Review* 106 (1988): 80-106. Reprinted by the permission of Regal Literary as agent for *The Paris Review*. Copyright ©1988 by *The Paris Review*.

Huggins, Godfrey. "Southern Rhodesia." *African Affairs* (1952): 51. pp. 143-149. Reprinted by permission of Oxford University Press.

Jollie, Ethel Tawse. *The Real Rhodesia*. London: Hutcheson & Co., 1924. Reprinted by Bulawayo: Books of Rhodesia, 1971. pp. 269-282.

Newquist, Roy. "Interview with Doris Lessing." *Counterpoint*. Chicago: Rand McNally, 1964. 413-24.

Pearson, Gabriel. "Africa—the Grandeur and the Hurt." [Review of Dan Jacobson's *Inklings* and Doris Lessing's *This Was the Old Chief's Country* and *The Sun Between Their Feet* (Volumes 1 and

2 of *Collected African Stories*)] *The Guardian Weekly* (April 14, 1973): 25. Copyright © 1973 by *The Guardian*.

Scott, J.D. "Man Is the Story." (Book review of Doris Lessing's *African Stories*.) *New York Times Book Review* (November 7, 1965): 4.

Sutherland, Efua. "New Life at Kyerefaso." 1957. Reprinted in *Unwinding Threads: Writing by Women in Africa*, ed. Charlotte H. Bruner. Exeter, NH: Heinemann, 1983. (Previously published in *The African Assertion*, ed. Austin J. Shelton. New York: The Odyssey Press, 1968.) Reprinted by permission of the Estate of Efua Sutherland.